BOUNTY HUNTER

BOUNTY HUNTER

E. C. HERBERT
with N. C. McGrath

Bounty Hunters

Copyright © 2014 E. C. Herbert with N. C. McGrath.

All rights reserved. No part of this book may be used or reproduced by any means, graphic, electronic, or mechanical, including photocopying, recording, taping or by any information storage, retrieval system without the written permission of the publisher except in the case of brief quotations embodied in critical articles and reviews.

Published by T and C Books, 2015

Because of the dynamic nature of the Internet, any web addresses or links contained in this book may have changed since publication and may no longer be valid. The views expressed in this work are solely those of the author and do not necessarily reflect the views of the publisher, and the publisher hereby disclaims any responsibility for them.

Any people depicted in stock imagery provided by Thinkstock are models, and such images are being used for illustrative purposes only. Certain stock imagery © Thinkstock.

Library of Congress Control Number: 2013923677

Printed in the United States of America.

CHAPTER 1

On the morning of April 9, 1865, at the Court House in the village of Appomattox, VA. the landscape which was usually emerald green, and alive with the sounds of birds singing, dogs barking and an occasional rooster crowing, was now a solid blue and gray as fighting soldiers from both the Union and Confederate armies gathered to witness the signing of declaration ending the war.

No gun shots or cannon fire interrupted the quietness of the crisp morning air.

RJ Murdock, wearing his battle-worn Grays, had taken a spot close to the Court House and with a tear in his eye witnessed his commanding officer, General Robert E. Lee signing the declaration and terms of surrender to General Ulysses S. Grant ending the bloody war known as the War between the States, or the American Civil War, which took the lives of over 750,000 men and boys and had pitched brother against brother and family against family.

"Well R.J, what are your plans now?" The voice was that of his best friend Calvin. The two had met on the battlefield and had become fast friends right from day one and had covered each other's back on several occasions, and now with the war over, it was time to make some decisions about the future.

"I'm headed for home," whispered Calvin as if his voice would somehow disturb the morning's quiet. Looking off in the distance at all those gathered here, and speaking to no one he continued. "Don't rightly know what I'll find when I get there. We saw what was done to Richmond, so I don't plan on finding much."

Before RJ could say anything, General Lee emerged from the McLean House, and standing on the front porch, drew his sword, held it high into the air and officially discharged his men one last time. With that, the war came to an end, slavery was abolished, and it was time to start re-building, an effort that was marred just five days later by the assassination of President Abraham Lincoln.

Even though there were several thousand men gathered here, it was as quiet as the inside of a tomb and RJ wondered if anyone else had picked up on just how quiet it was.

As a Term of Surrender, the confederate soldiers were allowed to keep their weapons and their horses, if they had one.

"I have nothing to go home for or to either," exclaimed RJ. "I received a letter awhile back informing me that Grandma had passed and my two younger brothers were selling what was left of the farm. The Union Army had just about destroyed it completely, burning down the barn and setting fire to the fields. I think I'll head west and see what I can find for work."

"Why not stay around here, there's plenty of rebuilding to do?"

The offer from Calvin basically went in one ear and out the other side as RJ had made up his mind to head west and had secretly hoped he could talk Calvin into joining him.

"As good as that sounds, I always wanted to head west someday and now that Gram is gone and my brothers are selling what's left, there is nothing keeping me from following that course." As a second thought he added, "I would imagine they'll be headed that way too."

"I always knew this day would come when the war ended," said Calvin, watching all the men solemnly walking away with their heads hung low. Some men could be heard crying, knowing they were now heading home after years of fighting, and having no idea what they would find but knowing their homeland had probably been destroyed by the Union Armies.

"How ya doing RJ?" A voice came from behind him. Not recognizing the voice, RJ and Calvin turned around.

A smile instantly lit up RJ's face as he set his eyes upon the face of Micah, another soldier, he had befriended at the beginning of the war and one he had heard was dead.

"I always knew that the dead could rise!" exclaimed RJ embracing Micah and giving him a couple healthy slaps on the back. As he stepped away, Calvin did the same adding a couple powerful back slaps himself and receiving a couple in return. Calvin's unbridled enthusiasm caused Micah to lose his balance, but a couple quick steps kept him upright.

"My Gawd, Calvin! I know you're happy to see me, but you could kill a man with your fervor."

"We heard you got yourself shot dead several months ago," Calvin said, as he looked at a frazzled Micah.

Both saw a much older Micah. His face was lined with wrinkles, his hair, once jet black was now lined with gray and un-kept. His eyes had taken on a gray, black color and were set back in their sockets.

"So tell us what happened?" Calvin and RJ listened as Micah told of the bullet wound that grazed his head and had knocked him unconscious.

"When I came to, the battlefield was empty except for the dead and the dying. It was dark, so I just started walking in a direction I thought was where my men had gone, only to find out that having walked through the night, I had gone in the wrong direction, and wandered into a Union camp where I was immediately taken prisoner. They had a sawbones there who doctored up my head." Turning and pointing at some of the Union soldiers who were walking away, he continued. "Three days ago, the unit I was being held by, packed up camp and started marching, stopping only long enough to start a small fire, make some coffee and then marched on, stopping only once we reached here."

"Was there anyone else being held with you?"

"Yeah, there were ten of us. A couple of times we almost made a run for it, but we were treated fine and they even fed us some pretty tasty vittles so we decided to hold off running." Pausing in his storytelling, Micah waved at a soldier passing, who waved back.

"Do you remember that fella we met during the Battle of Big Bertha? You know, he stuttered so bad that you could hardly understand a word he spoke?" Both RJ and Calvin acknowledged Micah. "He was one of the soldiers being held along with me, and you know he was so scared he stopped that stuttering cold."

The morning had quickly turned into afternoon, as the three walked along with everyone else.

"What are your plans now that the war is over?" asked RJ.

"Well, before this war broke out, I was what you'd call a Bounty Hunter." RJ and Calvin stopped in their tracks and looked at him.

"You, a Bounty Hunter?"

Even though the April temperature was still a little cool, sweat could be seen running down Micah's forehead. He used his shirt sleeve to wipe it away.

"Damn right! Bounty Hunting. How else do you get a chance to make one, five, ten thousand dollars at a clip? Once in a great while, you can even make twenty five thousand." Both Calvin and RJ's eyebrows shot up. "Twenty-five thousand dollars!
Did we hear you right?"

"Yup! Right now I'm heading for my old homestead where I buried some money when the war broke out with plans on fetching it after the war."

"Tell us about this Bounty Hunting?"

"Well, it is pretty simple. You go into any town and locate the sheriff's or marshal's office. You go inside and ask him if he has any reward posters for outlaws or murderers. Sometimes he has a board hung up outside his office where he tacks up wanted posters. I look at the ones who draw the most money and always make sure the poster says dead or alive." Micah saw a questioning look on their faces so he answered their blank stares.

"'Dead or alive' really means dead in my book. No one questions whether he has a bullet wound in the chest or the back, so it makes no difference."

"You mean you'd shoot a man in the back?"

"Listen, Calvin, the man who is wanted is wanted for crimes that range from murder, rape, bank robbery, where someone got killed, or shooting a lawman. The list goes on and on and the amount of the bounty depends on the seriousness of the crime.

RJ was taking in and trying to process all that Micah was saying.

"Once you find a poster, how do you go about tracking him down?"

Micah took a pouch of tobacco out of his rear pants pocket and rolled a cigarette for himself, then offered the makings to RJ and Calvin who shook their heads.

Taking a big drag, he continued, "Once I have the poster, I memorize one or two things about the face. Sometimes it's a scar, or might be really bushy eyebrows, and he might even wear an eye patch. Sometimes the sheriff will even let you take the poster, especially if it's someone wanted from his town."

The two were all ears as Micah once again continued his story.

"I look at how long the poster has been out, then I see where he is wanted, then I look at how much the reward money is. I go for the ones with at least five hundred dollar reward. Of course the distance I'll travel depends on the size of the bounty. Once I have my man picked out, I'll head to where he was last seen. Once in that town, I'll ask around, using the description from the poster."

Micah stopped and asked them both the question. "You know what I have found?"

They shook their heads.

"Whores," he said with a grin. "Locate the town's whores, toss out a couple of gold pieces, and soon you'll have enough answers that will lead you right to him."

Taking the last drag from his cigarette, Micah dropped the butt on the ground and crushed it out under the heel of his boot.

"No one knows who you are so, once you locate him, it's easy to get close enough to shoot him."

"How can you just walk up behind a man and blast him in the back? Don't the people around, jump you? I don't think I could just shoot a man in the back." RJ said, shaking his head.

"Well RJ, I didn't think I could either, that's why the first outlaw I went after was wanted for the rape and murder of a mother and her fourteen year old daughter. Once that one was done and I was holding five thousand dollars in gold coin in my hand, you bet your sweet ass the next one was easier. I don't always shoot 'em in the back. Depends on how mean they look." Micah responded with a smile on his face.

"You paint a pretty picture by tossing in the reward monies, but it seems pretty dangerous to me," RJ said.

"Sounds plenty dangerous to me too!" Calvin added.

"Ok, tell me boys, just what are you two going to do now? Go back to your homes that you'll probably find burned to the ground?"

All the while he was speaking, Micah was forming a plan in his head. He had been pretty successful before the war with his bounty hunting and could see the dollar signs if he could get RJ and Calvin to join up with him.

"I already know my homestead got destroyed and my two brothers by now have sold off the land and gone west someplace."

"Well, there you have it. Nothing to make you go back home for."

"You're right there!" RJ smiled.

Calvin looked at his friend and saw that smile and knew that he was giving some deep thought to what Micah was telling them.

I've seen that look on RJ's face way too many times not to recognize what's on his mind. Within seconds, Calvin's thoughts went back to the first time he had witnessed that sinister smile, he and RJ were pinned down in a ditch by five Union soldiers.
The rest of their squad had retreated, not realizing they'd left two behind.

As they lay there the ground around them exploded into showers of dirt as the lead balls hit all around them. Once the firing had ceased, they knew it would take about twenty seconds for them to reload their muskets. Calvin looked over at RJ for some kind of word as to what the heck they were gonna do now. RJ seemed to read his mind.

"If I'm right, there are five of them yellow bellied Blue Coats up there, but we have to know for certain so somehow we have to get them to fire so we can count the reports."

"How do we get them to fire without ending up dead in the process?"

"I'm gonna jump up and you gotta listen for the shots. Listen really well Calvin because my plan will depend on all of them firing and reloading at the same time."

Laying his weapon down and giving a thumbs up, RJ jumped up and put himself in plain view of the enemy. Within seconds, the quietness of the day was shattered by the POW, POW, and POW as three shots were fired. Another couple of seconds brought another POW, POW than once again quietness. By the time the first shots came, RJ was safely back out of sight.

"What did you count?"

Calvin held up five fingers.

RJ crawled closer to Calvin so he could speak softly. With that same smirk on his face, RJ laid out his plan.

When he had jumped up drawing fire, he also got a quick look at where the enemy soldiers were located.

"I say they can't reload in less than twenty seconds. I saw where they are located and I know that I can get to them before they can get reloaded." RJ spoke as he checked his revolver and instructed Calvin to do the same.

"Are you willing to bet your life on that? "Asked Calvin. "If you're wrong, then we're both dead men."

"Look around, Calvin. Do you see any other way to get out of here? Pretty soon they'll realize there are only two of us and will make their move to surround us."

"Why don't we do what you said to draw their fire, but afterwards we turn away and high tail it outta here?"

"Now, why would you want to run that way?"

"For one thing, your way puts us running towards those little lead balls that want to harm us, my way puts us running in the opposite direction of those little lead balls."

Thinking for a moment, then looking over and smiling at Calvin, RJ moved his head up and down. "For once you make a lot of sense. It would be a shame if this piece of ground was to be our final resting place, let's git outta here. What do you say?"

"I say, let's go." With that, Calvin jumped up and drew three shots from the clump of trees where the enemy was located, then turned to his left and like a scared jackrabbit was gone. RJ turned off to his right, and as he did so, he heard the last two shots fired.

There was no way that the Union soldiers could get reloaded so they just stood and watched as RJ and Calvin ran out of sight.

Before anymore could be said, Calvin spoke up. "Let's go home and if things are like what we think then we can move on to the west, but I need to go home."

CHAPTER 2

No one really knew how hot it was going to be that summer day as RJ and Calvin sat outside their freight hauling business, but it was so hot, that nothing in town was moving, not even Old Jake, the town's mascot, was nowhere to be found. He was always seen lying in front of Kincaid's barber shops, with his head resting on his outstretched paws. The heat spell had now gone on for almost a whole month, putting a dent in their hauling business.

After the war, they had gone home to see what was left of their homesteads. Micah had tried to persuade them into heading west with him and RJ almost did, but his best friend, Calvin, wanted to go home and RJ wanted to make sure his brothers weren't still around. Arriving home, he had found the homestead had been destroyed and both his brothers were gone, as he had thought. A close friend of his family was old man Oliver Wilson, who was still alive. He handed RJ a letter that his brothers had left for him, if and when he ever returned. Opening the letter, he read out loud that his brothers had just walked away empty handed. With the Union winning the war, the Confederate money was worthless.

"They've been gone for some time now." Oliver told RJ.

"I guess I was right when I told you there was nothing left for me to come home to, Calvin." He looked at his friend and hung his head and slowly shook it from side to side.

Old man Oliver spoke up. "What are you boys gonna do now?"

"Well!" Said Calvin. "RJ was talking about heading west, and by the looks of things around here, I guess he's right. Why do you ask?"

"Well boys, I'm ready to call it quits myself. Now I know it might take a little while, but before the war, this here freight hauling business made me a pretty penny, and I would bet my stock on it, that it will again."

"You heard me read my brother's letter, even if I had the money to purchase your business, it wouldn't be worth nothing."

"That's just it. I don't want your money, I just want someone to take the business over. As you haul stuff and start making a few dollars, you can pay me, say ten percent of your take." He paused for a moment, then patting RJ on the shoulder asked, "What'd ya say son? You have no money, and no way to make any to head west on. Haul a little freight, and once you have enough money and you decide you still want to leave, so be it."

Now as they sat in the heat of the day, almost five years to the day that they had left Virginia and took their hauling business to Colorado and with the lack of business quickly draining what savings they had accumulated, RJ's thoughts were once again focused on moving on.

RJ removed his hat, wiped the sweat from his brow and stared down Main Street. Nothing was moving in this heat. Slowly he turned to face Calvin who said, "Let's hear it? You've been sitting there fidgeting for going on an hour now and that was about the third time you got up to look down the street."

"I've been thinking. Remember those two riders who came through a couple of days back?

"You mean those two who spoke of a wagon train coming through and to be ready to feed a group of folks headed to a town in? What state did he say?"

Calvin took off his hat and scratched his head, trying to remember. "South Dakota, I think."

"Right, South Dakota. And a town one of them called Deadwood."

Looking at RJ and replacing his hat, Calvin said under his breath, "Deadwood, South Dakota. Don't sound like a very friendly place, if you ask me?"

"Listen, we haven't hauled any freight for three months now. We can tie in with the wagon train and go to this place called Deadwood and start up our freight hauling business there. With gold being found there it should be hopping with folks moving around and need our hauling business."

Calvin sat listening to RJ and had to agree with him. Oliver had left them the hauling business when he passed. For a few years they tried to make a go at hauling.

The east was rebuilding and everyone who had a team and a wagon became a freight hauler, so one day Calvin and RJ picked up shop and as RJ had always wanted, they headed west. The trip was a grueling one and when they reached Denver, Colorado and saw how it was just coming alive, they decided to stop for a while and see if they could get any business so they could replenish some of their money.

The first few years were okay and RJ and Calvin did all right, but then, just as in Richmond, things slowed down.

"Calvin!" barked RJ bringing him back from his thoughts. "Are you hearing a single word I'm saying here?"

"I hear you just fine."

"Well, what do you think? You got a better idea?"

Leaning forward, he stood up from his chair and doing the exact same thing he had watched RJ do, he looked down the length of Main Street. A minute later he reached out and slapping RJ across the shoulders which created a small cloud of dust, simply nodded and said. "Let's go get ready for a trip."

Over the next couple of days, as they were loading their best wagon, several of the town folk dropped by to wish them well, and two brothers, Hank and Tom Riley expressed a desire to purchase their other wagon and team.

"What are you boys thinking of doing?"

"Well, there is talk of finding gold in the Dakota's. Hank spoke to one of those riders who came through and was told there's a wagon train coming through on its way to a new up and coming gold town called Deadwood."

"We heard the same talk from those riders."

"I'll sell you the wagon and four mules for two hundred dollars."

"Two hundred dollars? You got a deal." Hank walked up to RJ and they shook hands. "Tom and I will be back here in a little while with the money."

RJ smiled as he watched them walk away, then turning back to Calvin asked, "Wasn't it Deadwood that Micah said he was headed to on the trail of an outlaw with a five thousand dollar bounty on his head?"

"I was wondering, just how long it would take before you remembered Micah coming through. Are you still thinking about the bounty hunting stuff that Micah talked about?"

"If we can't get any business hauling freight, it might be something to look into, don't you think?"

"Well, Micah looked like he was doing just fine. Did you see his boots and side arm?"

Seeing his friend and listening to some of the stories he told them, had started a small fire burning inside of RJ. The past years had taken their toll on him and he was ready to call it quits, as far as hauling freight went.

"Calvin, I am just plain tuckered out, hot, and getting older every day, and I feel like life has speeded up and soon they will be planting me in some no-name cemetery."

"I know the feeling," he spit out a stream of tobacco juice. "I Figured I'd be married by now and have a kid or two."

"Well, I thought you were going to hitch up with Claire."

He turned sharply. "You know damn well why. If you would have been willing to pick up here and move on out to San Francisco, Claire and I would have been married! After all, you always wanted to go west."

"Now, ain't ya glad I wouldn't? I told you from the minute she stepped off the train, she was only looking for a free ride to get her to the next destination, which for her was California. Besides, you could tell she was gonna be one big heifer when she got older, and you saw how fast she took up with someone else, as soon as you told her that you were staying here?"

As they stood there in the midday heat they saw two cowboys ride into town and hitch up in front of the Brown Palace Hotel.

RJ nudged Calvin, "Did you notice that neither one of them has a rope tied to their saddles? A telltale sign was the guns they were wearing low on their hips that they ain't cowboys, but gunmen, besides, I recognized one of them as being a wanted man."

"How do you know that?"

"I've been looking at the reward posters that sheriff Barnes has tacked up outside his office." Turning, and looking back towards the Brown Palace, RJ continued, "Remember Micah telling us to memorize something about the person in the picture? Well, I did just that on a man wanted for murder in Ogallala. He had a patch over his left eye just like the fella who just rode into town."

"So, what are you going to do?"

With a strange look on his face, one Calvin had never seen, he said, "I'm going to go over to the sheriff's office to get another look at that poster, and if it is him, then I guess I will go and tell the sheriff, but before I do that, I want to be sure we'll get the reward money."

"Do you think it's smart to do what you're about to do? What makes you so sure that gunman won't pull his pistol and start blasting away?" Then thinking for a moment said, "There were two of them."

RJ looked back at Calvin and beckoned him to follow.

Calvin a couple quick steps put him beside RJ.

When RJ and they reached the sheriff's office, Sheriff Barnes was just coming out of his office.

"Well howdy boys," he said as RJ and Calvin came over to him. "Why, you two look like you're in a god-awful hurry."

"We are Wesley. Two fella's just rode into town and tied up in front of the Brown Palace. I noticed one of them was wearing an eye patch and I'm pretty sure I saw a poster out on him. We were coming over to check him out."

"Let's take a look and see what we have. If he ain't here, I have more in the office."

"I never saw the ones in your office, so I know it has to be here." RJ took the nail out of the posters and started going through them stopping at one that showed a man wearing a black patch over his left eye, just like the man RJ had seen earlier.

"Says right here, that he has a five thousand dollar reward on his head, dead or alive."

Sheriff Barnes studied the poster, then looked at RJ and spoke. "Well, I guess I'll have to go arrest that there no-account murderer. Name's Jasper Watkins. Huh. Ain't never heard of him."

"Slow down there, Wesley. There is a reward on his head and I want a chance to claim it. I saw him first"

Sheriff Barnes looked at him and shook his head. "To claim that there reward money, you have to be the one to take him in and RJ, you don't even wear a gun. As a matter of fact, I ain't never seen you wearing one," he continued shaking his head, "neither does Calvin."

"Just because we don't wear one, don't mean we don't have them and know how to use one." The insinuation by Wesley had a burning effect on Calvin, and he started to speak but Wesley beats him to it.

"Listen here! Read the rest of that reward poster. See there where it says armed and dangerous?"

They read what he was pointing at.

"Why are you even interested?"

Before either of them could answer, Wesley answered his own question. "Easy money, I'll bet. Well, you'd better give them thoughts up before you get yourselves killed." Pointing to the half loaded wagon sitting in front of their office, he said, "Continue loads up your wagon just like you planned and when that wagon train comes through, both you fella's join up and forget about doing any bounty hunting, 'less you want to end up dead."

"What do you think Calvin? It's our reward money only if we bring him in."

So he thought for a minute and said, "Sorry Wesley, but I think I got a plan to bring that outlaw in that won't even require a gun, but I plan on wearing one anyways, just in case."

"Well, if you're bound and determined to do this, I won't stand in your way. But I want you to remember that I warned you against it."

"Noted," RJ said, walking away.

"What's your plan?" queried Calvin.

"Well, I don't think I can just walk in there and put a bullet into the man's back. I know I can't."

Pointing in the direction of the blacksmith shop, he continued with his plan. "Just because I can't shoot a man in the back, doesn't mean I can't bash in his skull with a piece of pipe."

As they walked into the blacksmith shop, he saw what he was looking for and went over to the bench and picked up a piece of pipe about twelve inches long. Holding out his hand, he slapped the pipe into his palm. "Yes'serrr, just what I was looking for." Reaching into his pocket, RJ extracted two small coins and handed them to "Blackie."

"What about me?"

"The way I see it, it's like this. When we walk in and locate them two, I'll walk in a direction that will put me to Watkins back while you circle behind his partner. When you see me bring up the pipe, you pull out your pistol and jam it into his friend's back, warning him against doing anything foolish."

"Do you think there is a reward for his partner?" Calvin rubbed his hands together in an unspoken gesture of greed.

"Won't take long to find that out."

"Let's go get our guns and get going before those boys decide to leave town."

It had been some time since either RJ or Calvin had worn their six guns and both remarked on it as they buckled them around their waists and tied them down.

"I guess we'll have to start wearing these all the time, don't you think?" Calvin, pulled his pistol from its leather holster and twirled it around on his finger before dropping it back into its holster.

"I would imagine it will depend on what we decide to do once we arrive in Deadwood." He had already made up his mind. Having these two ride into town at this time, and one of them wanted, acted as a dry run to see just what it would take to bring a wanted outlaw down.

"I'm glad we have that reward poster so we can claim the reward money right away and the bank has to pay us."

In the early days, if there was a reward on an outlaw, and you wanted to claim it, then you needed to show proof that you had indeed gotten the right person, so to do that you carried a poster on you so that you could get paid immediately, depending on if whether the bank had that much money, or else wait for several weeks as telegrams were sent and answers returned.

"Now I know why Micah said to only go after them that have a reward poster out on them, and to make sure you always carried it on you as proof that you got the right man and that he had a reward on his head." He took another look at the wanted poster before handing it to Calvin to look at. Folding it and tucking it in his pants pocket, he headed for the door.

"What'd' ya say, you ready to go make us some money?"

"You bet! I can almost feel the heat generating from that five thousand dollars burning a hole in my pants pocket."

"Com'on then. Let's not keep those pockets waiting."

It was still hot when they walked outside of their office. The heat hit them like nothing either could remember.

Calvin chuckled, and looking around to see if there were any ladies said, "It's hotter'n a witch's tit."

RJ laughed. "I'll tell you one thing," he ran his hand over his forehead. "I won't miss this heat, witch or no witch."

"Neither will I, although I heard that the Dakota's were just as hot this time of year."

As they walked towards the Brown Palace neither spoke. The only sound was of boots thumping with every step against the boardwalk and the sound of a pipe being slapped against a palm as they walked.

Before entering the Brown Palace, RJ slid the pipe up under the cuff of his shirt sleeve.

The Palace's dining room was almost empty, so it was impossible to enter without being noticed and such was the case now. Both Jasper Watkins and his companion looked up from their food and not sensing any danger went back to eating. Walking right up beside their table as if they were going to sit, RJ let the pipe slide down from his shirt sleeve and into the palm of his hand. Then, with an upward motion that was detected by Jasper a split second too late, he brought the pipe down squarely on the center of his head. At the same moment, Calvin drew his pistol and jammed it into the side of the other gunman who had started to kick himself away from the table, drawing his pistol as he stood.

"Don't do it!" he said in a loud voice as another gut wrenching sound was heard as RJ brought the pipe down again on the wanted man's head.

They weren't prepared to see his head split open, with the force of the pipe hitting the same spot twice. There was a shower of blood, flesh, bone and some brain matter sailing through the air, landing on all three.

"I'll take it from here." Calvin and RJ turned to see Sheriff Barnes beside them with his pistol drawn and pointing at Jasper's companion.

"Looks like you two earned some extra reward money today," Wesley told them, trading places with Calvin and putting his own pistol into the outlaw's side.

"This here fella is known as the *Nebraska Kid* and there's a thousand dollar reward on his head if taken alive." Pointing at the other outlaw, he continued, "He was a dead or alive one."

"I didn't see a poster on him and I went through all there were."

Sheriff Barnes took a folded up poster from his vest pocket and handed it to Calvin.

"I saw these two rides in. I knew that one's face, pointing his pistol toward Watkins, but this one I wasn't as sure of, so I took the poster with me to check him out." Wesley told the Kid to move on out and looked at RJ and Calvin and with a smile on his face told them, "good job."

With six thousand dollars cash money in their pockets, they had a big decision to make.

"Haul freight or hunt down outlaws?" This became the question as they finished packing their wagons and waited for the wagon train that was due in anytime now.

As the day wore on, two more riders came in from the south. These riders were from the wagon train and acted as second scouts and were only a couple miles ahead of the train.

"Well, looks like the waiting will be over in the next hour or two. Any last thoughts before we head on out?"

"Nope. Just anxious to be underway," then looking at RJ, he asked, "You saw how easy it was to make six thousand dollars, and how long it would take hauling freight to make the same amount, so my thoughts are on the future and what direction we should take."

The road to Deadwood would give them their answer

CHAPTER 3

At about five o'clock that evening, the long awaited wagon train entered the Main Street of Denver with much fanfare. Everyone was expecting the wagon train so they had stayed open, hoping that the people in it would spend some money. The boardwalks and streets were packed with the town folk as the thirty fancy, painted wagons made their way into town.

"Wow, would you look at that, what a sight that is," exclaimed Calvin! "I had heard of the Utter Wagons and their fancy paint jobs, but I ain't never seen one."

"That sure is a sight. That long haired blonde fella wearing the fancy buckskins must be Charles Utter."

As they stood and watched, the wagon train continued down Main Street. A large number of women riding in the wagons, as well as walking beside them was noticed by Calvin.

"Well, hot damn, will ya look at all those womenfolk? Why do you suppose there are so many, RJ?"

"Those ain't no ordinary women Calvin," answered RJ. "Look at the way they're dressed."

A big smile came over Calvin's face as he took a closer look at the fancy way the women were dressed. Their bright colors and ruffles stood out. Not to mention their low cut bosoms.

RJ looked at his friend and gave a wink. "Them there women are prostitutes." As he watched the moving train, he noticed a tall, blonde haired lady walking next to one of the wagons carrying an open parasol to shade her face from the sun which was quickly setting.

"Well, I'll be damned," RJ said, seeing someone he obviously knew and pointing in her direction said, "Lookie at the tall blonde. You know who that is, don't you?" he motioned for Calvin to come along, as he started to walk in her direction. The tall blonde looked up to see the two walking toward her and a big smile lit up her face as she recognized them.

"Son-of-a-bitch! Will you lookie there Oliver," she said to the driver of what would be her home until they reached Deadwood. Folding up her parasol and handing it up to Oliver, she turned and rushed into the welcoming arms of both RJ and Calvin.

As they hugged, RJ spoke up, "Hannah, what the hell are you doing out here?" There was a hint of surprise in his voice as he stepped back a step so he could look up into Hannah's face. Hannah had the nickname of "Too Tall Hannah" because she stood well over six feet three, which made her tower over just about anyone she stood next to, and RJ and Calvin were no exceptions.

"Where is that good looking fella you left with who was going to San Francisco?" asked Calvin.

"He took me to San Francisco alright, but three days after arriving there, he went and got himself shot in a poker game, leaving me penniless and no place to live. So I sold the wagon and team and had enough to rent a room for two weeks." Hannah stopped with tears in her eyes.

"It didn't take me more than a couple of days trying to find suitable work before I came to the conclusion there was only one thing that I could do, and there were plenty of men folk willing to pay top dollar for a tumble with 'Too Tall Hannah'." She chuckled as she continued on with her story.

"The money was good and, before long, I found myself able to buy one of the many saloons in San Francisco and hired several girls to dance and take care of the men. Within six months I had several rooms added on where the girls not only serviced the men folk but also called home. Oliver, here, was my bouncer and protector." She reached up and gave Oliver a pat on the leg. He gave her a big grin and a tip of his hat.

"What are you doing out here if you had such a good business going in California?" Before she could answer, a beautiful, blue-eyed blond stuck her head out of the opening in the wagon's cover and with help from Oliver climbed over the wagon's seat. Continuing, she stepped on the wagon wheel and Calvin extended a hand and helped her down to the ground.

"Let me introduce you both to Cora Hawkins." Cora extended her hand and they removed their hats and shook Cora's hand.

"Here comes Charlie." Oliver told them seeing Charlie riding up to their wagon.

"I hope you are securing a warm welcome for us," Charlie remarked to Hannah as he got down from his mount and faced RJ.

"My name is Charlie Utter," he said, extending his hand. "More folk know me by Colorado Charlie."

It was true. One couldn't live in or around Denver without having heard of Colorado Charlie.

"I'm RJ Murdock and my partner here is Calvin McCoy." They shook hands and Charlie said, "Did a couple of riders come by and inform you that we were going to be passing through on our way to Deadwood, South Dakota?"

"They sure did. That's why all the businesses are still open and the townsfolk are ready to serve you and your wagon train."

"Much obliged. We only want to replenish some supplies before moving on out. Shouldn't take more than a day or two."

As Charlie turned to leave, RJ spoke up, "Me and Calvin here, want to join up with your wagon train, and there are a couple of other fellas who also want to join up."

"The price is two hundred and fifty dollars a person. With that comes my guarantee that you will reach Deadwood safe and sound."

"That sounds reasonable," said RJ, turning to Calvin and giving him a thumbs up.

As he mounted his horse Charlie said, "I'll see you two before we pull out and you can anti up the money." As he rode away, he turned and said, "tell those other friends the price is two hundred and fifty dollars." With that, he spurred his mount in the direction of the rooming house where he could enjoy a nice hot bath.

"You two are coming along to Deadwood?" a surprised Hannah exclaimed!

"We've been giving it some thought when we heard about the wagon train passing through. Business here has been all but non-existent, and besides, once in Deadwood we might join up with another guy we had met during the war, a bounty hunter who we heard just might be in Deadwood."

"Bounty hunter, in Deadwood?" Cora asked, looking quickly over at Hannah.

"Cora went out with a bounty hunter on and off for about five years. He had built up quite a reputation for himself as a, 'Bring 'em in dead, not alive' bounty hunter. Some say he's mad.

As a matter of fact, he earned the nickname 'Mad Man Micah'."

"That's the same person we are talking about!"

"Well, as Cora said, she went with him for some time and can attest to his nickname. Besides, he would have to be mad showing his face in Deadwood. There is an unwritten bounty on his head. If you heard he was headed for Deadwood, don't be surprised that when you get there you learn that he's pushing up daisies. Don't mention what you're heading to Deadwood for to anyone on this wagon train, or you just might not reach there." He saw how seriously she looked at him.

"We'll make it a point not to mention that to anyone." he told her.

"You will get nothing but dead," warned Cora, first looking at Calvin then up at Oliver.

Oliver spoke up, "Listen to what you two are hearing. Deadwood is not a kindly city to lawmen, rangers, or bounty hunters. They don't even have the law there. It's every man for himself." Looking at Cora and Hannah, Oliver continued. "I have tried to talk these two out of going to Deadwood, but my words fell on deaf ears. Look around at all the women on this wagon train. Do you see anyone as good looking as these two? No, of course you don't. There will be lots of gun fights over them, take my word for that."

"Oliver, just what do you think our lives would be like back in San Francisco?" asked Hannah. "You yourself mentioned every day how much younger the girls were getting, along with how pretty they had become. Sure, we had a nice business going, but that was quickly coming to an end." Looking over at RJ she continued. "I've spoken to several of the women on this wagon train and several will be joining Cora and myself once we arrive in Deadwood."

RJ reached over and slapped Calvin on the shoulder and said. "Well, we'd best get the rest of our things loaded up so that when Charlie wants to pull out we'll be ready." Turning and giving Hannah a big hug, she gave him a kiss on the cheek. They excused themselves and headed back to their office.

"Let's go track down Tom and Hank and tell them they need to come up with five hundred dollars if they're wanting to join up with Charlie's wagon train."

Over the next day, the wagon train folks bought out just about all the town's supplies as they re-stocked their wagons and got ready for the remainder of the trip to Deadwood. RJ and Calvin took Hannah and Cora to supper that night, where they learned more about their bounty hunting friend Micah and their plans to open a Pleasure Palace along with a saloon.

"Are you two sure about what you are doing?" asked RJ, as they sat around the table sipping hot coffee and finishing off an apple pie.

"We've heard all the stories about Deadwood and how unlawful it is there, but that is where the money is to be made."

"You've seen the ladies on your wagon train. Most are younger than twenty five and you look to be forty and still beautiful."

"Listen, I know what I want and that's that. End of discussion. Cora and I are big girls and we don't need or ask anything from either of you two."

Cora spoke up. "Both of us have given this move a lot of thought." Before she said anything more, she looked over at Hannah for her approval before continuing. "Hannah and I have bounties on our heads. You would find that out sooner or later, so we are telling you up front, even knowing that you might take up with Micah and his profession as bounty hunters."

"I killed a man," confessed Hannah. They looked surprised.

"And I killed his brother, when he attempted to kill Hannah."

A sledge hammer blow to the midsection couldn't have been worse than what RJ and Calvin just learned. There was dead silence.

"I don't understand. Why haven't I seen any wanted posters out on you two?"

"Well, if they haven't hit here yet, there sure as hell won't be any in Deadwood," Cora said.

"Your bounty hunting friend, Micah, doesn't worry either of us. As we said earlier, bounty hunters are not in good standing in Deadwood, so I wouldn't mention the word bounty hunter on this wagon train or once you get to Deadwood if you want to stay alive."

"Cora! Tell these two how Micah finds and collects on his bounties."

"As I told you, I went out with Micah for some time and in the course of our conversations he told me his profession and how easy it was to collect the bounty seeing he never 'captured' one, but always brought him in dead." Cora continued, "Most of the time, Micah would find his man then wait 'til he saw him leave town and would follow him for some time 'til they were out of gunshot range from the town. Sometimes he would just ride up to the wanted person and, without warning, pull his pistol and blast away. Sometimes he would track him 'til he stopped and then stalked him 'til he was close enough to get a good enough shot at him. You see, he won't try anything in Deadwood, if he finds someone with a price on his head, he'll just wait 'til the time is right."

RJ and Calvin listened intently as Cora told of her knowledge of Micah.

Hannah interrupted Cora as she told everyone she was calling it a night. Cora was also leaving.

RJ and Calvin stood and offered to walk them back to their wagon. Hannah puts her arm in RJ's and they walked from the dining room out onto the street. The street was lit up with the many campfires that were blazing, and the night had a buzz about it as the wagon folks were still in the process of purchasing goods and some of the women were talking to some of the town's single cowboys in hopes of maybe making a couple of dollars.

"Well RJ, it sure was a surprise running into you here, and knowing you'll also be joining the wagon train."

As they reached Hannah's wagon, she whispered into his ear while giving him a kiss. "That man I killed was the brother of the local judge." Looking over at Cora she continued, "The brother of the man I killed, whom Cora killed, was the Judge himself." Seeing his shocked expression, she continued, "There's a twenty thousand dollar bounty on us." As she spoke, RJ felt the barrel of a small handgun being jammed into his ribs and heard the double click of it being cocked. In the same instant, Cora jammed her own pistol into Calvin's ribs.

"What's it going to be guys?" she asked, applying a little more pressure to her gun.

"Looks to be, that you two ladies are holding all the cards here. What is it that you want from us?"

"We want your word that you won't be gunning out for us once we let you walk away from here."

"All we want is a chance to make a new life for ourselves," said Cora, looking over at Hannah to receive some confirmation from her. Hannah gave her a slight nod, so Cora took the pistol out of Calvin's side.

"Hannah was raped so viciously by Emmett Davis, that she miscarried their son. That's right, you heard me correctly, their son. Emmett was a low down drunkard, but for some reason, Hannah fell in love with him and all was ok until Hannah told him she was going to have his baby. Then the drinking got worse and the beatings began."

"Emmett came over one night, after drinking all day with his friends, and demanded that I service him and his friends. When I refused, he beat me and stripped me naked and then he raped me and also let his friends do it. I lost the baby boy that same night."

RJ reached out and took Hannah into his arms as she started to cry, telling of that night as if it had just happened.

The evening suddenly seemed very quiet as the four stood together.

Cora interrupted the silence. "Two days later, Hannah shot Emmett when she found him passed out on the floor of her bedroom having kicked in the door thinking she was there."

"They arrested Hannah and knowing she wouldn't get any kind of a fair trial because the judge was Emmett's brother, I decided that the judge had to die too, so I went to his house, and when he answered the door, put two bullets in his chest and broke Hannah out of jail."

Calvin and RJ were silent as they listened to Cora tell her story. Hannah had stopped crying and was silent as RJ held her. Finally RJ said, "So, you figure Deadwood will be a safe haven for you both?"

"Well, there is no law there and no one will know us." Cora told them, as she put her arms around her dear friend.

The sounds of the night's action slowly came back.

"You two ladies have nothing to fear from either of us."

Again, Hannah gave RJ a kiss on the cheek and gave him a loving smile.

RJ once again reassured them that they had nothing to fear from either of them as he turned away from her and motioned for Calvin to follow.

As they left Hannah and Cora, they walked off in silence, having thoughts of Deadwood, and wondered just what the hell they would find there.

They were awakened next morning by a loud rapping on the door of their office. Opening the door, RJ was confronted by Hannah, who carried a coffee pot full of hot coffee she pushed past him and entered. Spying a cup on his desk, she picked it up and seeing it clean poured it full. The steam sent a warming aroma into the air. An aroma picked up on by Calvin.

"What's that delightful smell, I'm smelling?" came a voice from the back room.

"Hannah is here with a pot of hot coffee she just made for us."

Walking from the back room, Calvin appeared, combing his wild looking hair with his fingers, and scratching his belly through his undershirt. In his hand he carried his own cup and holding it out, Hanna poured it full.

"Where is Cora this morning?" he asked, taking a sip from his cup, then looking towards RJ he smacked his lips in approval to the flavor of the coffee.

"She went, to the mercantile to pick up a few items we're needing."

"Charles says we'll stay here for another day." There would be one or two more stops before they reached Deadwood where they could purchase more supplies.

Nine o'clock the following morning Main Street, Denver was once again crowded with people and wagons. Charles had decided they were ready to pull out, and as the word was passed around, everyone was excited. Teams of horses were hitched up to the wagons with much fanfare. As the lead team became ready, it was moved to the end of the street and all the rest would line up behind it. Last minute sales were done and the items packed into the wagons.

Calvin and RJ moved their wagon to the end of the wagon train, followed by Tom and Hank's wagon. As the wagons rolled out of town, RJ and Calvin waved goodbye to friends who had gathered to be a part of the excitement.

RJ, looking at all the wagons and listening to all of the gaiety in the air, turned to Calvin and said, "We're in for a mighty fun trip. Yes, sir, a mighty fun trip."

CHAPTER 4

Everyone on the wagon train was in great spirits as they slowly pulled out of town. Young boys and adults stood on the boardwalk waving as the wagons passed by and yelling their goodbyes.

The hot morning air was filled with the sound of a piano playing a ragtime number and some of the women started dancing around their wagons as they continued their movement out of town.

Soon, the town disappeared from view, the music stopped and the only sounds heard were those of the horse's hooves on the trail and the creaking of the wagons.

It didn't take long for Calvin and RJ to realize that the back of the wagon train wasn't where they wanted to be. The dust that was kicked up in the air was stifling. Even the bandanas they'd wrapped around their faces, didn't keep out the fine dust and the smell of horse manure.

RJ stopped his team and turned and motioned for Tom and Hank to do the same. Pulling the bandana from his face, he spoke up.

"Let's hold back a little and let the wagon dust settle."

"I'm for that," said Tom jumping from the wagon and walking up to his team, he took his bandana and cleaned off his horse's face and eyes.

RJ, took a sip from his canteen, swished it around in his mouth and spit it out onto the dry ground. He poured some of the water over his hot head, then using his hat as a bowl, poured water into it so he could dunk his bandana in it to also wipe his horse's eyes.

"Go easy on that water RJ. Don't know where we will find more out here."

"No worry there, Calvin." It was Tom who spoke. "We have a full water barrel."

With a grin on his face Calvin looked at RJ and asked. "Why didn't you think about a water barrel, RJ?" Not to be out-done RJ simply said in a low voice. "Who do you suppose told Tom there to bring along one?" Tom and Hank were heard snickering as they finished up.

A short time later they saw a lone horseman riding towards them. It turned out to be Colorado Charlie. As he approached RJ, he tipped his hat and asked them if they were okay?

"Yep, we're ok. We were just eating a lot of trail dust all them wagons were kicking up and decided to hold back some."

"Well, just to be on the safe side, I'll send one of my men back to ride with you."

"Do you think that's necessary?"

"It's not that there is any danger out here, but if you should break an axle or have a horse drop dead it wouldn't take long before you would be left way behind."

"Well, Charlie, whatever you think is ok by us."

"You have paid for me to deliver you safe and sound to Deadwood. Just gonna make sure you get your money's worth."

Charlie turned and said, "The guy I'm sending back his name is Dutch, known as Four-Eyed Campbell to some."

"*Four Eyes?*" Calvin asked, but Charlie had already had ridden away.

"That name means he wears spectacles," RJ said then paused. Reaching up and scratching the overgrown hair on his chin, he repeated the name. "Dutch Four Eyes Campbell."

Calvin asked if he thought he knew him, or had heard of him.

"I saw a poster on him in the sheriff's office before we left town."

"Well, what do you plan on doing about that?" There was excitement in Calvin's voice.

"Well, Calvin, right now I'm going to have to formulate a plan that will give us the chance to get Dutch and to know about the price on his head and to be able to collect it without drawing attention to ourselves in the process."

"I don't see how we are going to pull that off without someone asking questions, do you?"

"Don't you go fretting yourself none, just leave all the details to me and you will see how smooth this is going to work out."

"You heard what we were told about there being no law in Deadwood, so what good will it do us if we can't claim the reward money?" Calvin had a good point and RJ listened to him as he continued to speak.

Pointing towards Tom and Hank, Calvin indicated they would be witness to anything they came up with.

"You know Tom and Hank as well as I do! Tell them there are a few bucks involved and they would crawl across a hog pen for it."

"What are you thinking?"

"I'm thinking they must be pretty much broke with the monies they've had to pay out so I'm gonna offer them each a couple hundred dollars to go along with whatever I ask them to."

"How much of a reward is on his head?"

"I'm pretty sure it was ten thousand dollars."

"Phew!" was the only response that Calvin was able to give after hearing how much of a reward was going to be paid out.

"Are you sure about that amount?" As he stood waiting for an answer, his mind was thinking of all the things he could buy with all that reward money.

They saw the dust rising in the air from far off before they could see the figure on horseback.

"I need to speak with Tom and Hank before Dutch arrives." Pointing to the cloud of dust, which looked to be maybe a half a mile off.

He turned and motioned to Tom and Hank to come here.

"What's up RJ?"

"We don't have much time, so I'll make this quick. You boys interested in making some money?"

"Hell yeah!" Came the reply from both them. "What do we have to do to earn that?" They had excited looks on their faces and that trailed over into their voices.

"In a few minutes, an outlaw will be riding up to stay back with us. He is one of Colorado Charlie's men and there is a reward on his head that I am willing to split with both of you. In return, I need you both to just act like you know nothing, simple as that."

Tom took off his hat and ran his fingers through his thick crop of jet black hair.

"How much money are you talking about here?"

Before answering, RJ decided that this one time he was willing to split the reward evenly between the four. Therefore, all of them would receive, $2500.00 each. Seeing the look on both their faces when he told them the total monies they each would receive, it was all he could do to quiet them down.

"Listen to me, you two! Between here and Cheyenne, Wyoming I will be taking care of Dutch."

"You gonna kill him?" asked Tom rubbing his two hands together as he listened to RJ confirming the fact that he would indeed be killing Dutch.

"God dang it! You're talking Bounty Hunting here, ain't you RJ?" Thinking back to some time ago, Hank remembered meeting RJ's and Calvin's friend Micah who rode into town on the trail of some murderer he had been tracking for six months.

"You've got a good memory, Hank." RJ wondered how he could use Hank in the future hearing him talk about Micah whom he had only met once.

"We'll get into more detail later on, but for now, all I need from you two is what I just asked from you two, your silence."

A few more minutes went by before Dutch arrived. RJ took close notice of the size of the man. Both man and horse were coated with the brownish-gray dust that the horse kicked up from the dry trail.

Without getting down from his mount, Dutch introduced himself, "My name is Dutch, Dutch Campbell."

"Folks around have the bad habit of calling me by the name Four-Eyes." Looking at the four through his spectacles, he continued, "I have been known to shoot a man for that mistake." Reaching into his vest pocket he removed a folded up piece of paper and slowly unfolded it. Once he had done that, he handed it to RJ who took it and saw that it was a wanted poster with a picture of Dutch on it along with the words: Wanted Dead or Alive. Ten Thousand Dollars.

Calvin, who had been standing beside RJ, read it loudly so that Tom and Hank could also hear. "Ten thousand dollars sure is a lot of money," Calvin said, looking over at Tom and Hank, standing there vigorously bobbing their heads up and down in agreement. RJ secretly smiled to himself at how funny they appeared.

Suddenly, in the next heartbeat, any plans that RJ had put together went up in smoke as Dutch, with lightning speed, whipped out his side arm and hit Calvin right in the temple. Everyone standing there heard the sickening sound as Dutch's pistol smashed into the side of Calvin's head, knocking him out cold. Instantly, Dutch turned towards RJ and cocked his pistol, to cover himself if RJ had made any move to draw his own weapon. "Any more remarks?"

Tom and Hank started to move forward to help the injured Calvin, who had fallen in a heap on the ground and wasn't moving.

"What the hell did you do that for?" RJ yelled at Dutch, who now had his gun cocked and pointing at him. "Put that gun away."

Carefully, he pushed Dutch's hand to one side.

"Just wanted you boys to know who's boss here." Pointing at Tom, Dutch continued, "And that one had a smirk on his face I didn't like one bit."

You don't know it right now, Dutch, but your time alive is quickly coming to an end. Who knows, you might not even see the sun rise in the morning. With that knowledge, RJ's face lit up. Dutch once again pointed his pistol at RJ. "Did I say something funny, RJ?"

RJ just shook his head and stepped towards his buddy who still lay on the ground with Tom and Hank standing over him.

"We need to get going," said Dutch, dropping his pistol back into the fancy leather holster. "You boys pick him up off the ground and put him in the back of the wagon." There was a harsh commanding tone to his voice that RJ picked up on.

RJ headed to the back of his wagon to prepare a bed of sorts for Calvin to be laid on. As he did, he saw the length of pipe that he had used to bash in the skull of Jasper Watkins and right then he made the decision that is how he would take care of old *Four Eyes. In his mind's eye, he pictured those spectacles hanging down lopsided from eyes that were dangling out of a cracked open head.*

Now that Calvin was laid in the wagon, everyone was ready to continue the journey. Dutch rode beside the wagon. RJ noticed the relaxed state he was in and decided to make some light conversation with him to kill some time.

"You look like you're molded to that there horse Dutch."

From the saddle, Dutch looked over at RJ, spit out a long stream of tobacco juice before he answered. "I learned to ride a horse before I could walk. My uncle Ted would have me out in the corral at sunup with a little pony named Blue" Dutch stopped speaking for a moment as he searched his memories to bring up stories of his youth.

"You know that a pony has to be broke just like a full grown horse, don't ya?"

"I guess I had never thought much about that."

"Well, they do. Uncle Ted would lift me up and set me down on the saddle. Once he saw that I was gripping the reins and having my boots shoved into the stirrups all the way, he would step away and at the same time give Blue a slap on the ass."

"That must have been a sight to see," chuckled RJ as he pictured what Dutch was saying.

"That's how I learned to ride, and now it seems like that's all I do. Don't mind it much no more, but I think this will be my last time riding any sort of distance."

Gonna be your last time for that and everything else. RJ thought as he looked at Dutch knowing that when the time seemed right, he was going to kill him. RJ knew that Fort Collins was coming up pretty soon and after that, Cheyenne, Wyoming. Having talked to Calvin earlier, they decided that Cheyenne would be the end of the line for Dutch.

"Cheyenne's banks should easily have ten thousand dollars to pay out, compared to a military base such as Fort Collins," RJ had told Calvin, "besides, there will be more opportunities in Cheyenne to turn in a dead Dutch without creating a big fanfare".

Their plan was pretty simple. When he had a chance he would haul out the pipe and bash in his skull. Dutch had ridden ahead of them, and this gave them time to plan on how everything was going to work out to give him the opportunity to kill Dutch.

"When Dutch comes back and is riding next to our wagon close enough for me to reach him, I want you, Tom, to start some sort of ruckus so Dutch will stop and turn towards you. When he does, he should be close enough to me that I will be able to hit him over the head by standing up in our wagon."

"Why don't you just shoot him?" asked Hank.

"A gunshot would easily be heard and then someone from the wagon train would be back here, pronto." Then, after a moment he spoke, "I guess that wouldn't matter much, we could say he got into an argument and he went for his gun and one of us shot him."

"Well, I know I can't outdraw him," said Hank.

"Neither can I," repeated Tom.

"I'll shoot the bastard!" came Calvin's voice from the wagon bed where he was laid.

Everyone turned in his direction as he started to sit up. Tom climbed over the wagon's seat, and with his arms around Calvin's chest hoisted him into a sitting position.

"Well, well, well. Will you look who finally woke up! Did you have a nice nap?"

"I wasn't sleeping, and you know it," came a sharp reply from Calvin, who had placed his handkerchief over the wound on the side of his head, and removing it, found that the bleeding had stopped.

"Help me out of this wagon, Tom." He motioned Tom to give him a hand. As his legs hit the dirt he suddenly found himself falling and Tom wasn't prepared to catch him so he fell to the ground.

Hank was next to them in a heartbeat, reaching down to give Calvin a hand along with Tom's.

"I can't feel my left leg," Calvin told them as they stood him up.

Hank had his arm around his waist and let him put his right arm over his shoulder and around his neck. He tried to take a step and discovered that he had no feeling in his leg and was unable to move it at all.

As they looked on, they first saw Calvin's eyes, then his whole face take on the appearance of a crazy man, and with a mighty scream he pushed Hank away and lunged forward, which, of course not being able to move his left leg, found himself quickly headed for the ground. All three watched as

Calvin started rolling around on the ground screaming like a little kid who just received a bare bottom whupping from his old man.

Calvin's screaming was heard by Dutch who came riding up and dismounted. Tying his reins around one of the wagon wheels, he walked over to where Calvin laid on the ground rolling around and screaming. He stood next to Hank.

Spitting out a stream of tobacco juice that landed dangerously close to Calvin, Dutch crouched down and just stared at him. RJ saw this as a perfect opportunity and slowly stepped back to his wagon where he reached over the sideboard next to the wagon's seat and felt for the pipe, which he had stuck between the floorboard and the seat. Having secured it, he slowly brought it up and held it behind his back as he started moving in the direction of where Dutch was still crouched down, staring at Calvin, who continued rolling about on the ground screaming and kicking up a cloud of dust.

RJ was hoping that Calvin didn't stop screaming 'til he had completed his mission of bashing in Dutch's skulls. Two more steps and he would be where he needed to be. One more step and RJ had started to raise the pipe above his head. At the very moment, RJ started to swing the pipe towards the back of Dutch's head, he caught Tom looking directly at him. This eye contact was picked up by Dutch, who turned his head sideways to look up. The pipe which was intended to bash in the back of Dutch's skull, now caught him flush between his right eye and ear. With lightning speed, RJ had lifted up the pipe and brought it down again and again onto Dutch's head.

RJ didn't know what, but something inside his head kept his hand swinging the pipe, and it wasn't 'til Tom reached up and caught his hand in a downward swing, was he able to stop.

"Enough!" barked Tom. "We need him recognizable if we want to collect that reward money."

"I'm okay," RJ told him pulling his arm free of Tom's grasp. Calvin had stopped his screaming and having crawled over to where Dutch lay on the ground, had reached into the grapping hole in the side of Dutch's head and had scooped out some of the gray brain matter. It took all three a minute to realize what Calvin was about to do. Before they reached him, he had put some of the brain into his mouth.

"No," shouted RJ grabbing Calvin's hand and removing it from his mouth, but not before he was able to eat some of the brains that were once inside Dutch's head.

RJ gagged.

"Who are you?" That question took him back as he looked into the eyes of his friend.

"It's me Calvin, RJ. Don't tell me you don't know who I am?"

"Of course I know who you are, RJ." Having said that, RJ smiled at his best bud as he put his arm under his and stood him up with the help from Tom.

"Is your left leg still not working?"

"I feel it coming back to life. Just feels like it is waking up. Got pins and needles." Looking down at his foot, Calvin was able to pick it up and shook it. "See that?"

"You took quite a hit to your temple from Dutch's pistol. For a little while there we weren't sure if you were going to come around or not."

As he finished talking, all three jumped at the sudden howl that came from his mouth.

"What's the matter with you guys?" he asked, completely unaware of what he had just done.

"You mean you don't know what you just did?" Tom looked at RJ and then at Hank in disbelief.

"What are you talking about?" asked Calvin looking at RJ but questioning Tom.

"Let's talk about it later, for now let's get Dutch in the back of your wagon. What about you Calvin, feel up to riding in the seat or do you want to lie down for a while?"

"I feel okay to ride in the seat with you. I need to get this leg woke up."

"Well, let me help you up there and then we'll get under way."

Within five minutes they were rolling.

"Do you think Charlie will be riding back here or having someone else ride back here checking up on us?"

"With your injuries we will say that the two of you got into a fight and Dutch lost."

"There is no way in hell that Charlie will ever believe that," and pausing for a second to gather his thoughts, he continued, "Especially once he sees the damage you did to his head with your skull buster."

"I guess I got a little carried away there, didn't I?"

"Yep! You might say that."

"I don't know what came over me. Once the first blow struck and I knew that I had to hit him again, I lost all ability to stop on my own."

"Good thing Tom stepped in and grabbed your arm when he did or else Old Dutch there might not have had a head and that would have been a little hard to explain. How would we be able to claim that ten thousand dollar reward?"

"We'll be in Cheyenne the day after tomorrow and that reward money will be ours, don't you worry about that none."

"Not worried about that, but you have to be thinking about that much money that will soon be in our pockets."

"We don't want to make a big show in Cheyenne when we get there. I think we need to keep Dutch covered up and ride right for the livery stable where we'll leave the wagon and go fetch the sheriff and bring him to the body instead of the other way around."

"Let's tell Tom and Hank our plans and have them fetch the sheriff."

"That's a good plan, Calvin. That will keep us from having to expose ourselves to anyone."

All RJ and Calvin were hoping for was that Charlie wouldn't come riding back or send anyone back to check up on them.

As the sun started to set, RJ turned to Tom and Hank and motioned that they were planning on stopping.

The evening sky was starting to turn into a blanket of reds, yellows, pinks and the deepest blue-purple that RJ had ever seen and he was lost in looking at its beauty.

"Will you look at that sky?" He said out-loud and directed to no one in particular. Looking around at the landscape, he saw it to start to take on the majestic colors of the sky.

RJ's thoughts were suddenly interrupted by a very loud. . . . "Ooouuuuu, Ouuuuoooo, Ooouuuuu," sounding in his right ear.

Chapter 5

RJ jumped from the wagon seat when Calvin did his wolf howl, scaring the crap out of him. A loud oomph escaped his lips when he landed on the ground rump first, then choking on the dust from the large dust cloud he created. The next sound he heard was the loud laughing and hand clapping coming from Tom and Hank, who had witnessed Calvin's sudden wolf call and RJ's reaction

"What in the hell are you doing down there on the ground?" Calvin asked, looking down on RJ who sat there surrounded by the dust cloud. He looked up at Calvin through the dust and was about to give him a piece of his mind until he saw his face and realized he didn't have a clue as to what just happened.

Hank jumped down from their wagon and extended his hand to RJ. As he reached up for it, he could see that Hank was trying very hard to wipe his grin from his face, but was doing a poor job of it.

"Oomph!" RJ groaned as he was pulled to his feet and at once felt the pain in his rump which he grabbed with both hands and rubbed vigorously, an action which caused more dust.

"Want me to rub yer ass for ya?" Hank laughed, extending his hand in a motion of dusting off RJ's butt.

"Git outta here you fool," RJ yelled, knocking his hand away.

"Here's your hat." Hank said, bending down and picking it up off the dusty trail and giving it a slap or two to clear the dust off it. Taking his hat, RJ looked, first at Calvin then back to Hank and slowly shook his head from side to side before replacing his hat.

"He doesn't have a clue as to what just happened, does he?" His question didn't need an answer. It was obvious that there was something wrong going on inside Calvin's head.

"No, it would appear not." Hank answered as he looked up at Calvin who just stared down at them.

"I think that when Dutch hit him in the head with his pistol, it had some effect on his brain." RJ looks up at his friend, knew that he needed some sort of medical attention.

"When we get to Cheyenne, if there's a doctor there, I'm gonna have him look at his head wound." RJ reached up his hand for Calvin to grasp and as Calvin was pulling him up, he let go and RJ was once again sitting in the dust.

"What the hell did you do that for Calvin?"

"What?"

"You just let go of my hand."

"I did not."

"Oh my God," RJ bowed his head for a moment.

He sat there for a moment, wondering if his friend would ever be the same. Hank came over and helped RJ to his feet

"Whenever you're done playing your little jumping off the wagon game, we can get going." Once again RJ simply shook his head as he stepped onto one of the wagon wheel's spoke and pulled himself up onto the seat.

The day had turned into dusk and RJ motioned they were ready to call it a day and stop for the night, he wanted to light a campfire and boil some water for a nice cup of coffee and maybe make a tin of biscuits.

"How's your ass?" were the first words Hank said as he walked up to their wagon and helped RJ take a granny sack from the side compartment.

"I'm glad that it didn't happen earlier in the day or I would have had to sit longer." He reached back once again and rubbed his rear end. "And don't you dare make another offer to rub it either." Both RJ and Hank gave off a little laugh.

The evening air was soon filled with the smell of burning wood and the aroma of boiling coffee. Tom had made the biscuit dough and set the pan on the outer rim of the fire on a bed of the coals that he had pulled out from the fire.

It's dark enough now that there won't be no one coming back to check up on us. This thought brought relief to RJ as he sat looking into the fire and sipping on his coffee.

"You really don't know what happened today Calvin?" asked Tom.

"I told you Tom, that I don't remember a thing other than RJ jumping from the wagon." Calvin once again closed his eyes and tried to picture what had transpired that caused RJ to jump from the wagon, but once again his mind was blank.

"Catch, Calvin."

Calvin heard the word and looked up just in time to see a flying biscuit go past him. He just watched it go sailing by and landing in the dirt.

"Calvin why didn't you get that biscuit? I yelled catch."

"I did see it. See?" and he held out his hand with an imaginary biscuit in it.

"Oh Gawd, Calvin." RJ shook his head and walked back to where the wayward biscuit landed. Picking it up, RJ brushed the dust from it and took a bite.

Another flying biscuit was caught by Calvin this time.

"I have a little surprise for you boys," RJ said, getting up from the ground and going to the wagon. He opened up the side box and came up with a small metal can. Before sitting back down, he handed the tin to Hank, who removed the lid to discover the tin was filled with strawberry jam. Hank got himself a biscuit and spooned out some of the jam, then passed the tin to Tom, who took some before passing it on over to RJ. Calvin just sat there looking straight ahead. RJ puts jam on the biscuit in

Calvin's hand. "Eat it, Calvin."

"Okay."

"Tell us some about this bounty hunting stuff," Tom asked before taking a bite of his jam coated biscuit.

"Don't know much about it, other than what I was told by a guy I met during the war. His name was Micah and before he joined up, he was a bounty hunter. Sometimes at night sitting around the campfire, just like now, he would start telling us about some of the wanted men he had tracked down and brought them in for the reward money that was being paid for their capture alive, or for their bodies."

"I don't understand why someone would pay out money for a dead body, unless they wanted to be rid of him and were willing to pay money for it, but why would they want him alive. I could see paying to find someone and get back whatever he stole."

"That's just it. The wanted person wasn't always wanted for stealing something, but also for killing someone, or raping a woman."

"What was Dutch wanted for?"

"A little bit of everything vile, that's why the reward money was so high."

"What's your interest in knowing about bounty hunting? Are you planning on becoming one?"

"Who knows?" Tom said, looking over at Hank and shrugging his shoulders. "I just saw how easy it was to make twenty five hundred dollars, and how much freight would have to be hauled to make that same amount."

"You have to remember one thing!"

"What's that?"

"A freight wagon don't shoot back at ya."

"I didn't see no shooting here today!"

"This was a lucky day. Everything happened the way we planned it. Dutch even showed us the poster. He never believed we would do anything about it, until it wasn't always be that easy."

Calvin perked up and said, "Why don't you tell them some of the stories Micah used to tell us when we could have a fire and didn't have to worry about being attacked by the Union army."

"Let's hear some." There was excitement in Hank's voice, and RJ could see already, that he might have made a mistake getting Tom and Hank involved.

"Sitting around the campfire one night, Micah stood up and opened his shirt and pointed at two round scars. One just over his left nipple and one in the left side of his stomach. He turned around, showing us his back. We all expected to see where the lead shot had exited. To our surprise there were none."

"You mean that he still has those bullets in him?"

"Well, he told us he did." RJ rubbed his head trying hard to remember. "I remember him, saying that he was ambushed while he was on the trail of an outlaw wanted for a bank robbery where two female customers were shot. One of them died of her wounds. Do you remember what he told us his name was, Calvin?"

"Sure do. His name was Johnny "Big Ears" Howard. He was reported to have the biggest ears anyone had ever seen." Laughing a little, Calvin looked around the campfire and cupping his hands behind his own ears puffed them out, which made his head look deformed so everyone started laughing. "Just like a donkey." Calvin made a heeee haaaaw sound. After a minute or so, RJ continued his story.

"There was a Twenty-five thousand dollar reward on his head and on the wanted poster, it was stated more 'dead than alive. The woman who died was the bank president's only daughter who was married with two little ones. He had put up the reward money himself and had no qualms about the 'dead' part."

"Twenty-five thousand dollars is one hell of a lot of money for any one man to have, much less to offer it to anyone who killed that bank robber-murderer."

"Twenty-five thousand dollars is a lot of money Tom. That's why I've been doing a considerable lot of thinking about giving up freight hauling and to try this bounty hunting thing. Dutch, there, is the third wanted man that we will collect a reward for and in all three cases, didn't have to even fire a shot."

"Well, let's hear some more of the story you were telling. Sounds to me that it can also be dangerous, if not deadly." Hank had been taking it all in and was starting to get interested and maybe also to becoming a bounty hunter if it was something Tom also wanted to do.

"Okay. Where was I? Oh yeah, I remember now. Micah said that he easily picked up Johnny's trail solely on the fact of his huge ears, and even though in most cases, a month or so had passed, and although he had his picture on a poster, he hadn't had to show it to anyone. As soon as he mentioned his ears everyone seemed to remember them." he paused for a moment to take a sip of his coffee and then to refill his cup.

"I'm pretty sure it was in Abilene, Kansas that Micah said he finally caught up to Johnny. He had been in Abilene before on a number of occasions when tracking someone, so he was known by a few of the town's people, especially the bartenders. As soon as he pushed open them Swingin' doors and stepped inside, he came face to face with the big eared Johnny, who paid no attention to him other than to look him up and down before

turning back to his beer on the bar."

"What happened next?" Hank couldn't hide the excitement in his voice as he listened to RJ tell his story.

"Let's see, Micah thought that he was safe and he would be able to get Johnny later on until the bartender looked up and said, 'Hey there bounty hunter!' Micah said that in a split second, upon hearing himself being called bounty hunter, all he could remember was, seeing out of the corner of his eye, the glass mug that Johnny had in his hand as it landed against the side of his head. At the same time, he had drawn his pistol and jammed it into his stomach and pulled the trigger. As he stood there, he watched as the room grew darker and his legs became weaker, than the feeling of falling. His ears picking up the popping sound of another shot before feeling the sting as the lead entered his chest."

RJ looked around the campfire and realized how much he enjoyed sitting there and telling a story.

"Remember all the stories we used to tell, Calvin, just like we're doing now?"

"I sure do. Seems like a long time ago, though." Calvin appeared to be back to his normal self.

"This brings back memories for me too," said Tom. "Our Pappy would build a campfire in the back yard, Momma would bake some cobbler and then we all would sit around that fire eating cobbler and listening to Pappy tell of his many adventures growing up on a cotton farm as a kid and later on, having left the farm, he traveled to Texas where he meet our momma."

"We'll have a couple more nights out here before we reach Deadwood so you can tell us some of those adventures." RJ wanted to get back to his story as much as he wanted to hear some of Tom's and Hank's.

"Micah said that two things saved his life. One being that the shot he had taken in the stomach went through his oversized belt buckle which he always wore. That slowed the bullet down so it only went about halfway through his body. If it had gone through it, it would have hit his spine, which might have crippled him or killed him. The second was the shot he took in the chest. The reason it had sounded like a little pup was, that for some reason it must have had only half a charge of gunpowder in it so that there wasn't a lot of power in the shell and, upon entering his chest, it lodged between one of his ribs." "Why didn't the doctor remove the lead?

"Micah said he came to the next day, but it wasn't until a week later that the doctor returned and by that time the wounds had closed and were starting to heal over. The doctor wanted to operate, but Micah wouldn't let him."

"Well, that answered my earlier question about the lead still being in him." Curious as to why Micah didn't want the doctor to remove the bullets, he pressed RJ to continue.

"I asked Micah about that, knowing the bullets were made of lead and many a man had died from the infection caused by a bullet left inside the body."

"What did he tell you his reason was?"

RJ thought for a moment, took another sip of coffee and continued, "Well, Micah started telling me about some guy in the Holy Book named Peter who had some kind of thorn in his side that caused him a lot of discomfort but, at the same time kept him remembering what his purpose in life was."

"I don't understand. What kind of a thorn and why couldn't he have just removed it?"

"The Holy Book don't tell ya what the thorn was in his side for, only that Peter had asked the Lord to take it out a number of times, but he was told no, and to live with it, so he would remember what his mission was."

RJ stopped for a minute and remembered reading about Peter and decided to purchase another Holy Book once they got to town.

"What are you thinking about, RJ?" It had become very quiet once RJ mentioned the Holy Book and started speaking about someone named Peter, and now it would appear everyone was waiting for him to continue.

"Micah told me that those bullets left in his body would be his reminder not to ever let down his guard, to always stay focused on his mission whenever he was on the trail of a wanted person, or just relaxing."

About two miles ahead of them, Charlie was debating whether to send one of his men back to check up on Dutch and the two wagons. He passed the idea to his brother Steve, who'd just rode up to inform him that the wagons were all settled in for the night. Steve listened to his brother, then reassured him.

"Dutch would have come up here if there was anything happening with his charges."

"Still, first thing in the morning I want you to mosey on back there and check them out."

"Once we start up in the morning, I'll ride on back. I need to have a chat with Dutch anyway, before we hit Cheyenne." Turning his mount around, Steve headed back to the wagon train in hopes of spending some time with a whore named Libby whom he had taken a fancy to.

Charlie sat on his mount and watched as Steve galloped back to the wagons. Sitting atop his own horse, Charlie thought about Cheyenne which they would reach tomorrow evening, providing they didn't run into any trouble. Being the size of the train they were he didn't expect any.

Can't wait to get to Cheyenne and have me a hot bath. Charlie thought and reached forward to give his horse a couple loving slaps on the neck, then spurred him toward the wagons where he would get something to eat and maybe a couple shots of Ole Red Eye.

About two miles back, sitting around their own fire, RJ was just putting the finishing touches to his recollection of Micah's story.

"So, do you think Micah has taken up religion and now is a deacon bounty hunter? Or maybe a traveling man of the cloth and is no longer bounty hunting?"

"We'll have to wait 'till we get to Deadwood and if Micah is there we'll just have to see for ourselves."

"You don't really think that Micah could be a deacon or a preacher, do you?"

"You never know about such things, Calvin. I would imagine anything is possible, although where Micah is concerned, I wouldn't believe that would ever happen. I would think he'd be the last man to find God. I think it would be more like him finding the devil."

RJ smiled at the picture he formed in his mind of Micah wearing a pastor's collar, carrying a Bible instead of a gun, and preaching, Thou Shalt Not Kill. Then again, I can picture him with horns, a long tail, forked tongue, red glowing eyes and carrying a pitchfork.

"In the line of work he's in, it doesn't hurt to believe in something or someone that will look out after you. I just can't picture him believing in God. That would be a real miracle."

"Have you come up with a story to tell Charlie tomorrow concerning the dead body of his friend when we see him?" Tom looked at RJ and continued. "You have to know that sometime in the morning either he, or maybe his brother Steve will be finding us to make sure everything is okay."

"I guess I'll have to tell him the truth, with a little doctoring up some."

"Well, if you ask me, whatever you come up with has to include the reward poster and the price on his head. Anyone would believe killing another person for what he had done and with that kind of money on his head, would have to think that it was those reasons, only, that caused you to bash in his head. Heck, he even pulled out the reward poster he carried on him."

"We'll have to see what happens in the morning. If Charlie does come looking to see how we fared through the night and were ready to continue the journey."

As the campfire burned down, and the darkness settled in, RJ had a lot of questions that he didn't have answers for. Looking through the low flames of the campfire, he observed Calvin, just sitting there, knowing that there was something definitely wrong with his head. Not only was he a little quieter, but also were those sudden bursts of a wolf call. *I wonder what goes through his mind when he has one of those moments. Hopefully there will be a good doctor in Cheyenne that can help him or at least tell us what can be done.*

Tom and Hank sat looking at the fire as it started to burn down. This journey to Deadwood would mark the first time they did any distant traveling from their home in Denver. So much had happened already and there were so many more miles to travel.

"Do you think there will be trouble in the morning, Tom?"

"I don't rightly know, brother. I would imagine it will depend on the story RJ comes up with and if Charlie buys it or not."

Somewhere in the distant darkness came the eerie call of a lone coyote.

Ouuuuuuuuuuuu. Ou, Ou, Ouuhooooooooo.

The neck hairs on both brothers stood up on end.

CHAPTER 6

Sun-up the next morning found RJ and Calvin ready to go. Tom and Hank had just finished putting some stuff away in their wagon, but both were lagging about.

"You should have been moving rather than just standing around." RJ told them. It was plain to see that Tom and Hank were not ones to rise and shine.

As the sun reached high noon, RJ knew then that no one was going to show up back here. They had passed the spot where the wagon train had made camp the previous night.

Calvin suddenly stood up in the wagon and pointed to a makeshift cross that was stuck in a pile of rocks next to the trail.

"Lookie there," Calvin said.

"Wonder who's there?" RJ said, stopping next to the mound of rocks.

Calvin spotted something hanging from the wooden cross and stepping down off the wagon, walked over so he could see what it was.

"It's a set of rosary beads," he said, taking them off the cross and examining them before draping them back over the cross. Also next to the mound of stones was a small carrying case, obviously belonging to a woman. He went to open it, but Tom called out, "Leave it be, Calvin. It's none of your concern."

"Yep, I guess you're right, no need to go disturbing her belongings." With that, Calvin set the case back next to the grave.

"I wonder who it was."

"Does it really matter, who it was?" He nodded, and said a little prayer for the person. *It really don't matter,* he agreed, as he walked back to the wagon. Stepping up onto a wheel spoke and not paying attention, he started to pull himself up onto the seat when all of a sudden he whacked his head on one of the bolts securing the seat.

A loud searing scream escaped Calvin's lips. Tears of devastating pain formed in Calvin's eyes before running down his cheeks. All RJ could do was just sit there and watch, as his best friend went through what must be some horrible pain.

It took a few minutes before the pain began to subside and Calvin was able to lower his hands from his head. He slowly removed his bandanna and wiped the tears from his face.

"What caused all that?" asked RJ as Calvin slowly came back to a normal state.

Calvin looked at RJ and motioned for him to get moving. "We need to be moving," he said.

"Are you sure you want to move right now?" All RJ could think about was the jarring of the wagon on the rough trail road and how that might affect Calvin's head.

"I'm alright now. I started to have some pain when I climbed down from the wagon, but it went away, and then when I jumped up onto the seat and bumped my head, it hit me like a bolt of lightning." Once again, cradling his head in his hands, Calvin asked in a whisper, "What's wrong with me, RJ?"

This time, RJ didn't have an answer. In the past, he would have made a note of it so that when he had the time, or given the chance, he would look it up or ask someone 'til he got his answer.

RJ clicked his tongue, and snapped the reins. The wagon started off with a jolt. RJ looked over at Calvin but didn't see any expression of pain on his face.

"When we get to Cheyenne, if there's a doctor there we'll have him take a look at that head," he told Calvin, who just sat there like he didn't hear a word that RJ said to him.

RJ looked at his friend with a concerned expression and his thoughts ran deep.

All the years we've known each other and the battles we have fought back to back, nothing serious had ever happened to either of us. There is something going on inside his head that needs attention. Turning his eyes slowly to the heaven, RJ said to himself. *I'm not much of a prayin' man, Lord, but I'm askin' ya to make my friend well.*

RJ's thoughts were interrupted by Tom, who stood up in his wagon and yelled out, pointing to the trail in front of them. "There she is! Cheyenne!"

Cheyenne was still about two miles off. As RJ looked he could pick out the last wagon as it entered town. Gunshots disturbed the otherwise quiet of the day as several happy cowboys let off some built up steam.

"How come we never hauled freight to Cheyenne RJ?"
"Because everyone and everything was going to California? Stop and think how many trips we made to California when we first came out here."

"What do you really think our chances are of being successful in Deadwood?"

"Don't rightly know. We sure didn't have any freight to haul there from Denver." As he spoke, RJ's thoughts weren't on hauling freight out of Deadwood, instead it was about what was gonna happen once they entered Cheyenne and faced off with Charlie concerning the death of Dutch.

"Thinking about what your story's gonna be once Charlie confronts you?" It was a question even RJ hadn't answered, not even to himself.

"I guess I'll have to tell him the truth. He was going to draw and kill you so I came up behind him and hit him over the head with a piece of pipe, not meaning to kill him."

"Didn't mean to kill him? That would be kinda hard to believe seeing his bashed in skull, wouldn't ya think?"

Before he could answer, and in a move that scared the beejeezzzeees out of him, Calvin suddenly jumped from the wagon and landing on the dirt road, started rolling around in the dirt. As the three watched him in awe, it was pretty hard not to laugh at him, and given any other time they probably would have.

A cloud of dust and flying dirt soon filled the air around the figure as he continued rolling and thrashing about. As quickly as he had started, he stopped abruptly and stood up. As the three looked on, he spoke.

"No one can smell me now, can they RJ?" He walked over to RJ and extended his arm and ran it under RJ's nose. "Nothing. See, I told you there was no smell so we have nothing to worry about." RJ thought, *he must have been worried that Dutch was starting to stink*. With that, he turned to the others and said, "Let's get into town boys."

All three stood and looked at each other curiously as they watched him walk on past the wagon. It looked as if he planned on walking to Cheyenne, as he walked away, not once looking back to see if he was being followed. The air was soon filled with the most beautiful sound of whistling. RJ turned around and looked at Hank and Tom, who had stopped talking and was also listening to the whistling sound coming from Calvin as he walked along.

Tom jumped down from his wagon and ran up to RJ's. Reaching out a helping hand, RJ pulled Tom aboard. "What do you make of that, RJ?"

"That right there is the damn'dest thing I think I've ever witnessed. As many years as we've been together, he has never, once whistled."

Tom and RJ looked at each other and then sat quietly listening as Calvin continued whistling some honky-tonk number he'd heard coming from the piano player at one of the many saloons in Denver.

"Something to do with that hit to his head, wouldn't you say?"

RJ didn't hear Tom, instead he sat quietly as his thoughts went back to Charlie and what his response would be once they got to town and Charlie learned about the death of his friend.

The remainder of the ride into Cheyenne was a quiet one except for the whistling coming from Calvin. As they continued, RJ had a new thought, and it was one he would talk to Calvin about. *Why haul only freight. We could advertise and lead our own wagon train.* Then expanding on that thought. *Why only from Denver to Deadwood? Why not Deadwood to California? Denver to California? California to Oregon? The list was endless.*

Before they knew it, they were entering town. All the sounds of laughter and singing, and all the happy sounds, descended on their ears.

RJ looked around at all the buildings and was amazed at the size city Cheyenne was. Storefronts displayed every kind of goods and wares one could imagine.

RJ looked around for the doctor's office and for the undertaker's. He didn't see either.

"Hey Tom. I saw the livery stable so I'm heading there to keep this body sorta hidden until I can talk to Charlie. Why don't you and Hank see if you can find out where the doc is and also the undertakers?"

"If we find the doc, shouldn't we get Calvin over to him as fast as we can, I don't believe that the wagon train will be in town long?" RJ never answered him as he headed for the livery stables.

RJ realized he had never asked Charlie how long of a journey it was to get to Deadwood, with thirty-two wagons and so many women who walked rather than ride, it was a slow go.

At the livery stable, RJ unhooked his team and found an empty stall. Once he had them fed and bedded down, he went looking for the owner of the stables to pay for their keep and to ask where he could find the undertaker and a blacksmith.

The street was noisy with the many wagons and their owners.

Looks like no one is going to bed their horses at the stable. The only thing was, the body had begun to stink. He hoped that no one would look in the back of his wagon and see the dead body. As he moved about he spotted the sheriff's office and decided to see if he was in. Sheriff Samuel Collins was just walking out the door when RJ stepped up onto the boardwalk in front of his office.

"Are you the sheriff?" he asked, as he stood face to face with a man looking to be in his early forties with a wrinkled leathery looking face.

"What makes you think that I'm the sheriff of this un-godly place?" Before RJ could answer, he said, "I know, this here badge gave me away, didn't it?" he said with a grin. He extended his hand and introduced himself. "Samuel Collins is my name, but folks call me Sam, and to whom am I speaking?" Taking his hand, RJ introduced himself.

"So you're headed to Deadwood, I understand." Dropping his head down a little, he shook it as he spoke. "No law there," he uttered with a voice that was meant to be listened to. "Mark my words, that town will not survive. I give it less than five years."

The sound of gunfire was heard over the street noise and both RJ and Sam turned in that direction. In the street they saw two men, pistols drawn, taking turns shooting at the feet of an old drunk, making him dance.

As they walked in their direction, the sheriff took out his six-gun. RJ realized he was defenseless as he didn't carry a gun. His kills were from a piece of pipe and he didn't even have that with him. As they approached, they could see the drunkard's blank stare at the two cowboy's faces, along with hearing their loud laughter.

"That will be enough fun, boys." Sam said in a loud voice that got their attention and both stopped and turned to face him.

"Put those guns back where they came from boys. We'll call it a night and no one gets hurt or dead."

As RJ watched, the cowboys looked at each other and then with a wicked smile, they turned from the drunk to Sam not putting their guns away.

RJ was startled as two shots rang out from a drawn six-gun. At the same moment, he saw the two pistols go flying through the air having been shot right out of their hands. Both screamed in pain, grabbing their hands.

"Dang-it fella's. You just had to go and do that. Now you'll cost the town some money to get those hands looked at. Then we have to feed ya! Now, on the other hand, maybe you should just be shot dead and not cost the town a cent."

"Don't you carry a gun?" Sam asked RJ looking him up and down. Not seeing one, he reached in his trouser pocket and came up with two pairs of handcuffs. Handing one set to RJ, he took the other and cuffed one of the cowboy's hands and nodded for RJ to do the same to the other. In a couple of minutes both cowboys were cuffed and being led off to jail.

Once the two were locked away, Sam motioned for RJ to follow him.

"Let's head on over to the doc's office and tell him he has a couple of gunshot patients in the jail cell."

"Is the Doc a good one?" asked RJ. "I have a friend with a head wound that needs tending to."

As they walked along the boardwalk, RJ noticed that the action in the streets was dying down some as the folks started turning in for the night.

"Looks like Deadwood is getting a new supply of women along with gamblers and rich merchants who'll give people the simple necessities of life that they'll give an arm and a leg for." This was the case in any boom town that sprouted up with the discoveries of gold and silver.

"Sam!" a loud voice was heard behind them. Stopping and turning around to see who had spoken his name, both were confronted by a large man dressed in buckskins. He had long blondish hair and a considerably large mustache.

"Hickok, what the hell are you doing out and about? That's not like you. The gaming tables are probably screaming your name!"

"Now Sheriff Collins, you know that I'm a straight gambler and have blessed this town of yours with my presence."

"That you have, Wild Bill." Looking over at RJ, Sam repeated, "that you have."

Bill had only been in town a short time, after having learned that his friend Colorado Charlie was leading a wagon train of merchants to Deadwood, South Dakota and was going to team up with him.

"RJ, this is Wild Bill Hickok, I'm sure you've heard of him, having lived in Denver."

Extending his hand toward Bill, RJ introduced himself.

"I've often heard your name mentioned, Bill. I'm RJ Murdock." The two shook hands and RJ was surprised at the toughness of Bill's hands, and their size.

"Have you seen Charlie yet, Bill?"

"Yup, but only for a minute. We're meeting in the morning to work out the arrangements."

"Did he give you any idea as to how long he plans to stay here?" RJ knew that sooner or later, Charlie would be looking for Dutch and that would bring him around asking questions and demanding answers from him.

"He told me that he had some things to settle and then he will be ready to get under way. And with Charlie that, 'things to settle', could be anything."

Yeah, "things to settle" could be the strange disappearance of Dutch. A thought that had a disturbing effect on RJ.

"Well, you know Charlie better'n anyone Bill, so give us your educated guess?"

"We'll be out of here tomorrow."

"Okay! That's what I wanna hear."

Bill smiled at the excitement he heard in RJ's voice and gave him a warning. You've never been to Deadwood have you RJ?" Bill had put his hand on RJ's shoulder and looked at him directly. "Put a herd of gold hungry drunks, and women chasing men, together with loose guns and no law to control or break up a fight, and you have Deadwood." Looking him up and down, he ended the warning with, "Not a place for a person to be that ain't wearing a gun."

"Never wore one, don't intend to start now."

Releasing the shoulder hold on him, he said, "Your funeral."

Sam and RJ watched as Bill walked down, waving at the call of his name. Cheyenne had been a home for Wild Bill on several occasions and he had befriended quite a number of town folk. As they watched, RJ noticed the sure steps he took. Knowing exactly who he was, showed in his walk as well as the way he carried himself.

"Bill's right when he warned you about going to such a lawless place as Deadwood not wearing a gun." With that, RJ remembered what he needed to do and, changing the subject, asked Sam where the blacksmith shop was.

"Blackie's shop is located just outside of town. We've never had a fire in Cheyenne and I think it's on account of keeping that one business out of town."

The news of a fire that destroyed Idaho City, Idaho had reached Cheyenne and also Denver and the town folk all got together and built "Blackie" a new shop outside of town.

"Just keep walking the way you're going and you will run right into it. Graham is his given name, but he likes "Blackie""

"Thanks." RJ shook Sam's hand again and thanked him for the information. As he walked away, he caught sight of the undertaker's sign that hung over the elaborate display of caskets in the shop's window.

As RJ entered, he was met by a well-dressed young man who introduced himself as Newton Bell. "How can I assist you, sir, in your time of sorrow?" Words that were spoken softly and with a certain amount of sadness.

"I have a dead man over at the livery stable in a wagon that needs attending to."

Twenty minutes later and fifty dollars shorter than what he walked in with, RJ left the undertaker's office with the hope that Newton would get the body before Charlie had a chance to discover what had happened to Dutch.

As he continued to the blacksmith's shop, RJ was working out in his mind what he was hoping could be made before they had to leave.

That piece of pipe needs to have some finishing touches to it. RJ had been thinking from the first time he had used that pipe and it was what he would carry instead of a gun.

As RJ continued to the blacksmith's shop, he was unaware that Charlie had just started asking questions concerning the disappearance of Dutch.

CHAPTER 7

Deadwood, South Dakota lay some three hundred plus miles North East of Cheyenne and just as the streets of Cheyenne were alive with the wagon train pulling out of town and the town folk cheering and singing and a few gunshots were fired into the air, so were the streets of Deadwood but for a different reason.

A lone rider galloped from one end of town to the other.

Behind the horse was the naked form of a woman with her hands tied together and being dragged by a rope tied around her ankles. It turned out she was a prostitute who had gone thru the pockets of her "John" who just happened to be Micah. He had heard from several of the men who visited her that when they woke in the morning there was money missing from their pants' pockets, so he had set a trap to catch her and to put an end to her stealing.

Micah marked some bills to be used as evidence, so that if she stole from him it would be the marked bills. Sure enough, the next morning after a fun night, Micah noticed some of the bills gone from his pants and Miss Abigail not in the room. Dressing, Micah went looking for her and found her at the *Nuttal & Mann's* saloon, where he grabbed her and reaching down into her brassiere came up with his marked bills.

Two other prostitutes who had been accused of the same act were rounded up and forced to watch as Micah dragged Miss
Abigail to death. The dry dirt of the street caused a lot of dust, which very quickly filled the mouth and nose of the dragged

whore, making it unable for her to breathe. The rocks, tearing her flesh from her body caused excruciating pain, but she was unable to scream because of her dirt-filled mouth.

But the screams were heard and everyone turned in the direction from where they came from. The two prostitutes were being stripped of their skimpy clothing and soon, right there on the dirt street, in front of the folks who had gathered, both men, women and child, both were raped repeatedly by anyone wanting to take his turn, and there were plenty of heated up young cowpokes and old prospectors who hadn't found any gold and couldn't afford a bout with the *Doves of Deadwood*.

Micah sat side saddle atop his steed and watched the action for a couple of minutes. Taking his eyes from the rape he looked down and back at the dead, naked, torn and bloody body of what used to be a woman.

This sure is my kind of town. Micah thought to himself, letting go of a loud sinister laugh that was heard by most. A laugh that was well known by the town folk and everyone stopped what they were doing and turned to see what "Mad Man Micah" was going to do next. This was a name that sort of branded him because of his evil laugh and actions. As the folks watched, they saw him go over to where the two were being held down while the rapes were going on. Letting out another laugh, this one making some standing there cringe back in utter fright, they watched as Micah reached down and grabbing one of the men who was in the middle of his rape, pick him up off the prostitute and fling him through the air, private parts and all, as if he was nothing more than a rag doll. Staring down at the whore, who was bleeding from not only the rapes, but from the many blows she had been given. For a second, everyone thought Micah was going to have some mercy on this whore, but those thoughts were quickly quelled as they watched him drop his trousers and take his turn with the woman. Hollering as he finished and at the same instant, with no warning, he reached for his gun belt. He then drew out his pistol with a smooth action, cocked it, and putting the barrel under the chin of the whore, pulled the trigger.

There was an instant of quietness, then the air was filled with the screams and shouts from the men and many of the women who had watched the rape. The dry dirt street just above the whore's head was now red with splattered blood from the bullet as it exited her head.

Returning his gun to its holster, Micah stood up, reached down and pulled up his trousers. "Sorry boys," he said to no one in particular, "looks like you'll just have to make do with sharing that one," indicating the naked whore that was still being held down. There was a look of horror on her face as she turned her head in the direction of her dead friend. In the matter of a few minutes she was once again assailed and the rape commenced.

With that, Micah walked over to his horse, and putting his foot into the stirrup hoisted himself up. Turning once again to the body he had dragged, he untied the rope from his saddle horn, dropped it to the ground and spurring his mount, rode off filling the air with the laugh he had come to be known for. As he reached the city's outer limit, a lone shot was heard.

"Guess everyone was done with their playing." Micah told his horse reaching forward and giving him a couple hard slaps on the neck, creating a couple dust clouds and a loud neighhhhing from his horse who at once broke into a lively gallop at the spurring from Micah.

Micah couldn't believe what he had ridden into that first day he'd arrived in Deadwood. Before he had made it half way through town, he had witnessed two shootings which had left three people dead, two were men and a good looking red head whom he thought he had seen somewhere before. He saw another woman, this one half naked with only bloomers on, being chased by an old guy with a vicious looking bull whip whose loud crack made his horse jump almost un-seating him.

It didn't take Micah long to find the man whom he had heard was here in Deadwood, only it would take him some time to figure out how to kill him and collect the five thousand dollar bounty on his head without being labeled a bounty hunter which would not be a good thing in this lawless city. Micah's plan was pretty simple. Having lots of money, he opened a mercantile store where his comings and goings wouldn't be questioned by anyone. That way, when his prey left town, he would follow him and, after killing him, transport him to the next county where he would turn over the body and collect the reward. Sharing some of the money with the local sheriff would guarantee that no word would get back to Deadwood, and so a partnership was struck up between Micah and Sheriff P.K. Tuttle. Micah's business actually became very profitable and it wasn't long before Micah's dark side surfaced, being fueled by the fact that Deadwood was without any kind of law and a person could do just about anything, except raping any of the married women. Hell, there were so many whores who were available anytime and for any price, a married woman was considered off limits and, if you were unlucky enough to be accused of having anything to do with one, then it would be you on the end of Micah's rope.

Prostitutes were considered nothing more than an outlet for the men and basically had no other value and were treated as such. You steal someone's horse or his money and that was reason for a hanging; kill a prostitute and it went unnoticed. No one paid any attention to it.

So Deadwood became home to Micah. If you were wanted anywhere, sooner or later you ended up in Deadwood and if there were a wanted poster with reward monies paid for your skin, soon enough you would be on Micah's list and your days would be numbered, ending when you decided to leave town. The shadow of death, in the guise of a man on horseback, followed you out of town.

Al Swearengen who owned the Gem Variety Theater, which was one of the wildest establishments in Deadwood, saw and knew all that went on in and about in Deadwood. Al had built the Theater as a place of entertainment and bringing in at least a couple of thousand dollars a night wasn't un-heard of. Everything from prize fights to the many saloon girls, who were brought in under the false pretense of a job and forced into prostitution and were yours for a price, could be found there.

The Gem was a vicious place for a woman to work there under servitude to AL as a whore. Along with Al's foul temper, which could explode at any time, his two associates, Dan Doherty and Johnny Burns were known to beat a prostitute or two at times. Along with the beatings they were humiliated and sometimes even murdered by the two, which no one paid any attention to. Al, himself, was responsible for the murder of several of the whores who had complained of the harsh treatment they received from some of their clients. This complaining called for a death sentence.

It didn't take long, if you were a single woman, to realize that your chances of finding a legitimate job in Deadwood were few and far between and because whether you were sent for or brought here, this was the end of the line and not having any other means of support you soon took up the life of a whore. As long as you were pretty, you could expect to make some okay money, but your future was bleak and you aged quickly, losing the bloom of youth. In most cases, if you weren't murdered or committed suicide, then you succumbed to venereal disease, or in some cases a drug overdose. In any of these cases, the life of a prostitute in Deadwood wasn't glamorous.

Al was the worst, there was, as far as his treatment of whores whom he brought in. Public beatings, rapes, and all sorts of harsh treatment were punishment for complaining, resistance or disobedience.

Al had formed a friendship with Micah shortly after he had come to Deadwood. When Al saw that he feared nothing or no one, and walked the narrow line of being downright crazy at times, he knew that he had found the right person to keep his prostitutes and other business partners in line.

One afternoon, after the two had finished enjoying their favorite whores, Al and Micah sat around in the front of the Gem sipping on some of the finest whiskey that was brought in from the west coast. Puffing on a good cigar, which had become one of Micah's favorite pastimes since making Deadwood his home, and savoring his friendship with AL, as the two sat there, Al looked at Micah and cleared his throat before he started to speak.

"I've been watching and noticing that your business is doing pretty well." A statement that brought a nod of agreement from Micah. "I've also noticed that most think you're one mad and crazy person at times." Before he could continue, Micah's whole facial expression changed and his shoulders started to bunch up, which Al noticed and immediately held up his two hands, saying, "Whoa, there Micah, I didn't mean to insinuate that I think anything by that statement."

"Glad to hear that, AL. I'd hate for our friendship to end before it had time to blossom." Micah said these words using a soft womanly type voice, said through clenched teeth, which was followed by a smile that told AL that Micah had taken the remark for what it was.

Leaning back in his chair on two legs and sucking in a mouthful of smoke, Micah tilted his head back and slowly expelled the smoke, watching it slowly rise into the air headed for the ceiling. Looking back at AL, Micah motioned for him to continue with his earlier conversation.

"I would like for us to do some business together."

Micah raised his eyebrows and slowly lowered the chair's front legs back on the floor. AL didn't wait, but continued, "I need someone who has no objections to beating women or killing them for that matter. I have a large number of prostitutes and from time to time I need one or two of them to set an example to the others as to what happens when you don't do my bidding. I want it to be something done in public and for everyone to know why." Stopping to take a sip of whiskey, AL once again continued, "As you can see, Marshall Seth Bullock has no authority in my section of Deadwood. He stays out of my business. He has no power or even cares to have any here, on the east side, so you'll have nothing to fear."

"I fear nothing," came a whispered reply to a statement that needed no reply.

"Are you interested?"

"I must say AL, you have my attention. Just what is in this for me?"

"What do you want?"

Micah had been sitting there, knowing what AL was getting at with his line of conversation and had already knew what he was going to ask for, taking a big chance on the outcome. Taking a look around to make sure that there was no one within hearing range, because what he was going to say could mean a sudden bullet in the back either now or later, but it would come. A bounty hunter's life would be zero here in Deadwood.

"Let's hear it, Micah."

Exhaling loudly, Micah began. "For the past few years I have been a bounty hunter."

Al's cigar dropped from his mouth and landed on the floor, and his eyebrows raised above bulging eyes. Quickly recovering from the surprise, when Micah stopped to see if there were any reaction, Al managed to plaster a smile on his face. Micah had seen his first reaction, but he also had seen the recovery, therefore he continued.

"As you know, my life would be over if that were to become known. Since arriving here in Deadwood on the tracks of a wanted man, and one I did get, I have watched thousands of dollars ride in and out of town simply because I couldn't chance the kill."

"How have you operated up 'til now?" What he was hearing from Micah put thoughts in his head and he could make it work for him.

"I would go on one of my buying trips and visit the local sheriff's office where I would pick up at least five wanted posters of outlaws with at least a five thousand dollar bounty and memorize some feature on the picture that were easy to pick out, then just kept my eyes open 'til someone that I recognized rode into town."

"Where or how can I help you out in return for you working for me?" AL was surprised by what he was just told by Micah and knew that his life was also on the line if Micah ever thought he was betrayed in any way.

"Well AL, you know a large number of people, so I would say you get word pretty quickly when an outlaw rides into town." Al listened to Micah and agreed with him that he did get word when a bad guy rode into Deadwood but it was a different reason than what Micah was asking him to do.

Micah went on. "You know Sheriff P. K. Tuttle, so you should be able to get into his office and look at some of the wanted posters and maybe even be able to pick up a few to bring back to me so that I can then be on the lookout. You could have a couple of your whores also look out and inform you if they see one of them. I wouldn't be against paying a whore for information, which has the potential of putting thousands in my bank account."

As Micah laid out his plans, AL listened and at once realized the benefit of doing business with Micah.

"You know the reputation I have in this town? I need to change it into something more refined, because pretty soon I'm going to get into something else and will need a calmer attitude." Al was getting tired of always having to take care of the business of keeping his whores in line. As Deadwood grew, so did the number of his whores and the need to keep them in line. He had lost the desire to beat up a woman and wanted to keep out of the limelight as much as he could, plus he needed someone who had no soul or qualms about beating or even killing a whore when needed.

And so, the partnership was sealed that afternoon with a handshake. Since then, Micah had designed what he thought would be the most forceful way to deal with the prostitutes whom AL would tell him who needed dealing with from time to time and left it up to him as to the punishment he wanted to dish out.

Micah had seen the results of one of the whores getting beaten in public or shot. Having body parts cuts off them in public and even the gang rapes.

The gang rapes were probably the most visual form of punishment. This was carried out with the whore being stripped and tied to stakes spread eagle in the town's square, and would be carried out over a weekend. Once complete, the woman was left in such a bad condition and in pain, she usually committed suicide or begged someone to put her out of her misery. Most weekends would find someone tied up in the square and soon it lost its impact on, not only the prostitutes but also on the town folk.

Micah's bank account grew and no one suspected him of anything other than being a successful businessman.

One day, after he had stripped one of the girls and was preparing to stake her out, when another thought entered his mind. No one was paying much attention to him except for a couple of young cowboys and two old drunks. Wanting to get the attention of the folks walking by, Micah suddenly rolled back his head and gave out one of the most bone chilling evil sounding laugh that at once brought people to stop dead in their tracks and focus their attention on the town square where Micah was standing over a naked girl. Telling the two cowboys to keep the girl pinned down, he gave off another laugh and started running toward the livery stable. Within minutes, he returned riding his horse. One of the cowboys was already into action when Micah rode up, dismounted and removing a rope from his saddle horn, tied a loop in one end and bending down and dragging the cowboy off her, grabbed one of her legs and tied it around her foot. Turning, Micah mounted his horse.

One more blood curdling laugh and putting spurs to horse flanks took off on a gallop dragging the woman behind him.

"I've got the town's attention now." Micah said aloud as he reached the end of town, stopped and turned around to drag her back down through town. Looking back and down to the woman, Micah saw the effect the dragging had and it wasn't pretty. The short distance he had dragged her some of her skin had been scrapped off from the rough surface and the dirt had stuck to any place where she was cut and bled. He watched as she tried to clear the dirt and horse excrement from her mouth and face. It was hard to believe that only a few minutes ago, this woman was one of the fairest and most sought after prostitutes at the Gem, and now you couldn't even distinguish her features.

Once again, Micah let out another bone chilling laugh and headed back through town where most of the town folk still stood with their eyes on him as he came galloping by them. Looking back, he saw there was no movement or sound coming from the dragged body. You could see where big clumps of skin had been torn off and the blood darkened the dirt which covered the now dead prostitute.

Everyone stood there staring in horror at the body.

"Sheeeeeeeee'….deadddddddd,…..sheeeeeeeee's…deadddd dddddd!" Micah screamed into the silence that had befallen the shocked town as they watched him dragging the whore through the street. Throwing the rope on the ground and with one more chilling laugh took off towards the livery stable.

It wouldn't be until the undertaker got the body that it was learned that she had died from choking, her being unable to breathe through her mouth, throat and nose, being caked full of dirt and horseshit, which wouldn't even allow her to scream. The pain she must have gone through before she succumbed to not being able to take a breath was hard to imagine.

Over time, Micah would add some different twist to how he dragged them. His favorite was letting the victim stand up with hands tied behind her back and his dragging rope tied around her ankle. He had started using a twenty foot long rope so this would let him get up some speed before the rope tensed up and violently pulled the legs out from under the whore, slamming her into the ground. He would then head for the boardwalk where he would drag her over the wood. The board's roughness tore off flesh, staining the wood red with her blood. This had the lasting effect of burying itself in one's memory in stark detail as the blood stains were visible longer. Town folk complained about this, so Micah had a mock up boardwalk built in the alley next to the Gem, so he had something to drag their bodies over. This quickly became known as Blood Alley.

Some three hundred miles away, a wagon train was pulling out of Cheyenne headed for this lawless town known as Deadwood.

CHAPTER 8

Charlie had accepted RJ's story about the death of his friend Dutch which gave RJ a big sigh of relief. Calvin looked at RJ and saw his face relax at Charlie's acceptance of the explanation of Dutch's death and was even more surprised when Charlie reached out and gave RJ a couple slaps on the shoulder as he turned and walked away after telling him they were going to set out within the hour. Calvin had also seen that RJ was holding his right arm in the position to drop down his weapon if needed. RJ had designed the pipe weapon and had a leather type holder made that could be strapped to his forearm to hold it, a sudden downward motion of his arm and within a heartbeat he could be holding it in his hand.

Hot was the only way to describe that morning. A person could become soaked in his own sweat just standing still and the time seemed to drag by waiting for all the wagon teams to get hitched up and in line to take off. Joyful sounds could be heard everywhere. Dogs ran freely barking and stirring up dust and spooking the horses. A yelp was heard from time to time as someone made good his kick at one of them.

RJ waited until the wagon train had departed before he brought the wanted poster of Dutch to the sheriff for the bounty. Two hours later he was counting the reward money.

Alongside the wagons walked the many women who would become prostitutes. Wherever there were men and money there would be "Ladies" willing to sell their charms for a price. These Ladies would be responsible for bringing into the many saloons and gambling establishment's lots of big spenders and an array of shady characters. A prostitute's life span was around five years unless she was killed by one of her customers, got a disease, or committed suicide. One of the women walking beside a wagon that morning was a high spirited gal by the name of Dora, who would go on to become the most well-known Madam in Deadwood. Dora would go on to marry a gambler named Joseph Dufran and expand her business to Sturgis and Rapid City and Belle Fourche.

Leading the wagons out of Cheyenne was Charlie, who had changed into more practical riding clothes, although one would still say he was *fancy dressed*. Alongside him rode Wild Bill Hickok.

"What do you make of Charlie and his always washing his hands and changing his clothes several times a day?" Calvin asked RJ.

"Well, Calvin," responded RJ. "Sometimes a person has what we would consider a strange habit because it's something we ourselves wouldn't do, but seems normal to the person doing it. Charlie probably doesn't even realize that he is doing anything out of what he considers normal and probably has thoughts about the rest of us not washing often and changing."

The wagon train slowly pulled out of Cheyenne with RJ and Calvin along with Tom and Hank hold back until the dust that was created by the many wagons and horses had time to settle.

RJ couldn't help noticing what a big fan fare this was for the folks who lived here. Once the dust had settled and RJ slapped the rumps of his team he figured they were approximately two miles back.

Once out of town, RJ dropped his arm and his newly designed skull crusher, which was a slightly curved piece of one inch round pipe with a handle of rawhide which had been wrapped tightly around it, he handed to Calvin, who, inspected it carefully while slapping it against his opened palm causing a dull thud.

"Wow," said Calvin. "You were serious when you made the decision not to use a gun to bring down outlaws." Calvin continued slapping the piece of pipe in his opened hand and suddenly with great force and speed brought it down against the side of the seat which created a loud *whaaap*, which spooked the team into a fast gallop, with the jolt sending both RJ and Calvin tumbling over backwards landing in the bed of the now racing out of control wagon.

Hank and Tom were able to control their team and watched as RJ's wagon raced away. If it weren't for the road being fairly straight at this point, the outcome could have been tragic, but because it wasn't, RJ was able to quickly gain his footing and stepped over the wagon's seat where he was able to grab the reins and bring the team to a halt.

RJ was on the ground inspecting the horses when Tom and Hank pulled up.

"Well! That was exciting," Hank stated as he also jumped down from his wagon and walked up beside RJ to help him with his inspection.

A couple of minutes later, RJ was back in the seat and they were once more underway.

"How's that head of yours?" asked RJ, whose thoughts were once again focused on his friend?

Calvin sat there staring straight ahead, not hearing RJ's question. Tapping Calvin on the shoulder to get his attention and seeing the blank look in his eyes as he turned toward him, RJ at once knew something was dreadfully wrong with his friend.

"How's that head of yours?" He repeated.

"Why are you slurring your words?" Calvin asked. "And I know I should know you, but I can't put a name to that face."

"It's me, Calvin! I'm your friend, RJ."

RJ looked at Calvin for some sort of head movement, but Calvin just sat there with a faraway stare on his face.

"Calvin." RJ repeated again. Still looking eye to eye with his friend.

"What's up?" answered Calvin. "And why are we stopped?" RJ thought for a couple minutes before answering.

"Just giving the team a little breather." RJ had decided not to let on what had transpired a few short minutes ago. He had taken Calvin to the doctor in Cheyenne but because Calvin was having no symptoms at the time of the visit, the doctor couldn't tell them what was the matter, only to keep an eye on him and if he were to have a fit when they were near a doctor, take him in then. RJ didn't know what kind of doctor they would find in Deadwood.

Calvin said, "They look rested enough. If we don't get going night time will soon be on us and we should travel as far as possible while it's still light."

Hank had returned to his wagon and was waiting for RJ to start moving.

"Git-up." RJ said, as he snapped the leather reins down across his horses' back sides.

The sky was starting to take on all shades of red, yellows, and gold against a background of navy blue and purple. Dusk was quickly gaining on the daylight and once again "The Maker" was finger painting the sky. RJ looked at the colorful sky and was in awe once again.

Soon, the sounds of music and the mumbled sound of voices caught RJ's ears as they came around a curve in the road and found the wagon train had pitched camp for the night.

Bringing his team and wagon around next to the last wagon. RJ reined up and motioned for Tom and Hank to do the same. Once settled in, they joined the rest of the wagon train folks who were all sitting around one large campfire. Some had cups in their hands as they sipped some of the coffee boiling in a large pot set on the top of some of the fire's hot coals. A couple of the men were passing around a whiskey bottle.

RJ, Calvin, Hank and Tom picked out a place to sit and taking hold of the pot filled their metal cups with some of the steeping hot coffee.

Charlie and Wild Bill were also seated around the fire. At once, someone asked Wild Bill to tell some of his travel stories.

As Wild Bill spoke, RJ couldn't help but respect the man for his life's story telling. RJ was just getting ready to git up to leave when Wild Bill spoke up.

Pointing at one of the men sitting there, Wild Bill asked, "Aren't you Adam Hall?"

All eyes followed Wild Bill's finger as it came to rest on this one cowboy who probably wasn't much older than twenty one or so.

"What if I am?" he said as he started standing up in case there was going to be some kind of confrontation.

At once, the only sounds that were heard was the crackling of the fire as all eyes were on this young cowboy starting to stand.

"Sit down, boy!" Wild Bill said in a commanding voice which put everyone more on edge. "No lawmen here, so if you are the 'Adam Hall' whose wanted poster I saw while in Cheyenne, you have nothing to concern yourself with. Just want to know the folks I sit around a fire with, drinking coffee."

With a smile on his face the cowboy sat back down, and looking towards Wild Bill, spoke, "That poster you saw there in Cheyenne was of me. Did you see that they have a ten thousand dollar reward on me alive or dead?" He didn't wait for an answer, but continued as he gazed around at the rest of the folk sitting there, now relieved knowing there wasn't going to be a gunfight.

"Killed myself a dirty, rotten, stealing whore, only thing was that her lover was the town's Marshall and he challenged my hand and I had to kill him. Just the fact that he was a lawman took precedence over the fact it was in self-defense that I had to shoot him."

RJ sat and listened as he told his story and all the while working out a plan in his head on how to collect that reward money without anyone having to know that he was in it as a bounty hunter.

RJ got up and left the group and went to look for Calvin and come up with a plan. Calvin was found in the company of one of the prostitutes in the back of Tom and Hank's wagon. The three must have worked out some kind of deal with the young lady as they sat around their own campfire awaiting their turn.

"I'm sure she wouldn't mind a fourth," Tom told RJ. "Only a dollar!"

Calvin was surprised to see RJ, when he appeared from the wagon attaching his suspenders and wearing a big grin. As Calvin approached the fire, Tom got up and rushed to the back of the wagon where he disappeared.

"What's up, RJ?" asked Calvin, sitting down and filling a tin cup with some Arbuckle and taking a sip.

"I was over with Charlie and Wild Bill sitting around listening to one of Bill's stories and the damn'dest thing happened. Seems there is a wanted outlaw on this train by the name of Adam Hall and there is a ten thousand dollar reward on his head, dead or alive."

The crackling of the fire was all that was heard for a few moments as Calvin and Hank listened while RJ finished telling them about Bell.

"What kind of man does this person appear to be, RJ?"

"Well, Hank. I would say from what I saw that he is sort of a hothead who is more apt to draw on a man and ask questions after."

"You mean there is ten thousand dollars sitting right over there just waiting for us to go and get it?" Calvin stood up and was pointing in the direction of the large campfire. Hank, being a little slow didn't get what was being asked by Calvin but liked what he had heard concerning ten thousand dollars.

"Ten thousand dollars!" Calvin sat back down and looking at RJ saw that look he had seen before when RJ was trying to work something out in his head.

"We lucked out once with Dutch, do you think we can do that again here?"

"Tomorrow we will arrive at Fort Laramie and I'm sure that Hall will stay well-hidden for fear of someone recognizing him or one of the wagon people turning him in. If we are to claim that reward money, he will have to be killed tonight and in such a way so as not to attract suspicion of any kind that his death is related to the bounty money placed on his head."

RJ was about to lay out his plan when Tom approached the campfire and Hank got up and left. All thoughts now were on pleasure and the ten thousand dollars could wait. While Hank was gone, RJ filled Tom in on what was happening. After hearing what RJ had to say, Hank spoke up.

"Why don't you let Tom and me have this one, RJ?" Both RJ and Calvin placed their attention on what Hank was about to say.

"I think that this might be a plan that will work and not expose you or for that matter Tom and myself as bounty hunters. Tom and I will take our pistols and simply walk over to their fire and walk up to him and blast away. But before we actually pull the trigger we will yell out that he murdered our sister. No one there will be the wiser that we aren't related to whoever it was he murdered. Then when we get to Fort Laramie we can put in for the reward money and split it four ways."

As RJ sat and listened to Hank, it seemed to him like a good enough plan. *After all, who is going to question them?* He thought.

As Hank finished, Tom came walking up to the campfire with a very satisfied look on his face. RJ noticed the perkiness to his step. *AHHHHHH to be that young again, he thought.*

As Tom reached the fire, RJ saw the woman who had just finished and was not surprised to see that she was of Chinese decent. What did surprise him was that she looked no older than fourteen or at the most sixteen. He had heard all the stories of men bringing Chinese girls stateside with the promise of work only to keep them as prostitutes or sell them to others.

This young girl, in three years from now, won't be recognized if still alive. RJ had seen it all over the years and in a way felt sadness toward this young girl as she walked away from the wagon.

"Tom, Tom, listen to this!" Hank almost shouted out loud enough to be heard all the way over to the other campfire. Tom listened and then agreed to the plan.

"When should we do this?" asked Tom, looking at RJ.

"I think you two should go get your pistols and do it now. After all, I just returned from there and it will make the story of Adam murdering your sister more believable."

"I think you and I should mosey on over there and be prepared just in case things don't go as smooth as we hope them to." With that RJ and Calvin checked their guns and headed out.

"I'm a little nervous." Tom said to Hank as he inspected his pistol and spinning the chamber dropped it into the leather holster which he buckled around his waist.

"How are we going to do this?"

"Well, we walk over there and see if the cowboy that RJ described is still sitting around the fire, and if he is, we just walk up to him and blast away just like we said earlier."

Tom and Hank started walking toward the wagon train and by the light of the big fire was able to pick out their quarry. Looking at Tom, Hank gave him a signal, and together they walked into the group sitting around the fire. A couple looked at them as they walked by.

Tom noticed RJ and Calvin, who looked at them and indicated with a nod in the direction of Newton.

Bounty Hunters

Charlie, Wild Bill and Adam looked in the direction that Tom and Hank were walking and Bill was in the middle of saying something when Tom and Hank suddenly drew their pistols and shouting out Adam's name, and together, pulled their triggers. Adam was in the process of standing, when the first lead hit him in the stomach. He heard their voices, but the pain in his stomach overshadowed their words. The next bullet eased his pain by hitting him in the face and ending his life. Charlie and Wild Bill were in the process of drawing their weapons when they heard a warning of "DON'T DO IT". Those words came from RJ who, along with Calvin, had stood up and had their pistols pointed at them. Everyone around the campfire had watched as the cowboy dropped to the ground dead.

"What's all this shooting? And why are you two pointing pistols at us?"

Dropping their pistols back into their holsters, RJ turned to speak to Charlie.

"Tom and Hank are traveling with us to Deadwood. Earlier I was over here when you questioned this Hall person about being an outlaw with a price on his head. I went back and told Tom and Hank that the person who had murdered their sister was sitting over here. I couldn't stop them so I took Calvin and myself over here to do exactly what I foresaw was happening."

"I hope your boys realize how close they came to joining old Adam there."

"And you must realize how lucky you were. If you hadn't listened to me, I would have put an ounce of lead into your chest and I really didn't want to have to do that."

Looking over at Tom and Hank, Charlie told them that there was a ten thousand dollar reward on his head and that he would act as witnesses as soon as they arrived at Fort Laramie.

Pointing to a couple of guys sitting there, Charlie spoke. "Ben and, Harry, you two pick up Mr. Hall and carry him to Tom's wagon. Tomorrow when we arrive at Fort Laramie I'll go see the commander and see what is needed for you to claim the reward monies."

"Appreciate that Charlie." Tom said as he and Hank turned from the dead body and head back to their wagon being followed by Ben and Harry carrying the corpse.

The body was covered with a tarp which should keep the body from decaying and smelling too bad.

It would be quite some time, after lunch, before they arrived at Fort Laramie. Two hours after arriving at Fort Laramie, Tom and Hank were four thousand dollars richer as were RJ and Calvin. Two thousand dollars was paid to Charlie and Wild Bill Hickok would once again meet up with an old flame, Calamity Jane.

Chapter 9

Calamity Jane had heard that a wagon train led by Charlie Utter and his brother Steve was on its way to Deadwood, South Dakota, but what she didn't know was that Wild Bill Hickok was also on the wagon train, so Calamity made arrangements to join up when it arrived in Fort Laramie.

The day that Charlie's wagon train was due into Fort Laramie was a troubling one for Charlie. During the night someone had entered Jeddah Kings wagon and had slit his throat and had removed his money belt which everyone knew he had. Normally, Charlie would have done a lockdown of his train and searched everyone's wagon and person, but he didn't want to slow down his schedule. Jeddah was traveling by himself with enough cash to build a saloon and dance emporium where he was also going to employ several of the prostitutes that were on the wagon train.

RJ was also concerned about the murder which had occurred that night.

"What do you think about Jeddah being murdered last night?" Calvin asked as he walked up to RJ.

Calvin was feeling extremely tired this morning. His head hurts and it was another hot morning and he woke up soaked with sweat.

"How did you know about the murder?" RJ asked as he eyed a sweaty Calvin and looking worse than he had at any other time since he was hit on the head. Obviously, he didn't get much sleep during the night. RJ worried about him.

"I heard you telling Tom and Hank a while ago." Remembering what else he had heard RJ telling Tom and Hank that morning, he now questioned RJ.

"How much money did Jeddah have in the money belt?"

"Charlie wasn't sure, but he thought it had to be thousands because he was planning to buy or build a saloon and dance emporium once he reached Deadwood. He was said to have also talked to some of the women and had secured them for his venture of having a stable of whores."

Thinking about the money now, RJ knew that a man couldn't possibly carry too much money on him, especially in a money belt, so that meant that there had to be a secret compartment built into his wagon someplace.

"So what is Charlie going to do about it?" Calvin asked and at the same time ran his hands over his head to get rid of the sweat rivulets that had accumulated there.

"Wow. How did you get that cut on your hand?" RJ asked, reaching for his hand to examine it.

Before Calvin could answer, Charlie's voice was heard instructing everyone to climb aboard their wagons and move out. This time not only Charlie and his brother Steve were leading the wagon train out of Fort Laramie but in the front wagon which used to belong to Jeddah was Bill Hickok and sitting beside him was Calamity Jane.

RJ, Calvin, Tom and Hank watched as Charlie's Shutler Wagon's passed through the gates of the fort. The gaudy painted wagons brought a variety of remarks and laughter from the soldiers who watched them pulling out through the fort's gate.

With the excitement of once more being under way, gone were the unanswered questions concerning the murder of Jeddah and the cut on Calvin's hand. The wagons would now make good time with no other cities or towns to stop at and that was fine with RJ as he wanted to get to Deadwood. Once again, he held back so that they wouldn't have to deal with the dust, which made quite a cloud by the thirty wagons with their teams and even from those who walked next to the wagons. The journey would be long now with the heat of early,

As RJ was waiting for the dust to settle, a woman that appeared to be in her early thirties and a widow, walked up to him as he was doing one last check before pulling out, and asked if he would be willing to let her join them.

Calvin, Tom and Hank all stood there staring at this attractive woman and waiting for RJ's answer. Before RJ could answer she continued, "I can cook, do laundry," and lifting her billowing skirts, showed off a nice pair of legs and stated that they hadn't been wrapped around a man since her husband was killed, and for a lift to Deadwood she would be willing to let them all samples her charms.

Calvin looked at Tom and they both smiled at each other.

Martha Kelly was the name she gave RJ. Her husband had brought her from the east coast out west when he was given a promotion that included the command of Fort Laramie. He had been killed with his first encounter with a small group of hostile Indians who had been raising hell with the settlers who chose to build homes outside the safety and protection the fort offered. The Lakota Sioux were getting more and more worked up from the many settlers taking Lakota land for their own.

That was how Commander Kelly's life came to an end, and why Martha Kelly was now offering herself for a ride out of this place that only offered bad memories which had haunted her dreams since his death. She also had grown tired of the many soldiers who tried to interest her in a little fun, and the new commander that had taken over the Fort's command, lately had been demanding her charms, to the point she was actually worried that one of these nights he would break into her room and rape her. As she stood there telling her story, RJ observed the way she wrung her hands together and paced in small circles

RJ looked at Calvin, who had stood and listened as she told her story and nodded his head in agreement to let her come along.

"We would be honored to have you along." RJ told her.

Martha immediately rushed into his arms and burst into tears.

"Oh, thank you, thank you," she sobbed.

RJ was taken aback by her sudden movement into his arms and visualized in his mind what the days and nights must have been like since her husband's death. If the heat of the day didn't make his shirt wet with sweat, her tears did. Her being so desperate to leave the fort that she would offer herself to him, a complete stranger saddened him. Whispering in her ear, RJ reassured her that everything would be alright from here on out. He felt her trembling body relax and heard a shallow sigh escape her lips.

Taking hold of her shoulders RJ gently pushed her away. He locked eyes with her and told her to go and get her things and they would wait. Rushing away with the promise that she would return quickly, RJ looked over at Tom and Hank and simply shrugged his shoulders.

As promised, fifteen minutes later Martha returned, hauling a large case. Calvin, seeing her struggling to carry it, ran to her side and removed it from her hands

"Is that all you have to bring?"

"That's all I want. I need to leave everything behind that reminds me of this place."

RJ saw that Martha had changed and was now wearing men's clothes. The trousers had been taken in to fit her figure and in doing so, exaggerated her rounded behind.

"Your husband was entitled to his horse, saddle and arms." RJ told her. "Even if you don't necessarily want them, they will fetch you some money."

Martha just looked despairingly at RJ and he immediately understood. Motioning to Calvin to stay with her and the wagon, he lit off in the direction of the Commander's office.

"RJ is a really nice man." Martha said to Calvin as they both watched RJ enter the Commander's office. Five minutes later, RJ walked out of that office and walked to another building marked ARMORY. They watched him enter and when he exited this time he was carrying a rifle, sword and a pistol in a holster.

Walking over to Calvin, RJ handed him the weapons and headed out in the direction of the stables. RJ was gone a little longer, but when he appeared he was leading a beautiful pure black stallion wearing a fancy saddle, with some of the most beautiful bead work and shiny silver trim conches he had ever seen.

"Wow, "was all that Calvin could voice as RJ walked up to them.

Tears were rolling down Martha's face as she once again saw the magnificent stallion with its beautifully handmade saddle that his men had given to him as a welcoming gift the first day on duty, and now seeing it for the first time since his death, brought back memories of his love for the horse and saddle.

Martha said, "Commander Kelly loved that horse and that saddle was the most beautiful thing he owned." A smile crossed her tear stained face as she went on to say that he told her she was really the most beautiful but that he didn't *own* her.

"Here is the story Martha. The livery man says he will give you twelve hundred dollars for this horse and saddle. I told him that it wasn't mine to sell but would be glad to ask the owner."

"Neither is for sale." Martha told him shaking her head. "I would like for you to accept them as a gift from a very thankful woman, RJ."

A whistle escaped Calvin's lips as he ran his hand across the horse's sleek neck.

"You don't have to do that," was all that RJ could muster, being left speechless at the gift he had just been given.

"I know that RJ." Then walking to him reached out her arms and putting them around his neck, pulled him down so she could plant a kiss on his lips.

That kiss was the most tender that RJ had ever received, and he wrapped his arms around her waist and pulled her in against his heated body.

Martha couldn't believe how her body responded to being drawn in so close to a man again and the feel of his lips on hers, and the hardness of his body and the tenderness of his hug.

And then as they both realized what had just happened, they separated so quickly that one would have thought that a handful of hot coals had been dropped between them.

"That was interesting." Calvin said with a wicked grin, giving RJ a swift slap on the back.

Helping Martha up onto the wagon's seat, he motioned for Calvin to join her.

"I think I will ride horseback for a while," Calvin said with a big grin on his face.

I ain't never ridden such a fine animal before, were RJ's thoughts as he lightly touched the Stallion's flanks and took off like his ass had been stung by a bee. RJ knew that the custom made saddle would take some getting used to. As he reined the stallion to a stop, he noticed a slight stain on the saddle horn and wondered if it was made by the Commander's blood. A question he would never get answered simply because it would never get asked.

As RJ rode back to the wagon, he noticed for the first time the blueberry colored eyes of Martha. This time, though, she had no tears in them and they sparkled like the stars at night, kissing the dark sky.

For some reason, RJ's stomach felt like he had swallowed a dozen butterflies. A feeling he hadn't felt for a long, long time now.

"I couldn't help but notice you ride the same way Johnny did." RJ just looked at Martha at the mention of her dead husband.

"Johnny used to have such a smooth way of riding the horse that they seemed as one even when he would spur him into a fast run."

RJ knew just what she was talking about and he saw Calvin nod his head in agreement.

The dust had settled so RJ told everyone that it was time to be under way. With one last look around, RJ tipped his hat to the few that stood around and spurred his new friend into a slight trot.

As they passed by the undertaker's they saw a new wood coffin being loaded onto a flatbed wagon and watched it make its way to the cemetery. Charlie had forked over the money so that Jeddah would have a proper burial and headstone, rather than being buried in Boot Hill.

Once again, RJ's thoughts were on Jeddah's murder and the money he was said to have had in the stolen money belt.

The first day back on the trail was uneventful. RJ noticed that Calvin showed no signs of his head injury. Late in the day he felt a soreness in his rear and knew that it was time to either get out his own saddle or ride up there in the wagon next to Martha.

The day's sun was quickly turning to dusk and it wasn't long before they rode up onto the wagon train. Charlie had stopped for the night.

That first night, Martha went over to the Chuck Wagon to help out Cookie. It was something she would not do again. As she walked by Cookie, he reached out and pinched her behind. This brought an immediate reaction from Martha as she reached for the first thing she could get her hands on. That was a large cast iron skillet and as she turned with it, only at the last minute changing its course from the side of his head, which would probably have killed him, to lowering it a few inches so that it hit his left shoulder.

There probably wasn't a person around that didn't hear the breaking of a shoulder bone, and the loud anguished scream from Cookie.

Grabbing his shoulder wasn't the smartest thing for Cookie to do as Martha swung the skillet once again. This time landing on the hand that Cookie had grabbed his shoulder with, which was also the one used to pinch Martha's behind. Once again, the sound of breaking bones echoed through the camp along with another scream of pain from Cookie.

All this was followed by a loud burst of laughter. RJ knew that he had to step in before Martha decided to swing that skillet again. Rushing up behind her, he wrapped his arms around her waist and lifted her off her feet, which caused the group to laugh even harder. Seems everyone wanted to see more of this woman's temper or they were so sick of Cookie's chow they wanted him out of action.

Arms swinging and legs kicking, the four lettered words coming from Martha's mouth burned RJ's ears but excited the group. As he carried Martha, he noticed how slim her waist was. It was several more minutes before Martha had calmed down enough to the point where RJ released his hold on her.

"That son's-a-bitch pinched my behind. No one pinches my behind, no one!" Martha had calmed down, but her voice was still loud and no doubt overheard by everyone as more laughter was heard.

"Charlie and Wild Bill are on their way over." Tom told RJ walking up beside him and Martha.

"Well, now," said Charlie, "I guess we have a problem here that this young lady is responsible for causing."

"No one gets away with pinching my behind and walks away in one piece." There was still anger heard in Martha's voice.

"What do you have in mind, Charlie?" asked RJ, releasing Martha.

"Well, while we were at the Fort, I was told that this young lady was noted for making cakes and on some occasions did some cooking for the troops. Now with Cookie injured, we will need someone to take his place and I have no one to replace him with. Stopping for a moment he eyed his men and turned back to RJ and Martha and asked. "What do you say Martha. Come and be our cook and I promise you that there will be no more behind pinching or anything else out of place." He turned to the group. "Right men?"

Hesitating, then responding with resounding, "RIGHT," came the reply.

"What do you say, Martha? Will you be willing to come help out?"

"Under one condition. You tell these folk that no one lays a finger on me."

"I think I just made sure that doesn't happen again." Charlie said as he turned away and started walking back to the wagon train.

"If Charlie gives his word, it's set in stone," was all that Wild Bill said, before walking away following Charlie.

RJ watched as they walked away, turned and put his arm around Martha's shoulder and simply put his cheek next to hers.

"Looks like I should have brought some of my cake pans." Martha stood on her toes and planted a kiss on RJ's cheek.

Chapter 10

Over the next few weeks, RJ and Martha grew closer together. She stayed back with him until about three o'clock every afternoon. That is when she would leave the wagon and get on her horse and together they rode to catch the wagon train which stopped every day at four, so that everyone had ample time to themselves to wash the trail dust from their faces, and get the big camp fire started. Martha would go to the chuck wagon and start to prepare some grub for everyone. Cookie would help the best that he could and as promised by Charlie, no one attempted to lay their hands on her.

There was a double lined wood box that served as a holding place for any varmints shot along the trail that could act as part of the supper chow that Martha prepared. Today when she raised the lid, she was surprised to see two turkeys and a couple of rabbits. As she removed them, Hilda and Sue Ellen walked up and greeted her.

Sue Ellen was a small, blue eyed, blond of seventeen who had left her home after her ma and pa were killed by an Indian raiding party. She had survived by hiding in the root cellar under the kitchen floor. It had been hard on her, hearing her ma screaming and then her pa's loud voice before it turned to a gargling sound as his throat was slit. Another loud scream from her ma was heard. She would hear that scream over and over again throughout the night, only guessing at what was being done to her. There had been enough stories told and printed about such attacks and what the savages did to the white women, before killing them. She heard later, that a small Indian raiding party was captured by the Cavalry. One of the Indians had tied to his horse's mane a long blond ponytail with a yellow ribbon tied to it. Sue Ellen knew, from finding her ma scalped and her ponytail gone, that this was her Ma's. She had asked the Fort's Commander about it and several weeks went by before he located her and gave the ponytail to her. She now kept it in a little fancy beaded pouch.

Hilda, on the other hand, was cut out of the same cloth as Martha, the only difference was Hilda was a prostitute, and at thirty two years old, knew that her years of working were numbered. She was in hopes of going to Deadwood and maybe finding some older prospector who had a claim and who needed a woman around to make his nights more comfortable and to feed him some good food. Up to now, she had been lucky. She had been stabbed twice and had lain close to death for two months. It was Martha and Sue Ellen, who had taken care of her at the Fort's Infirmary which consisted of a row of six cots, a cabinet holding some bandages and salves, and rubbing alcohol used to disinfect open sores, gunshot wounds and an array of different cuts. Although the Fort had a halfway good doctor, it was Martha and Sue Ellen, who had nursed Hilda back to health.

Tonight as the sky darkened and a bright moon lit up the sky Martha noticed for the first time the business of the train. Like herself, everyone had a specific job to do. Brushing the horses, inspecting the wagons, hauling buckets of water from the water wagon back to theirs. She saw that there weren't many children. Hell, there were more dogs running around than kids.

As Martha gazed around the camp, her eyes stopped on Sue Ellen and she saw for the first time her innocent features and decided to make some conversation with her.

"What are your plans Sue Ellen when we get to Deadwood?"

A big smile lit up her face and there was excitement in her voice. "Hilda wants me to come to work for her as a dancer."

Martha gave a quick turn of her head looking Hilda right in the eyes. "Have you told this young lady just what sort of dancing you expect from her?" asked a concerned Martha and that concernment showing in her voice.

Before Hilda could answer, Sue Ellen put her hand on Martha's shoulder. Martha turned and looked at her. "She told me." Sue Ellen said with the same excited voice.

For a moment, Martha felt sorry for Sue Ellen and wanted to speak, but Hilda spoke up.

"There are worse things for such a pretty young thing." Hilda said. "What kind of life do you think she would have on her own in Deadwood?" Stopping for a minute to give thought of what she wanted to say next, she continued, "Everyone saw what you did to Cookie. Suppose that was Sue Ellen's rump he pinched. What would she have done? Huhhh? Tell me? At least with me she stands a chance of surviving."

Martha knew what Hilda was saying was true. If it had been Sue Ellen instead of her, she would have ended up being Cookie's plaything for the night.

"Just look at her." Hilda said. "Right now, I've seen a lot of the men on this train look at her with evil grins, wanting nothing better than to run their hands over those luscious curves. As to demonstrate what she had said, Hilda ran her hands lightly over the bare skin of Sue Ellen's arms.

"We'll get along just fine now won't we Sue Ellen?"

Before Sue could answer, there was a voice from behind them asking, "How's them birds coming, ladies?"

Turning around at the sound of a man's voice, Martha saw it, was that of Steve, Charlie's brother.

"Good," said Martha. "As a matter of fact, you can give us a hand." Reaching for the long spits she jabbed them through the bird's backside and out through its neck and handed them to Steve.

"Here," Martha said, handing the birds to Steve. "Go over and pass each of them through the fire a few times and burn off all those feathers and brown their skin up some, then bring them back to me."

The large cast iron pot of water that sat in the corner of the fire had just started to boil. Martha picked up several of the peeled onions and walked over and dropped them into the boiling water. Almost instantly the hot, dry air was filled with the welcoming smell of food cooking. Two skinned rabbit carcasses were thrown in next.

The night's air was soon filled with the odor of tobacco, cooking food, and the music of someone playing a fiddle. All the smells and the fiddle playing had a calming effect on everyone. Even the livestock and horses were giving off their own form of speech, as they were fed and bedded down for the night, and as always the howwoo, howwoo, howwwwoooww of a couple of coyote's, also enjoying the coming darkness and the end of another day.

The two turkeys and rabbits would only go so far, so it was up to everyone to make a dish to share. These dishes were placed atop a makeshift table of two boards placed on a couple of wooden crates. There would be some small towns on the way to Deadwood where staples would be re-stocked. Charlie had done his homework well and so far the wagon train headed to Deadwood hadn't encountered so much as a heavy rain.

Having gotten the rabbits starting to cook and the turkeys on a spit, Martha made her way back to the smaller campfire that RJ had started. She immediately spied the coffee pot and the steam rising from it.

"Would you get me a cup of that coffee I see boiling?" RJ immediately fetched her cup and poured her a steaming cup of the strong brew. He was used to her routine and watched for her every evening. Knowing her love for the strong brew, he always had her cup ready and lived for the smile she rewarded him with as he handed her the cup. He had never met a woman who enjoyed a cup of Arbuckle as much as she did, and silently wondered what else she enjoyed.

I can't imagine in such a short timeframe what I've come to feel for this woman. RJ knew that once they arrived in Deadwood, that he would have to confront his feelings for Martha. After all, he wasn't getting any younger.

RJ stared into the fire as Martha sipped on her coffee.

Calvin saw the looks that went back and forth between RJ and Martha and knew that he was slowly losing his best friend to a woman and his stomach did a slight flip flop at the thought. *You're more than a best friend, RJ. You are family.*

Calvin's thoughts, were interrupted by the presence of Tom and Hank, who told Martha that they had cooked up some stew.

"I can see that." Said Martha. "Why, thank you, Tom," she said, bringing the bowl to her nose. "Smells delicious!"

"RJ has told me you boys bought his hauling business, but decided to leave Denver for Deadwood. "I've been at the fort for some time and not once did I ever see or hear of any freight wagon haulers."

"Now, don't go discouraging them, Martha! They'll want to sell the hauling business back to us." Calvin and RJ looked at Tom and Hank and it was Calvin who spoke.

"You wouldn't really do that, would you boys?"

There was a short silence where the only sounds heard were the snap, crackling of their fire and the sounds coming from the wagon train.

"No, of course not." It was Hank who spoke up. "You two already know that there are some other ventures we are considering."

Both, RJ and Calvin gave Hank a dirty look and silently hoped he wouldn't blab out just what that consideration was.

"Not to worry, RJ. We made a deal and plan on keeping it."

Before anything else was said, Sue Ellen appeared with a tin plate on which was some pieces of turkey and a hind end of one of the rabbits.

"Cookie sent me over with this food."

Everyone looked at the slices of turkey and the rabbit and smacked their lips.

Setting the plate down, Sue Ellen turned to leave.

"Wait, Sue Ellen." It was Martha who spoke. "I want you to meet these people." With that, Sue Ellen was introduced to RJ, Calvin, Tom and Hank. Once introduced, Sue Ellen turned to leave.

"Let me walk you back to your wagon," offered Tom, who had stood up and removed his hat when introduced to her.

"I'd like that," came Sue Ellen's reply.

Tom was a few years older than Sue Ellen but had instantly been awed by her beauty. Tripping over his own feet, Tom stumbled his way to Sue Ellen's side where he offered up his arm. Putting her arm through his, they walked away with six eyes following them.

"Sue Ellen has befriended a woman named Hilda who wants her to work for her as a dancer once they arrive in Deadwood." Sitting down and sipping her coffee, Martha continued. "You all know what kind of job that really means don't you?" she asked? No one had to answer.

"Deadwood isn't gonna be a very nice place for such a beauty as Sue Ellen."

"No, it won't be RJ," came Martha's reply to his statement.

Word of life in Deadwood had reached most cities. Everyone knew what life was like in a "BOOM TOWN", especially for that of a young woman such as Sue Ellen.

No more words were spoken as they sat around the night's fire, listening to the sounds around them and gazing into the flames until their eyes started to close.

The fire was nothing more than a pile of embers when Tom returned. Calvin, Martha and Hank were asleep and RJ was in a semi state of sleep and was aware of Tom's return. With a smile on his face, RJ rolled over on his side and put his arm around Martha. Feeling her warm body next to his, closed his eyes and was fast asleep within minutes.

Martha, being half asleep herself was also aware of Tom's return and felt RJ's arm and the warmth of his body as he snuggled up next to her. Her thoughts were the thoughts of a woman who was quickly falling in love and the tear that ran down her check was one of happiness instead of sadness.

The noise of the night was quickly fading, as the night wrapped them all in her darkness.

As the wagon train slumbered, many miles away in a town called Deadwood, people and businesses were just starting to come alive. Those who had worked hard all day, were now ready to play.

CHAPTER 11

Five weeks into the journey to Deadwood found the travelers still in good spirits. No major happenings so far. Sue Ellen was now riding in the freight wagon with Tom and Hank. Both had taken a shining to her and her to them. Martha kept a watchful eye on both Tom and Hank but so far they were nothing but gentlemen toward her.

Calvin had been having some terrible headaches which were more frequent as the trail became less traveled and bumpier. At these times all he wanted to do was to lie in the bed of the wagon with his arms wrapped around his head.

"What are you going to do about Calvin?" asked Martha, looking back at him curled up on the wagon's bed. This time the headache had been going on for two days straight and Calvin had been those days without food or water and Martha was getting worried about him.

"Not much to do for him until we get to Deadwood. We will come across a couple of more towns but neither one is large enough to have a doctor, unless we are lucky enough to have a traveling doctor there." In these days those towns that couldn't keep a doctor were visited by traveling ones.

"Tonight when I go to cook, I'll ask around and see if anyone has any kind of medicine that might be of some use for his head."

All thoughts stopped with the arrival of two men on horseback.

RJ noticed right away the low slung holsters and the dried bloodstain on the right arm of a young blond boy. For a minute, RJ thought them to be brothers and was a bit surprised when they introduced themselves and he learned they were in fact father and son.

"Names Harvey Lewis," the older of the two spoke with a grin that showed off several rotten black teeth. "Folk that know me call me, Heavy Harv."

RJ eyed him up and down and it was an obvious nickname seeing his size ranged from extra-large to humungous. "My son there is Travis."

Both RJ and Martha extended hello's followed by their own introductions.

Heavy Harv spoke up. "We heard that there was a wagon train headed to Deadwood." Turning in his saddle and looking back and forth at the two wagons continued. "I wouldn't suppose you're that wagon train?"

"We're with that wagon train which is about two miles ahead of us. We joined late, so we were at the back eating too much dust so we dropped back a couple miles so it could settle some."

"How bad is your boy hurt?" It was Martha that spoke looking at Travis then back at Harv.

"Nothing to concern yourself with, ma'am," Harv said, tipping his hat, looking at his son, he gave him a nod, then putting his boot heels to his horse's flanks, the two galloped away without saying more.

For a couple minutes, RJ and Martha sat and watched as the two galloped off in a cloud of dust.

"Wonder what or who they are running from?" Martha questioned, finally.

"Don't know, but we will probably find out once we settle in for the night." Turning to gaze back at Tom and Hank, RJ lifted his arm and motioned that they were moving. The jerk of the wagon brought a loud moan from Calvin. Martha turned and stepped over the seat back and sat down next to Calvin and as softly as she could, lifted his head and placed it on her lap.

Calvin, with a look of pain on his face, opened his eyes and gave her a slight smile before once again closing them and wrapping his arms around his head trying to make the pain subside.

"Tonight I need you to find out all you can about those two," said RJ, speaking over his shoulder at Martha. "There is something about them that sticks in my craw."

"I had the same feeling. Did you see the dried blood on the kid's shirt sleeve?"

I did," answered RJ. "I would say he was either shot or stabbed."

The heat of the noonday sun was starting to affect the team as some froth started showing up around their mouths and one could see the sweat appear on their hides.

"We need to stop and rest the team." RJ sensed that Charlie was putting on as many miles a day now that he could without wearing out many of the wagon teams. They had only crossed one river over the past few days and the water barrels were getting close to empty as the heat sapped the strength from the horses.

RJ knew that Beaver Creek was up ahead and was sure that is where Charlie would settle for the night.

About the time that Martha was getting ready to leave RJ and head out for the wagon train, laughter and singing was heard from the trail in front of them. Rounding the bend in the road, they saw that the wagon train had come to a halt beside a large river.

"Must be Beaver Creek," RJ said.

Pulling up behind the last wagon RJ pulled his team to a halt. Martha stepped down and headed for the chuck wagon with instructions to find out all she could about the father and son.

Calvin sat up and by the look on his face RJ knew he was still in some pain, but a lot less than previously.

Tom and Hank set about making a fire and boiling water to make some coffee. Campfire smoke filled the evening air and mouths started to salivate knowing food was soon to be tasted. "Won't be long before the pot's boiling," Tom remarked, then turned to RJ and spoke. "Them fella's out on the trail. Suppose they are wanted killers? Maybe have a price on their heads?"

RJ sensed a little excitement in Tom's voice. "I don't rightly know, Tom! We might know a little more once Martha has a chance to ask around." Tom nodded his head, acknowledging RJ's words.

"Not much we can do about it anyways," RJ continued.

"You're right about that, but it would be a plus to know something more about them. Here comes Martha now."

Looking in the direction Tom had motioned, RJ was surprised to see Martha walking towards them. In her hand she was holding a small bottle.

As she approached the campfire, she gave a big smile to RJ, and standing on her tip toes planted a warm kiss on his cheek. Both knew they were falling for each other and it was all RJ could do not to wrap his arms around her waist and continue that hello kiss.

"I have some medicine for Calvin," Martha said, holding a small bottle out to RJ. Taking the bottle from her outstretched hand, RJ took off the cap and held it to his nose for a smell.

"Holy crap! What the hell is this stuff?" RJ remarked, holding the bottle at arm's length and rubbing his nose on his shirt sleeve.

"Something they call laudanum and I was told to give Calvin only a spoonful at a time."

"I've heard of that stuff." Hank spoke up. "Mostly made up of morphine and opium and can be addictive if not taken wisely. Many a person had fallen into the hell of addiction if not careful." RJ had also heard of the stuff.

RJ handed it back to Martha. Taking a spoon from their cooking kit, proceeded to pour some out and told Calvin to open his mouth.

"Holy Mother of God!" That was the reaction from Calvin once he swallowed the liquid. It burned his throat all the way to his stomach, where it immediately felt like he had swallowed a mouthful of hot coals. His eyes teared up and his nose ran. After a few minutes, Calvin felt the pain in his head subside, and for the first time in a week, RJ saw Calvin's old familiar face.

Calvin's eyes became clear and full of life. Gone was the hazy look of pain that he had felt since receiving the pistol blow to the head. All of Calvin's sensors returned in the short time span it took for the laudanum to have its effect.

"RJ, I'm leaving this bottle with you. Don't let him have any more for at least an hour or two , and not even then, if he doesn't need it." She handed the bottle to him and he took it. "I got that from Mr. Wilson, who is a dentist. He will be around a little later for his five dollars." Seeing RJ's eyebrows rise, she informed him that was the price for two bottles, one of which he would be bringing with him. Kissing RJ's cheek, Martha left. RJ watched as she walked away and he felt that old manly feeling and could hardly wait for her return.

Doc Wilson, just as Martha had told him came around shortly after dark once evening chores were taken care of. Although a dentist by trade, Doc Wilson had been traveling around in a wagon he had decked out and had fancy lettering painted on the outside of it. All sorts of items were listed for sale and the wagon had been his traveling home. He had all kinds of elixirs, Magic cure medicines, Granny remedies promising to cure whatever "ailed ya", and even some pots and pans and other utensils for sale.

RJ at once recognized him from his short stay in Denver. He smiled at remembering that the town folk had wanted to string him up and he and Calvin had talked them into not doing so if he would agree to do some free dental work for the town folk. Seeing it was that or having his neck stretched, he agreed. Now here he was again, but under different circumstances.

"Why, I'll be a son-of a gun! Is that you, RJ?"

"Wha'd' ya say Doc." RJ took the extended hand and the two patted each other's shoulders as if they were two long-lost brothers.

"That woman, Martha, didn't tell me who it was that I gave her the Laudanum for." Having now released hands and facing each other, RJ was the next to speak.

"Not for me Doc, but for Calvin here."

Doc Wilson took Calvin's hand and shook it.

"Why do you need something as strong as Laudanum?" He asked?

"Some time ago, another man hit him in the head with a pistol and he has been having terrible headaches and acting strange from time to time." RJ went on to tell Doc all the strange things that Calvin had done since receiving the horrible hit to the head.

"By the sounds of things, I'd say Calvin here needs to see a real doctor."

"He will, just as soon as we reach Deadwood, but in the meantime, he needed something for the pain, and by the looks of him right now, that Laudanum has done the trick."

Calvin was aware of both RJ and Doc talking about him, but for some reason their voices tended to echo in his mind as though he was hearing them from far away. It was quiet now as he looked first at RJ and then Doc.

That man standing beside RJ looks awful familiar. Blinking his eyes a few times to get them to focus, where they had been blurry, Calvin remembered the face and a smile lit up his face for the first time in a long while.

"Is that you, Doc Wilson? Shoot, I figured that some of the town folk followed you out of town and strung you up. Can you believe it, RJ?"

Doc Wilson reached into his vest pocket and took out another bottle and handed it to RJ. RJ in return handed the five dollars to Doc who waved it off.

"Keep your money. Tomorrow evening come by my wagon and I will have something else for him to take till you can get him to a doc in Deadwood. That stuff there, nodding to the bottle of Laudanum, is pretty strong and he could become addicted to it."

"We'll keep a close eye on it."

A little more small talk and Doc bid his good-night and headed back to his wagon.

"Shucks RJ! Did you think we would ever see that guy again?"

"Can't say that I did."

"What's that medicine he gave Martha to give to me?" Calvin had started to feel the head pain coming and told RJ he needed to take another spoonful. The Laudanum didn't taste half as bad this time and within a matter of minutes, Calvin felt relief from the pain as the morphine that was in the medicine did its job.

It's easy to see his relief from the pain, but I wonder if it will relieve him of the sudden outbursts that he has? This was a question that only time would tell, and RJ was hoping that it would. For now anyway, RJ was happy for his friend and the relief he was finally getting from the awful headaches.

As Calvin walked over to the campfire, RJ noticed that the bounce he once had in his step had returned.

Back at the chuck wagon, Martha and Sue Ellen were busy cooking the skinned deer that awaited them.

"Cookie. Did you see two men ride in today?" Martha figured that if anyone knew them, Cookie would.

"Yup. Why do you ask?" Came his reply.

"Just curious, that's all. They stopped by our wagon. It looked like the younger one was hurt."

Cookie eyed Martha before he spoke. It didn't do anyone any good talking about others and one had to watch his words and look out for ears which always seemed present.

"They came riding up and without asking any questions, rode right by all the wagons and rode right up to Charlie. A few minutes later they rode right over to Doc Wilson's wagon where the young blond haired kid got down from his horse and jumped aboard Doc's wagon.

Martha listened as Cookie went on to tell her that once they had stopped, Doc and the kid disappeared in the wagon.

"He was still in Doc's wagon when you arrived."

Looking Martha up and down, and stopping with his eyes fastening on her bosom, Cookie asked. "You wanna know who they are, don't ya?"

Martha let Cookie have his look before turning from his gaze, offering him a nice long look at her backside which she made sure to swing a little extra.

"I didn't know who they were but I heard Hickok telling Jane that old man Lewis and his son had arrived so they must have been expecting them at some time or another."

Martha only shrugged her shoulders at the mention of his name.

"You don't have any idea who Heavy Harvey Lewis is do you?"

"Nope." RJ had noticed that the boy had dried blood on his shirt sleeve, other than that we didn't pay much attention to them."

"Harvey and his son are wanted in several states for bank robbery, holding up a stage where the driver was killed and two women passengers were raped and also shot. One of the women lived to give a description of the two. Wasn't hard to figure that it was Harvey Lewis and his boy. Not too many fella's around that fit the description of old Harvey."

"How much reward money is offered?"

Bounty Hunters

"Don't know. Like I told you, I didn't know them, Hickok does. Go ask him."

"I don't much care who they are to ask him."

Martha didn't dare ask any more questions. She knew that Cookie had no more information to give, and there was no way she was talking to Bill Hickok.

If RJ wants to know more he will just have to come visit with Bill.

"Well. If it isn't the woman I met earlier," came a voice from behind her. Turning, Martha now stood face to face with Heavy Harvey Lewis and up this close he looked huge.

Standing there, she could feel herself break out in a cold sweat and a creeping feeling that started from her feet and crept up her spine, as the hair on her neck stood on end. She started breathing shallowly. Of all the people she had encountered in her travels, she had never had this reaction and had no idea what it meant. Instantly, she pictured this slob of a man, in the act of violating one of the women Cookie had just told her about and felt that if she had a pistol she would use it the same way one had been used on Calvin, but then she thought that she would just put a bullet right between the fat bastard's eyes.

Maybe he had done the women a favor by shooting them once he and his son had their pleasure. She shook her head, trying to rid her mind of that picture.

"What do you have cooking back there?" were the next words she heard him ask, "Smells mighty fine."

Mustering up every ounce of courage she possessed, Martha was determined to not show her disgust for this man, but to see if she could get any information from him to give to RJ later on.

"Some of the boys shot a deer today and that is what you smell cooking."

Harvey's eyebrows, which Martha noticed were probably the bushiest she had ever seen, and went straight across his nose with no stop, now rose up as he opened his eyes wide.

She noticed some spittle run from the corner of his mouth, black from the large ball of chew which puffed out his left cheek It was obvious to her that these signs meant that he was hungry and the smell of the deer had started to affect him or did he smell her own sweaty body. The thought of him leering at her in that way sent a shiver up her spine.

Looking at him she asked. "Where's the boy who was with you earlier?"

Without giving the question any thought, Harvey started to tell her. "The boy was shot in the arm a couple days back. He and I were standing outside this trading post back in the hills and there was this kid doing all kinds of pistol tricks when it went off and the lead hit my boy Travis in the arm." Turning slightly, he gestured in the direction of one of the wagons and told her. "He's over there in that wagon. That's where I took him.
Some traveling Medicine Man."

Before Martha could ask any more questions, they both saw Travis step from the back of the Doc's wagon. Harvey mumbled under his breath, something Martha couldn't quite make out before saying he had best go see Travis. As he turned to leave, Martha couldn't help but notice the awful stench coming from him and a shiver rippled through her as once again the thought of him violating the women Cookie had told her about. She turned her head and gagged, not wanting anyone to see her, she put a handkerchief up to her mouth to capture the awful tasting bile which invaded her mouth and made her eyes water.

The meal was over and Martha was walking back to RJ's wagon with some of the deer stew, when she heard stealthy footsteps behind her. Turning her head, she saw Harvey coming up quickly behind her. She hurried up her steps, but he was too fast for her despite his size.

"Hold up there, little lady," he said huffing and puffing, "I wanna ask you somethin'."

"I'm sorry, but I'm in a hurry to get back to my wagon before this food gets cold. I've got some hungry men there, and they wouldn't be too pleased if this stew arrived cold."

"Yeah, I'm still kinda hungry myself." He had a nasty grin on his dirty face and he stepped closer, causing Martha to instantly have a bad feeling as to what was about to happen.

"You've already had your food mister." Martha told him trying to keep her voice normal.

"I'm talking about dessert Missy! You!" Two large, unclean hands came up and reached out for her.

With that, Martha took off running. Harvey lunged at her and grabbing hold of her blouse, he threw her to the ground.

The food she was carrying to RJ went flying and the wind was knocked out of her as Harvy threw himself on top of her, mauling at her blouse and skirt which had flown up as she was tossed to the ground exposing her lacy bloomers.

The darkness was hiding the violation which was about to take place, if Martha didn't get her wind back enough to scream to RJ.

"It's been a while since I've had me a woman!"

Martha looked straight into the face of Harvey and saw the lust in his eyes.

"Noooo," she managed to gasp as his hands ripped her blouse away, exposing her charms to his lust inflamed eyes. Her hand came up and clawed at his face.

"Oh, now is that any way to treat a man who wants you so bad," he held down her one arm as he fumbled with his pants. He managed to get his pants down, but was having trouble with the bloomers when he heard a loud voice next to him, "That's enough mister. Let that gal up," and at the same instant, heard the click of a gun.

"Uh, uh, I'm getting'.' He started to rise, but was having trouble with his pants around his ankles.

The next thing he knew there was the spat of a gun and a bullet went through his 'John Henry' shredding it and leaving a bloody stump pumping blood all over Martha. She screamed and she wasn't the only one, as Harvey bellowed and screamed, his hands covering his crotch as he stumbled and fell tripping over the pants which were still around his ankles.

Back at their wagon, RJ had heard the scream. Flexing his forearm, RJ now held his pipe weapon in his hand and was running toward the scream he had heard.

Calvin just stood there with a smoking gun. Lucky for Martha, he had been taking a walk when he came upon the rape scene. "I guess that's the end of your raping days, Harvey. In fact, I would say that's the end of your having any pleasure from a woman at all. With all the whores in camp, why did you pick on the one decent woman who wasn't one to get your pleasure from?"

With that, Calvin put his arm around Martha and told her it was time to go get RJ.

"What about him? We can't just leave him there Calvin. He'll bleed to death if we leave him."

"So what! Maybe I should just put another bullet between his eyes and put him out of his raping days."

"I can't have that on my conscience despite what he tried to do." Martha and Calvin heard some voices of men coming toward them from the direction of the wagon train.

Calvin shrugged hearing them arrive.

As Calvin and Martha stood there facing in the direction of the oncoming men, they also heard the thumping, running steps of RJ coming in from the opposite direction.

All this time, Harvey lay moaning on the ground, his hands still covering the bloody remains.

Charlie headed up the five men who arrived from the wagon train. Now they all stood around the moaning figure lying on the ground with bloody hands cupping his private parts.

"Oh my God, what did you do to him?"

"I guess you can see what I did to him. That son of a bastard tried to rape Martha and would have if I hadn't been out walking around."

Doc was one of the five men who were called by Charlie to come along hearing the single gunshot and knowing someone might be in need of medical attention.

Charlie shook his head and went to bend down with the others. He started to pull aside Harvey's hands to view the injury when he was pushed aside by RJ.

Having pushed Charlie aside, RJ walked up next to the figure of Harvey still lying on the ground moaning, and before anyone could stop him, he raised the pipe above his head and the night air was filled with the horrible sound of a person's skull being caved in as RJ brought the pipe weapon down squarely on the side of Harvey's head silencing his moaning and another whack to make sure he wasn't going to be around to rape again.

"Well, Charlie," said RJ. "I heard you mention a reward was posted for this man." Pointing to everyone standing there he continued, "You all are witness as to who killed this man and deserving of that reward." Everyone shook their heads in agreement.

"What about his son?" Martha spoke up.

"Doc is fixing him up. We'll keep him chained up until we get to Deadwood. There we will have a trial and a hanging." Turning to face RJ, Charlie had a very stern look on his face when he said. "You can claim the reward for that there fella, but the son's is mine." With that Charlie instructed the others to hoist Harv up and bring him back to the wagons.

"Thank you Calvin." Martha walked over to him and gave him a big hug, then turned and wrapped her arms around RJ, who returned the hug along with a ravishing kiss which left them both breathless.

"Half that bounty money is yours Calvin," RJ said and reached over and gave his friend a loud slap on the back.

Calvin smiled to himself. He always felt proud anytime that RJ made any kind of fuss over him. Where RJ looked at their friendship as that as brothers, Calvin looked at it as father and son. And what son didn't like praise from his dad.

DEADWOOD, SD circa 1876

In 1874 on an expedition into the Black Hills of South Dakota, Colonel George Armstrong Custer announced the discovery of gold and with that announcement a migration of some 5,000 people infested the Black Hills and the illegal town of Deadwood was started.

Charles Utter and his brother Steve would lead a thirty wagon train to Deadwood from Colorado in 1876. Wild Bill Hickok and Calamity Jane would be on that wagon train.

Deadwood would go down in history as the place where Wild Bill Hickok was murdered by Jack McCall while playing his favorite card game. The term "Dead Man's Hand" referrers to the last card hand that Hickok held when he was shot in the back of the head. Aces and Eights, and to this day it is still called the Dead Man's Hand.

As Deadwood grew, lots of money was made and lots of money was lost.

Prostitution, Opium, and the liquor trade were the mainstay of Deadwood. Everything and anything goes in this lawless town.

With the women that were brought into Deadwood by Charlie Utter, Madam Dora Dufran's brothel would soon become the largest and most profitable one in Deadwood.

Another brothel run by Madam Mollie Johnson would also host some of the nicest looking prostitutes in Deadwood, she would also become quite wealthy.

Saloons and drinking emporiums were also top money makers for their owners.

Tom Miller opened the Bella Union Saloon, which would be a top money maker in Deadwood.

Al Swearengen, who ran the Opium trade in Deadwood, was owner of the Gem Variety Theater, which was a front for his Opium business.

On Charlie's wagon train were several Chinese. Wong Fee Lee would become a wealthy and prominent merchant, but most Chinese who came to Deadwood worked in the service trade or as prostitutes.

Deadwood would suffer two major fires from which many called it quits and moved on to other towns to continue their businesses.

Deadwood's population today is approx. 1,270.

Chapter 12

Two days out from Deadwood, all hell seemed to break loose. The wagon train was hit by three incidents, two of which would have future ramifications.

First. . . . a broken wagon wheel would kill two of the travelers. Dale Peterson, who was traveling to Deadwood to start up a Blacksmith shop, and the Lovely Lilly, who was going to work in one of the many brothels that she and the other prostitutes had heard about.

There was no doubt that the wagon was overloaded with much iron and tools of the Blacksmith trade. That night, the accident could have been prevented if Dale had checked his wagon over. At least ten of the wagon wheel spokes were showing large cracks. As was the custom on this trip, because of the summer heat, sleeping under a wagon was quite common. This night would find Dale and the Lovely Lilly entertaining each other when the spokes finally shattered, dropping the heavily loaded wagon on top of them, and crushing them to death.

"Well, all I can say is that Dale left this earth a happy man!" were remarks made by Charlie as Dale was laid to rest in a grave beside the trail. A few stones were piled over it as a marker. Dale's wagon was picked fairly clean of anything that might be of some use later on. Charlie emptied his pockets of any money he had and checked the wagon over before letting the others have at it.

"I wish I'd gotten to know him during this trip," came the voice of the one picking through Dale's stuff.

"Yep, it's a shame a man has to be buried out here, along the trail and no one knows it."

"I think I remembered him talking about a brother he was going to send for as soon as he got the shop up and running enough to generate some money for a train ticket."

Already, the morning air was hot and sticky. The second grave was dug and the Lovely Lilly, dressed in one of her pretty dresses was laid in it and covered with dirt.

"Now, there's the biggest waste known to man." It was Charlie's brother, Steve, who spoke. In the weeks spent on the trail, he along with several of the men had tasted the dessert Lilly had to offer.

"What was she doing under that wagon with that fella Dale anyways?"

"What the hell do ya think they were doing? She was a whore! Use your imagination!"

Steve had grown close to Lilly and was about to ask her not to continue on in her trade, but tie up with him and Charlie. Now she was dead and Steve hung his head as he walked from her grave. It would take more than Charlie's stories sitting around the night's camp fire to cheer him up.

The second thing to happen was the murder of Dr. Wilson and the escape of Heavy Harvey's son Travis.

The deadly Doctor Wilson was discovered by Martha, who had gone to purchase more medicine for Calvin. Ole Doc had, had his throat slit and because the body was cool, it was believed that it happened pretty early in the evening. There were pieces of rope that had bound Travis to the bed, his bloody shirt and a bloodied knife left in the wagon's bed. The Doc's money box was empty.

Charlie grouped everyone together to ask if anyone had seen or heard anything. No one had.

He also offered Doc's wagon and all the stuff on board along with the team of horses if anyone wanted to buy it. From the group assembled there Calvin spoke right up. I'll give two hundred dollars for it.

Well, I'll be damned, Thought RJ. *In all our years together he had he never spent a measly dime without talking to him first, and now, here he was offering some big money without first talking to him about it.*

Doc's Medicine wagon and horse team sold for six hundred dollars to Calvin. RJ was surprised that all through the bidding he hadn't once counseled him.

I wonder where he got his money. As always, RJ kept most of Calvin's money giving him whatever he asked for whenever he asked, now here he was paying six hundred dollars for a wagon and not having had to ask him for the money.

RJ's thoughts went back to the murder of Jeddah King and the fact that his money belt was stolen and his money box was empty just like Doc's.

I thought it was you back then, and now I can almost be one hundred percent correct in my thoughts.

A stiff slap on the back brought RJ back to the here and now.

"What do ya think of my purchase of Doc's wagon and everything on board?"

It was good for RJ to once again see the twinkle in Calvin's eyes and the broad ear to ear grin on his face even while suspecting him of the two murders.

"The Laudanum medicine sure has helped you these past couple of days?"

Still with a big smile, Calvin acknowledged RJ. "It sure has."

RJ had found an empty medicine bottle in the wagon and assumed that Calvin had been taking it without his knowledge. Finding Martha and questioning her as to what Doc had told her about the Laudanum, he became even more concerned for his friend.

"I think he is getting hooked on that stuff. Not only have I found an empty bottle, but he has been acting a little strange over the past couple days."

"I've noticed a change in him also," Martha said.

"Today, out of the clear blue, he started to bid on Doc's wagon."

"He what! Now, why would he do something like that?" Martha knew exactly what Calvin was doing bidding on the medicine wagon.

"I suppose it was to secure all the bottles of that Laudanum."

Martha thought for a moment and looked at RJ. "Where did he get that money?" This was the same question RJ had been asking himself and was now sure his friend had everything to do with the death of Jeddah King.

Wiping the beaded sweat from his forehead, RJ thought for a minute before confiding in Martha his thoughts. Turning to her, RJ started telling her his thoughts about the death of Jeddah, the missing money belt and Calvin having so much money to pay for the Medicine wagon and team.

"What are you going to do now?" asked Martha? Standing there next to him rubbing her hand across his shoulders. It was pretty easy to see the look of concern on RJ's face and the tenseness of his muscles.

"Since Calvin had that hit in the head, he hasn't been right. Some days I think that he doesn't even recognize me or for that matter even who he is. That medicine has helped a lot, but I'm scared for him. I have seen his eyes and I don't recognize them at times."

Again, Martha asked RJ what he was going to do.

"Tonight, after supper, I'm going to have a man to man talk with him. It has been a long time since he and I have sat and shot the sh. . . Crap."

"I'll bring you two over something special to go with your coffee."

RJ looked at Martha and he could feel those feelings once again.

Martha didn't need to hear any words at this moment, she could feel his thoughts as the tension left his shoulders and his lips met hers.

True to her word, later that evening, Martha showed up with some hot biscuits smothered in strawberry jam that she had gotten from Cookie.

Sitting around the fire were Tom and Hank, along with RJ and Calvin. As she approached, she heard an evil sounding laugh come from Calvin.

Martha walked over next to where RJ was seated and handed him the tin plate of biscuits. Now looking into Calvin's face, she sensed something wasn't right and turned and gave RJ a questioning look.

As the campfire flames leaped into the night, they cast an eerie shadow on all who sat there and Martha felt the hair on her arms rise up some. Before Martha could speak, Calvin set down his plate of biscuits and let out another sinister laugh, this one having an effect on them all.

Hank looked over at Calvin then at RJ. "Calvin! I don't know where you got the laugh, but I've just about had it with you."

Without any kind of warning, everyone saw the gun that suddenly was in Calvin's hand a split second before they heard the roar of it going off, stunned even more as they saw the lead hit Hank right between the eyes, killing him before he hit the ground. Another roar of his pistol and a big red stain appeared on Tom's left shoulder, knocking him to the ground screaming in pain.

Turning now to face RJ who had dropped his pipe into his hand and was ready to defend himself, Calvin leveled his gun and pulled the trigger. The round of lead hit RJ's hand and the pipe went flying into the night. Before Martha could even let out a scream, Calvin was at her side with one hand around her neck and his pistol's barrel shoved between her heaving breasts.

"Don't make me pull this trigger," Calvin warned, not at Martha but at RJ.

"No Calvin!" warned RJ.

At that warning, Calvin again let out his evil laugh.

"Just who do you think you're warning? Me? Don't look like I have much to fear right about now, does it?"

As quickly as this had all started, Calvin un-cocked his pistol and turned away from RJ and Martha. A strange look came over his face, along with a puzzled frown and Calvin asked, "What the hell happened here RJ? Who shot Hank and Tom?"

The night's silence which had been violated by gunshots were now disturbed by loud voices coming from the camped wagon train and headed in their direction.

"What do I do now, RJ?" Calvin's voice was now sounding like a small child who had been caught doing something he shouldn't have been doing.

Even though his best friend had just shot him and threatened Martha, RJ was beside him and put his arms around him. Calvin buried his face into RJ's chest and bawled like a new born baby. RJ removed the gun from his hand and handed it to Martha.

The voices of the men rushing in their direction were interrupted by the sound of a pistol being cocked and in the same instant another roar of a pistol shot. As RJ turned in the direction the shot had come from, he saw Tom curled up on the ground and Martha standing over him holding in her hand the smoking pistol he had handed her only moments before.

Martha looked at RJ and burst into tears. RJ released one of his arms from around Calvin and signaled Martha over next to him so that he could wrap his other arm around her also.

What the hell is going on here! RJ's thoughts went out to what he had just witnessed.

On the ground lay the two brothers. In his arms were the two most important people in his life. RJ knew things would never be the same between them. Gone was RJ's brotherly feelings he had had towards Calvin all these past years, now being replaced by those of a father for his son. Martha had told him a short while ago that Calvin's admiration for him was that of a son for his father and RJ now saw that in Calvin's actions.

I should have seen that. RJ now thought to himself.

Feeling the warmth of Martha standing so close to him, RJ knew that she was the woman he wanted and once they arrived in Deadwood he would take her for his wife.

I'll get Calvin the doctoring he needs and together Martha and I will get him healthy. Thoughts that now invaded RJ's thoughts. RJ's thoughts went back to that instant the bullet from Calvin's pistol blew the pipe out of his hand and for the first time realized how foolish his thinking had been. *Pipe against a pistol's lead? No contest.* He concluded.

As Charlie and the others approached his camp, he felt Martha release her hold and heard her telling them what had happened. RJ was surprised in hearing her put all the blame on Tom and Hank.

Charlie listened to Martha then motioned for the men to get some shovels and come back and dig some graves. As he was walking away, he turned and told them, "Tomorrow evening about this time we will be riding into the streets of Deadwood." With that, Charlie disappeared into the night. Calvin had quit sobbing, and Martha just stood there in a trance.

"I've never shot anyone before." Looking towards RJ, she said, speaking in a distant sounding voice, and with a faraway look in her eyes as though just realizing what she had done. Now, with lips trembling, she continued, "as a matter of fact, I've never even shot a gun before."

"Tom would have killed Calvin. You realize that, don't you?"

"I know, but that doesn't stop my brain from knowing that I just killed another person." Trying to hold back the tears, looking at the dead men as they were being carried away, she continued, "The man I killed didn't even start it!" Then looking at Calvin she asked, "What are you going to do with him? Can't you see now that he is getting strung out on Laudanum?" Martha watched as the men carried the two dead away to bury them and her thoughts went back to Calvin and what was going to be done.

Shaking his head as if he didn't want to believe what had just happened RJ said, "Yes, I guess I've known it for a while, but I didn't want to believe it and it still doesn't explain his behavior before that. He hasn't been acting right ever since he got hit on the head. To tell the truth, I didn't rightly know whether it was the laudanum or getting hit that was causing it."

Calvin just stood there looking off into the night with a blank look on his face. There was little doubt that he didn't realize what had just happened.

"Once we hit Deadwood, if there isn't a doc there that can help Calvin, we just might turn around and head back to Denver or even San Francisco. And if there isn't a good doc there, we'll find one, no matter where we have to go."

RJ knew that his plans on becoming a Bounty Hunter with Calvin would depend on getting Calvin healed.

As night settled in and silence blanketed the darkness, a lone coyote could be heard somewhere off in the darkness singing his song.

Chapter 13

BANG, BANG, BANG, KA-BOOM. The far off gun shots signaled the arrival of Charlie's wagon train into Deadwood. Deadwood's population had heard about the wagon train coming and with it some new business people and a new supply of *working girls*. The streets of Deadwood were alive with the local folk who had gathered to welcome them in.

"Sounds like the wagons are getting quite the reception in Deadwood." RJ had an ear to ear grin as he sat there next to Martha. Turning and looking back over his shoulder at Calvin driving the two horse team pulling the medicine wagon, RJ caught Calvin taking a long pull from one of the medicine bottles.

"What do you think Martha?" asked RJ who had a sleepless night with the shooting of Tom and Hank on his mind. He had grown weary, not only from lack of sleep but from the constant hot temperatures and the constant worry for his friend. *Denver could get hot, but nothing like this heat*. Wiping the sweat from his forehead with his bandana, RJ wrung it out then tied it around his neck.

"If you're talking about what I think will happen to him now, I don't rightly know. What we do know is that Deadwood has no real law to speak of so I wouldn't think anything will transpire. Hell, I doubt if Charlie will even concern himself with anything to do now that we are all here and he has his money."

Any responsibility he might have felt, he left at the entrance to Deadwood."

RJ knew that he had enough money to find a place or a piece of land, but would soon have to be either becoming a Bounty Hunter or setting up a legit business.

The noises coming from Deadwood were getting louder as they caught sight of it.

As they pulled closer to the wagon train already lining the main street, some of the town folk noticed them and several headed towards their wagon clapping and singing loudly.

RJ noticed that it was easy to tell that this was a 'BOOM TOWN' everything he had heard and read was alive right in front of him. The buildings were poorly constructed and lined both sides of the street. Shelters, shacks, and lots of tents welcomed them before they entered Deadwood.

"Those tents remind you of anything Calvin?"

Calvin nodded his head. He and RJ had occupied a two man tent for most of the war and those memories were as fresh now as when they were living them.

Charlie sure had the right idea coming here. Anyone getting in on the ground floor of this town would come up wealthy. RJ's thoughts were interrupted by the crowd that now encircled their wagon. Wild laughter, clapping and pistol shots filled the air. Martha had climbed down and was at once grabbed by several men who spun her around in circles. Fiddle and piano playing sounds filled the air. RJ kept a close eye on Martha, determined to make sure she was okay.

Calvin, stepping down from the brightly painted wagon was also surrounded by town folk who thought he was the doctor they had heard was with the train.

"Well, hi there fella!" came a woman's voice from behind him and at the same time he felt a hand pressing on his shoulder. Turning, RJ was faced by a woman he guessed to be in her early twenties and one of the local whore's. She was scantily dressed with overly large thighs and a big butt. Much of her cleavage was showing, but it was hard to tell where it left off because she was also about two hundred fifty pounds of pasty flab. RJ noticed right away she was missing a couple of front teeth, probably having them knocked out by some drunken cowboy or miner. Her blond hair was unkempt. The outfit she wore had several stains down the front, and she had splashed on way too much cheap perfume in the hopes that her rank body odor would not run off a potential customer.

Those girls that just arrived are in for a rough night, I would gather, if most of the whores here looked anything like this one did. RJ didn't have any more time to think as this woman was quickly yanked backwards and RJ heard Martha warn that he was off limits and if she didn't want a couple of black eyes to match her missing teeth, she'd best be moving on and to leave her man alone. RJ was seeing a side of Martha that she hadn't shown him before and he liked what he was seeing.

More of the town folk had circled them and were now walking with them toward the main street of Deadwood where several large fires had been lit lighting up the night sky and adding to the hotness of the air.

RJ made sure that he held tightly to Martha's hand as more and more town folk descended on them. A quick look back over his shoulder, told him Calvin was just fine as he had the arms of several girls wrapped around him.

"Looks like Calvin is going to be in for a rough night." Martha looked back at Calvin and laughed at RJ's remark.

"Something tells me he will be just fine, RJ." Martha remarked, locking her arms around RJ's waist.

The next thing RJ felt was Martha's soft lips on his. The kiss lasted for only a moment and then followed by a thank you. No other words needed to be spoken.

RJ caught sight of Charlie and Wild Bill. Both were sitting on a bench in front of a makeshift saloon, each of them drinking from their own liquor bottles.

"What do you think they will do next?" Martha spoke, trying to make her voice heard above the noise the crowd was making that had gathered around them.

"I talked some with Charlie. He told me that he has no plans of settling here in Deadwood."

"And now that you're here, what are your plans?" Looking into his face, Martha rapidly blinked her eyes and puffed up her rosy red lips and acted like a Damsel in distress.

"Well, the first thing I'm gonna do is collect that bounty money so that I'll have some money in my pockets when I ask a very special woman to be my wife."

There. I've come out and said it. RJ hadn't intended to ask Martha yet, but he simply got caught up in the excitement of the moment.

"I hope that very special woman you're planning on asking to marry is me!"

With a grin than looking all around, he said, "Well, I guess there are quite a few to choose from." She gave his arm a swat. Though they were being crowded and everyone around them were making so much noise that it was almost impossible to hear, RJ leaned over Martha and with his cheek pressed tightly to hers whispered into her ear, "Will you marry me, Martha?"

Stepping back out of his embrace, Martha searched RJ's face. She wasn't sure just what she was looking for but it gave her a moment to compose herself before answering his proposal. Finally, with blushing cheeks, she said, "Oh yes, RJ. I'll marry you!"

RJ felt Martha's rough hands as she reached up and pulled his face down close enough to join lips. Pushing herself away from RJ, Martha told him. "I'm going to go join in the celebration, you coming?"

The night was hot and sticky and RJ realized just how tired he had become over the last few days with everything that had happened on the dusty trail of death, so he told Martha, "You go ahead and have a good time and I'll see you back here later." As Martha turned to walk away, RJ called out her name.

Turning to see what he wanted, Martha caught sight of a figure rapidly coming up behind him. RJ immediately saw an expression on her face that reads, 'watch out, behind you'. Not having any kind of weapon, RJ spun around to his right so that he could get in a good swing with his left hand.

As the punch connected with the jaw of the one behind him, RJ saw that it was his old friend from the war, and bounty hunter, Micah. The blow dropped Micah to his knees, but did no damage as far as a broken nose or jaw bone.

Throwing his arms up over his head and waving them, Micah yelled with laughter, "Enough! Enough, friend!"

RJ was immediately at his side, helping him up.

"What in tarnation are you doing in Deadwood and where is that sidekick of yours, Calvin?" Both men stood there for a piece just looking at each other. Martha had stepped forward so that RJ could introduce her, all proper like.

"RJ has told me some about you." She said extending her hand, then added. Then, with a smile on her face she added, "He didn't tell me how handsome you were though." This brought a fun, spank on her bottom from RJ as he told her to run along to the celebration.

"Fine looking woman you have there, RJ." RJ nodded his head in agreement as they both watched her walk away. RJ longed now for time to be together.

"So, what brings you to Deadwood?"

"In a way, you did Micah!"

"How so RJ?" Micah was remembering what he had said to RJ and Calvin about the kind of money to be made bounty hunting.

Micah listened as RJ went on to tell him about the bounty he and Calvin had already collected on this trip from Colorado and what was still to be collected.

"You haven't mentioned your trade to anyone on that wagon train, have you?" A concerned look came upon Micah's face.

RJ assured Micah that no one knew what he and Calvin had done to secure the reward monies without giving themselves away as Bounty Hunters.

"I hope you're right about that RJ. Deadwood would not be a very healthy place to be if someone finds that out. Let's go get us a beer and I will tell you all about what I've been doing the past few years and what role I now play in Deadwood."

RJ and Micah found all the drinking establishments were now crowded with new faces and the prostitutes were already displaying their wares.

Wow! That didn't take long for all those women on the train to pop into action, and by the way they were being crowded upon, just goes to show that they were much needed.

RJ noticed how fresh and clean the women had made themselves and how dirty and scruffy looking the men were, and he couldn't picture why a woman embraced this trade.

"Pretty quiet there, ain't ya RJ?" Micah had gotten them both drinks and RJ realized he had been standing there for some time engrossed in his thoughts.

"Here's to whatever adventure the future brings to us."

RJ said, "Here, here," as he raised his glass to tap Micah's in a salute to the future.

Over the next hour or so, Micah told RJ all about his life here in Deadwood.

"So, my friend," said Micah, "What made you decide to come out here to Deadwood of all places, and where did you find such a fine looking woman?"

"Well, I was hoping that you and Martha would become friends." Taking a sip of beer, and wiping the foam from his upper lip, RJ continued. "Martha has accepted my marriage proposal." Not being one to beat around the bush, RJ came right out and said what needed to be said. "Martha will find out very quickly what you have done to some of the women here and there is no way she will ever speak to or have anything to do with you, ever."

Micah was about ready to speak when the music and the loudness in the place came to an abrupt halt as two men of Mexican descent walked in and drawing their pistols, fired two rounds into the ceiling.

"Stay cool, RJ," whispered Micah under his breath. "Juan Ortega and one of his henchmen."

RJ watched as Micah lowered his right hand so it rested on his gun handle.

"I hear that there is a Gringo here in town looking for me?" Juan spoke rather good English for a "Mex," and an old Mex at that.

Pointing his still smoking pistol at one of the patrons he asked. "Is it you Amigo?"

A violent head shake was the only answer he received. Continuing to scan the room, Juan reached down and took a glass of beer off the table he stood next to. Raising it to his lips, he drained it, set it gently back on the table top, and with his dirty shirt sleeve wiped off the foam that stuck to his long unkempt mustache. He gave out a loud belch, then pointed his pistol at another and again asked. "Is it you Amigo?"

Juan caught a movement out of the corner of his eye just as he finished his question, but a split second too late to respond.

At the word Amigo, two shots rang out in quick succession. Everyone, including RJ turned and looked at Micah standing there with his own smoking gun.

Looking at everyone staring at him, Micah shrugged his shoulders, holstered his pistol and trying to speak with a Mexican accent said, "I'm the Gringo who was asking about you AMIGO." This brought loud laughter from the bar's patrons.

"Drinks are on me fellas!" Micah reached out and gave RJ a solid back slap and pointed to a corner of the room where they could sit and talk.

On their way by the two lying dead on the dirt floor, Micah stopped and gave the body a solid kick to the face.

Micah, instructed a couple men to pick up the two bodies and within minutes, the place was once again alive with the sounds of a honky-tonk piano, lively stepping dancing girls the clatter of a roulette wheel and cards being shuffled. Micah pointed to a table in a corner where he and RJ could sit and talk.

"Juan had a ten thousand dollar reward posted on him. I've been on his trail enough times without success. I started asking about knowing that word would find him and that he would come looking for me."

"It looks like you have a pretty good thing going here."

"It is and I plan on keeping it like that, understand?" RJ noticed a warning in his words and setting his beer on the table questioned him on it.

"There is room for you and Calvin if you two choose this type of life. If you do, then everything will be done according to the way I want them to."

There was a couple of minutes of silence as RJ took in what Micah had just told him.

"Calvin and I didn't really plan on becoming partners with you or interfering with what you have made for yourself in any way. Don't really know if it is what we want to be doing."

"I'm just telling you in advance, if you want to do this type of business, it comes through me. If you have an issue with that, then find a different line of business or plan on moving on. No one here in Deadwood suspects what line of work I'm in, and it will continue to stay like that."

Seeing that Micah's glass was empty and so was his, RJ stood and reached down for his empty glass. As his hand touched it, Micah's hand grabbed his wrist. At once their eyes were focused on each other's. "You do understand what I've told you?"

"Yes I do and I think that we both need another beer and then over the next couple of days let's work out the details of our partnership. If you want to be the head here, I'm fine with that and I'm sure Calvin will be too."

"Good to hear that, RJ."

As RJ made his way to the bar with the empty glasses, his thoughts were on all that Micah had just told him and wasn't quite sure how to digest it, but knew that a partnership of sorts was something he had thought about the last few days before reaching Deadwood.

CHAPTER 14

Two weeks after arriving in Deadwood, Martha and RJ were married. It was a simple ceremony, held just outside of town beside a small creek that had a tent erected next to it. This would be RJ's and Calvin's home as they started building a real one, Martha would stay in town and RJ would bring her out on the weekends.

Any kind of supplies could be purchased in town if you had the money, and the selling of the wagon and team to Tom and Hank and the bounty money collected, RJ figured he would have enough to build his and Martha's home.

Calvin wanted to build a small house next to his.

"I have my own money," he told RJ showing him all the money he had acquired from the murder of Jeddah.

So I was right in my thinking that Calvin killed Jeddah and he had also found his hidden money.

To help speed up the building, RJ had hired a couple locals who were willing to swing a hammer, but just like anything else in this sort of town it cost him plenty.

The afternoon heat was almost unbearable. A dip in the creek from time to time helped some, but weighted them down until their clothes dried out some.

Both RJ and Calvin were in the creek when Micah rode up.

Eying the water, Micah almost decided to join them, but then changed his mind. Instead, he dismounted and motioned for them to come up out of the water.

RJ and Calvin plopped themselves down next to Micah.

"What's up?" asked RJ.

Stripping off his shirt and wringing it out some before putting it back on, RJ saw an excited look on Micah's face.

"Remember those two Mexican's I shot that first evening you all arrived? Well the bounty money was deposited into my account along with a telegram stating that Juan has a partner, who has a large scar across his forehead, who rides with him from time to time."

"Well, that other 'Mex' didn't have a scar so we know it wasn't him." Both RJ and Micah looked at Calvin, then at each other.

"Guess we'll have to start calling you *eagle eye*," said Micah, letting out a sarcastic little laugh.

Micah had their full attention as they listened to him describe the Mexican, with a scarred forehead, who went by the name, Chico Morales.

Standing and rubbing his hands together, he went on to tell them that he also had a ten thousand dollar reward on his head, *dead* or *alive*.

Looking over at Calvin, RJ saw a look come over him that he hadn't seen before.

If he was a cornered wolf, that would be the look on his face, thought RJ, but then the look changed and Calvin took on his regular appearance.

"Did that message give you any location as to where this Chico could be found?"

"Well, the message was two weeks old, but stated that Chico had been in Grand Platte, Nebraska on and off for the last couple of months."

"That sounds like he has made North Platte his stopping off place."

"North Platte's a pretty big city and has a railroad so it would be an ideal hold-up place and a move around area."

"Did the message say anything else?"

"Only that he rode with another Mexican named Arturo Sanchez, and when in town, he stays with a whore named

Bellarosa."

"What are your thoughts?" asked RJ curious as to what Micah's plans were.

"I'll send out a couple more men to help out with the building if you and Calvin wants to go and see if you can locate and bring to justice this Mexican dirt bag and anyone else he might be found with."

"So, what's the deal here?" RJ and Calvin had discussed bounty hunting together with Micah as the one in charge that would make all the decisions.

"What would you two say is a fair share?"

"All you're doing is supplying us with old information. We have to be away, on horseback, not only facing the elements, but when we find him, we'll be up against his guns and any other guns he happens to have with him."

"Remember boy's what I told you when we first talked? Your lives would be useless if anyone found out that you were bounty hunters. I might not be out there with you, but I'm still facing the same danger, if not more, getting the information." Searching their faces, Micah knew he had to take a strong stand and not let them decide but he had to.

"I'd say sixty-forty would be fair. You two get forty percent to split between you."

"Well, I doonnnnn'tttt." Calvin was stopped mid-sentence by the raised voice of Micah, who wasn't about to let them do the decision making, *If I'm getting the info for them then I will get my share*, were his thoughts.

"Listen. I'm the one taking the biggest chance here. Without me there would be no way for you to gather information without creating suspicion and as soon as that happened you both would be dead men."

RJ knew what Micah said was right. He had told Martha what he and Calvin were planning on doing. At first she was apprehensive, but the more she learned about the way he and Calvin would go about it, the more she was for them. She had started listening to talk whenever she was around the men who came in to purchase a meal. So far, she had nothing to report to RJ, which meant that getting info was going to be hard to do unless you had other sources.

"Listen RJ, when you boys ride out of here, no one is going to suspect you of anything for leaving, much less to go bounty hunting! Sixty-forty is a fair shake." Micah was ready to do some physical damage to Calvin if he opened his mouth again. He had nothing to worry about as RJ suddenly stuck out his hand and said, "Agreed."

"Agreed," resounded Micah taking RJ's outstretched hand. Calvin didn't make any attempt to shake hands with Micah, or he with Calvin.

Two days later RJ and Calvin were saddled up and bidding farewell to the men working on the house.

Martha stood next to RJ with her arms wrapped around his waist. This would be the first time RJ and Calvin would be away on the trail of some outlaw and she didn't know how she felt about that.

He's no gun fighter! She thought to herself as he and Calvin climbed up into the saddle. Martha watched as they rode out of sight, but the money that he could make in a short period of time intrigued her.

RJ was correct when he had told Micah that Martha would never have anything to do with him, and now her thoughts were on how she could gather information to give RJ so that he didn't have to partner up with him.

Martha's answer to gathering information came to her in the form of a little Chinese girl named Nuying and it happened strictly by chance.

Nuying worked at one of the bath houses, hauling water and towels for customers who had paid for a bath. Bath house girls were paid hardly anything, but they could make extra money, depending on what they were willing to do. Some prostituted themselves. Nuying, being educated had decided one evening, while hauling water for a customer, that when he offered her some money for some fun time she would take it and do what she had seen many bath house women do in the past.

They all seem to like it enough and I have seen them even kiss the fella, but mostly just lift up their dresses and bend over and let the man do whatever he wanted. Nuying made the sign she had seen others make and she had no trouble getting someone to answer her request. Holding the few coins in her hand, he followed her out back where she bent over a couple of hay bales and lifted up her dress. Feeling the man press up behind her, she changed her mind in a hurry, at the first feeling of pain, and started to stand up, pushing him away. He was not having anything to do with her change of mind and gave her a couple hard backhands to which she threw the coins at him and blurted out in English that he was a pig and to let her go. Martha just happened to be walking by when she heard the commotion and went to help the girl she heard yelling.

Grabbing a large piece of wood, Martha hit the man directly in the back of the neck, momentarily knocking him to his knees. Reaching out, Martha grabbed Nuying's hand and pulled her away from there and she led Nuying to her place.

"You speak English?"

"Some. I understand more than I speak."

"My name is Martha," and just like a man does, extended her hand.

"I'm Nuying." Taking Martha's out stretched hand just like she had seen the men do.

"I know something about your culture," said Martha. "What does your name mean?"

Looking kinda shy, Nuying whispered, "Female Flower."

"What a beautiful name, Nuying."

As they walked towards Martha's room, she had many thoughts go through her mind.

If she would be willing to, she could gather much information from customers not knowing she can understand English. She is just what I've been looking for so that RJ doesn't have to be involved with that scum, Micah, any longer.

Over the next couple of days, Martha and Nuying hit it off and Nuying agreed to help gather whatever information she could. Wherever she was, she would always be listening.

Upon Martha's request, Nuying talked to two other Chinese girls that were prostitutes who could understand some English to see if they would help gather information, for this they could make some extra money. Both agreed to help. When Nuying told Martha this, she warned Nuying to tell them to be very careful, along with herself. "Micah would just as soon kill you as to look at you," she warned.

Martha went to sleep that night with an added smile on her face, knowing her plans to get RJ away from Micah were coming together and all because she was in the right place at the right time. Reaching over to the empty side of the bed where RJ should be she said out loud, "Good night my love, sweet dreams."

Out on the trail, RJ and Calvin were also settled in for the night. The campfire had burned down to a pile of coals and RJ, using his saddle as a pillow, gazed into the heavens and attempted to count the twinkling stars.

The night was filled with the singing of a hundred different creatures.

"Do you hear that singing, Calvin?"

"I hear it RJ," Calvin answered as he rolled over onto his side to face RJ. RJ instantly caught a horrified look on Calvin's face just before he heard the gun blast and the muzzle flash which momentarily blinded him.

"Snake!" yelled Calvin.

RJ saw Calvin's mouth move, but didn't hear his words. No one wanted to be this close in front of the muzzle blast of a colt six gun. Twice during the war he had been deafened by being in front of a gun muzzle blast. Not only do you lose your hearing for a spell, but you would also pack a terrible headache.

The night wasn't going to be a good one for RJ, but at least he was alive. The snake turned out to be a Prairie Rattler and very dangerous to a human.

I've never seen a snake of any kind come out at night, but then I haven't been in South Dakota at night. There would be lots to learn if one intended to stay alive.

Even with the pain in his head, RJ relived what just happened and was dumbfounded with the speed and accuracy of Calvin's shooting.

Shaking his head violently, RJ tried to ease the roaring he was experiencing in his head, but it only made it worse.

Looking at Calvin, RJ saw his lips moving, but heard no sound as the roaring in his head blocked out what Calvin was saying.

RJ closed his eyes for a minute and when he opened them, Calvin was extending to him a bottle of the medicine he had been taking. Making a sign with his hand that he didn't want it, Calvin replaced the cap and tucked it back into his saddle bag, but not before taking a healthy swig.

Getting to his feet, RJ stumbled around some, but knew that he had to move around if he was going to get rid of the pain quicker. As he walked around, he felt a decrease in the roaring and the focus in his eyes returned to normal.

"RJ, are you alright?" He could now hear Calvin's voice, and turning around, he nodded his head and spoke, "Where did you learn to shoot like that?"

"Long story, but one you have to hear. Once your head is back to normal in a day or two I'll tell ya."

That's a story I'll look forward to hearing.

As he continued to walk around the camp, he suddenly felt very sick to his stomach and bent over and vomited up everything that he had just eaten. Being handed a canteen from Calvin, RJ took a sip of water and swooshed it around in his mouth before spitting it onto the ground.

If I was back in Deadwood, Martha could be taking care of me right now. Another sip of water and RJ started to feel normal once again.

"If you want RJ, we can go on back to Deadwood for a couple days till you're back to your old self."

"No Calvin. I'm feeling better and by morning I hope to be fine. We need to get to Grand Platte as soon as possible. Time was of the essence, even though while Chico maybe using Grand Platte as his home base, he could be just about anywhere. Micah had given him the name of a contact for him to look up once they were in town, and town was still a long way off.

RJ woke to the smell of coffee. Calvin had stoked the coals and coffee was ready. As RJ opened his eyes, he was surprised that the morning sun didn't affect his head at all. No, the rolling over or sitting up didn't cause his head to bother him, like he was afraid of.

"Well, well, well, will you look who decided to join the living," Calvin poured a cup of coffee and handed it to RJ, who brought it to his nose for a whiff before taking a sip.

"Always said you make the best damn coffee. God, that's good."

"My daddy always taught me, when he was sober enough and at home, that if you were gonna make a pot of coffee then it was worth making it drinkable."

"Your daddy was a smart man where coffee was concerned."

Looking off into the distance, RJ heard Calvin continue. "Too bad he wasn't as smart where the family was concerned."

RJ remembered what Calvin had told him about his childhood one night when they lay behind a fallen tree finding cover from the Union soldiers gun fire, and he now heard the same hurt in Calvin's voice.

Calvin's daddy was a drunkard and a wanderer. Seems he was only home for short periods of time, and when he was, he was usually drinking and it wasn't unlike him to take his belt to either him or even to Calvin's mom.

Calvin told him that when he was about twelve, his daddy came home from being away for several months and was in one of the foulest moods he could ever recall, and immediately started in on his wife with verbal abuse, which very soon lead to physical, with his daddy pushing his mom up against the wall, and backhanding her several times. He was watching from his bedroom where he had cracked the door a little, after being woken up by all the yelling and screaming. As he watched, he saw his daddy rip off his mother's dress and right there on the kitchen floor, he watched as his daddy raped his mom. This was followed by more slapping and ending with a punch to the face. Calvin ran into the room and jumped on his daddy's back. Being no match for his daddy, he found himself sailing through the air and knocked unconscious when his head hit the hard metal of the cooking stove.

When Calvin came to, the morning sun was shining in through the kitchen window. He sat up and shook his head a little. Gazing around the kitchen, he didn't see his momma, but saw some blood stains on the floor along with her torn clothes. He called out her name to no avail.

Getting to his feet on shaky legs, he walked around the house calling both his mother's and his daddy's name. Hearing his dog barking, he went outside and saw him standing in front of the open barn door. There was enough light in the barn for Calvin to see the figure of his mom hanging from one of the rafters. She was still naked. The body of his daddy on the floor with a shotgun by his side and half his face missing.

Calvin told sadly that sometime during the early morning his mom had gone out to the barn and hung herself and was found by his daddy who maybe, through guilt, turned the shotgun on himself. No one would ever know for sure. Calvin had told him that he lived through it all by thinking that she had shot him and then hung herself. Calvin told RJ that it was a good thing, either way that his daddy was dead because he was going to kill him himself when he had the chance.

Recalling all that now along with the head injury he had received, RJ could understand a little more of Calvin's strange behavior from time to time.

The voice of Calvin brought RJ out of his thoughts.

"Feel like saddling up and making some dust?" asked Calvin as he dumped the remainder of the coffee over the hot coals and extended his hand out to RJ, who latched onto it and was helped to his feet.

RJ's first couple of steps were a little shaky, but then he was able to maneuver just fine.

RJ would learn some more surprising things about his friend that he would never have known or given a notion to. Now when they stopped, sometime was given to practicing a quick draw and accuracy in shooting. It didn't take much convincing from Calvin for RJ to forget once and for all his smashing in the heads of those he was trailing, even though that method had stood him well for a time.

Much talk concerned Micah and what they were going to do, if they continued bounty hunting with him. Neither trusted him very much and for good reason. They each had a feeling about the man, and the more they learned about him, the greater the feeling persisted. They couldn't put a finger on it, it was just a niggling feeling that caused their stomach to quiver and the hair to stand up on the back of their necks. They looked at each other, knowing they shared this apprehension.

CHAPTER 15

About a two days ride from where RJ and Calvin were, sat the city of Grand Platte, Nebraska. At this very moment, the town folk were in the streets with their eyes to the west watching a spiral of smoke rise into the cloudless blue sky. They all knew that the only ranch in that direction this close to town was the McHenry's.

"Yes, sir. They are burning the McHenry's ranch." Jud, the town's know-it-all voiced loudly as he stood in the middle of the dry, dusty street pointing in the direction of the McHenry's ranch. In the stillness, you could hear some of the town folk gasp.

For a long time now, a Mexican, who went simply by the name of Chico and his right hand man named Arturo Sanchez had made the Grand Platte their home along with his band of two bandito's; one was Chico's brother Ricco. Although they mostly kept to themselves, Chico, who had earned the nickname of Scarhead, due to a nasty looking scar across his forehead, had been having some trouble with a local rancher named Cliff McHenry.

As the story goes, Chico had heard about a good looking woman with two daughters who lived just outside of town with her husband Cliff McHenry. Having left the whore Bellarosa and being half drunk, one afternoon he had decided to take a ride out to see for himself what he had been told. As he rode up the drive, Cliff, who was sitting on the front porch watching his wife and daughters, had seen a rider coming up the drive and had signaled for his family to come inside as he opened the door and reached around inside for his rifle

Before he had a chance to say anything or remove his sombrero in an official hello, Cliff walked out onto the porch and cocked his rifle which he cradled in his arms ever cautious of the stranger.

"What do you want Mexican?" asked Cliff in a very loud, unfriendly voice.

"Amigo, don't shoot!" he said, fanning his hat out in front of him and with a voice that sounded urgent. "I'm not looking for any trouble, I only wanted to ask if I could water my horse?"

"Move on, Mex, find someplace else to water that mangy animal you call a horse."

As Chico started to speak, a gunshot rang out and his horse dropped to the ground with the Mexican on-board, pinning, but not breaking, his right leg.

Out of reflex, Chico drew up his pistol, screaming in pain he tried to focus his eyes then his gun hand in Cliff's direction. This action brought a swift kick to his gun hand sending his pistol through the air and causing him even more pain as he heard bone breaking. Chico could not move out from under his dead animal or reach for the pistol which was several feet away where it had landed from Cliff's swift kick.

Knowing that he didn't have to worry about Chico for a few minutes, Cliff saddled up his horse and tying one end of a rope around Chico's midsection, stepped up on his mount and with a forward motion, pulled Chico out from under his dead animal, not stopping, despite Chico's pleading until he had dragged him all the way into town stopping in front of Doc Miller's place of business.

That had started a mini war between the two and now the townsfolk stood and watched the smoke from Cliff's ranch fill the western sky not knowing what was happening to Cliff and his family, but knowing they were not willing to confront Arturo and his small band of outlaws.

Once the smoke was about gone and a couple of hours had passed, several of the men rode out to Cliff's ranch to see the damage. No one was expecting to find what they did, although they all had witnessed in the past how savage Chico could become at the drop of the hat.

No one in Grand Platte had the guts to stand up to him so he did what he wanted to do, when he wanted to it and several of the townsfolk had been subjected to his savage behavior.

Before Bellarosa, he was prone to take any woman he chose, married or not. If it turned out to be your wife and if you interfered you received a well-placed bullet between the eyes, but only after you were made to watch as one after the other had their way with her.

"You Gringo's piece of crap!" he would say.

On two different occasions, Cliff happened to be near when one of these rapes took place and stepped in. The last time, Chico told him that he wouldn't be around long and to guard his family well. Cliff knew that no one in town would have his back and he would have to stand alone if any physical danger presented itself.

What the townsfolk witnessed that day as they rode up the drive to the still smoking ranch, would be burned into their memories for a lifetime. The lifeless body of Cliff was still tied to one of the porch's charred up-right post, smoldering from the fire that was set. On the ground right in front of him was a mattress which had been dragged out from inside the ranch. The lifeless, nude body of Cliff's wife, Delores, lay on top of it, her blood having soaked into it staining it a bright red. It was pretty easy to guess what had probably taken place here.

As the folks who had come out gathered around the two dead, one of the men spoke up. "I would say that Cliff was made to watch as Chico and his gang raped his wife before killing her and slitting her throat."

"What's that sound?" One of the men asked, raising his hand and waving it to quiet everyone down.

Looking towards the opened barn door small cries could be heard coming from inside. As the men's race to the barn they saw a trail of blood, which went through the open barn door. Inside they found both the girls, Prudence and Claire, huddled together, naked and bloody, in one of the horse stalls. The story they would relate made all the town's folk want to hunt Chico and his gang down and string them up, but they all knew that wasn't going to happen.

Since Chico had come to town with his small band of outlaws, he made it quite clear that he was in charge and to prove that point he brutally killed several of the older men and even a couple of the saloon whores. The town's sheriff was controlled by Chico and would not raise so much as his little finger to help anyone whom Chico sent Arturo after, but now, seeing McHenry and his wife dead and the shape of his two daughters, he made a silent oath against Arturo and his banditos. Sheriff Tom Callahan at that moment had no idea that this oath he whispered to himself was soon going to be a reality as RJ and Calvin would soon be there.

Both Cliff and his wife were forced to witness the rape of their two daughters along with the beatings and cutting that was inflicted on them, after which they were dragged into the barn and left there while they raped their mother on the mattress where just a few minutes ago, they laid and underwent the same treatment.

The air was filled with the screams of Delores as the brutality of the rape took place. Once they had satisfied their lust, Chico pulled out a large knife from his boot, he motioned for his men to stand her up and once done, he stepped up behind her and reached across her breasts and pulled the knife across them. Now both Cliff's and Delores's scream's filled the air. Plunging the knife into her belly just above her belly button, Chico pulled the knife upward, then out and then across her throat with so much force he nearly separated her head from her body. Stepping away from her, the body made an eerie thud as it fell to the now bloody mattress.

The two girls stayed huddled together with their arms wrapped around each other as they listened to the screams of both their parents.

About the time, the screams stopped, there was a new sound as pistols spewed their deadly lead into the tied up body of Cliff. The girls screamed in terror. Within a couple of minutes they heard the thundering of horses as Chico and his men's road out from the ranch, leaving them alive to recount what had happened here. Neither one moved until they were found by Sheriff Callahan.

On Wednesday morning, RJ and Calvin passed the burned down ranch and RJ mad a comment to Calvin.

"Kinda strange seeing one old porch post standing straight up from that burned down ranch."

"Wonder what started it?" remarked Calvin, reining his horse to a stop, then turning side saddle to just sit and stare at the pile of rubble.

Both horses seemed a little on edge because of the smell of smoke that still lingered in the air and with their keen sense of smell, there was another odor, one that only they smelled.

"Whoa boy!" said RJ reaching forward and lightly patted his mounts neck. "Let's move on."

As RJ and Calvin rode into Grand Platte, many of the folk on the street stopped what they were doing to watch the two strangers ride through town.

"Howdy," came the voice directed at them from Sheriff Callahan as he stepped through the swinging doors of the Silver Palace Saloon.

"Back at ya, sheriff." Both Calvin and RJ said at the same time while finger tipping their hats in a friendly gesture and reining their horses to a stop.

Sheriff Callahan watched as they dismounted and looped their horses' reins around the hitching post in front of the

Silver Palace and then stepping up onto the boardwalk and stood facing the sheriff.

"What brings you boys to Grand Platte?"

Not wanting to let on that they were bounty hunters, RJ answered, "me and Calvin here are looking for a Mexican who goes by the name Scarhead. Do you know this fella?"

Sheriff Callahan raised his eyebrows at the name and gave out a little snicker. In his breast pocket was a telegram which he had just received from Micah telling him about the two men who stood before him, named RJ and Calvin and to help them out in any way he could. Micah went on to say that Chico had outlived his usefulness and this would be a good way to get rid of him and his outlaw gun men.

"Hah! The whole town knows of Scarhead." Playing along he asked, "What're ya looking for him for?"

"He's done some bad things sheriff and it's about time for him to be retired."

Already knowing who they were, Sheriff Callahan squinted his eyes against the bright day sun and whispered, "You two Bounty Hunters?"

Looking first to his right then left and being satisfied there was no one around to hear him, RJ nodded.

Before they had left Deadwood, Micah had filled RJ in some about this Sheriff Callahan.

"He and I have done some business together on a couple of occasions." Micah went on to tell RJ that from time to time he would receive a telegram from him advising him of a wanted figure who had ridden into town with a price on his head.

"Callahan would take him into custody and hold him in his jail until I got there. Plans would then be made for the wanted person to be let out of the cell with a harsh warning to *get-out-of-town*. I would simply wait and gun him down on the trail and return him to town tied face down over the saddle and collect the reward. Five hundred dollars went to Callahan if I collected five thousand, he got a thousand if the reward was ten thousand.

RJ decided that he would have to get on Sheriff Callahan's good side by offering him the same deal that he had with Micah although it would mean another hand in the kitty.

"I thought as much from the first mention of Scarhead." Motioning toward the saloon, Sheriff Callahan indicated he was ready for a cold beer. Stepping through the swinging doors, RJ observed through the bluish haze, that there were only a couple cowboys sitting at a table along with a couple of whores sitting on their laps. They didn't even look up or in their direction as they walked by on their way to a table in the very back of the saloon.

"We can see all the action from back here," Callahan said, dropping his hat onto the table and kicking out a chair, spinning it around so the chair's back was up against the table's edge and sat on it with his arms draped over its back.

Seemingly out of nowhere, a tall, scantily dressed woman appeared at their table and bent down and gave Callahan a kiss on the cheek.

"What'll it be gents?" she said as she turned and smiled at both RJ and Calvin.

"Three beers," answered Callahan, giving the bar girl a playful smack on her backside drawing laughter from her ruby red lips.

A couple of minutes passed and she returned with the three beers and set them down on the table, gave Callahan, another playful kiss on the cheek, and was gone without another word. All eyes watched her walk away.

"Here's to money," said Callahan raising his glass in salute. RJ and Calvin did the same.

"So. You two are looking for Scarhead? What makes you think he is here?"

"We came from Deadwood where a good friend told us to look you up and you could probably help us out."

Smiling, then taking a sip of his beer and wiping the foam from his upper lip with his sleeve, Callahan whispered, "So, Micah sent you two, to take down Scarhead and his small band of outlaws?"

Faster than a striking rattlesnake, Calvin was out of his chair, gun in hand, cocked and the barrel pressed against Callahan's throat.

This action drew the attention of the others and jumping up from their table and ran from the saloon.

"Don't you think we can, Sheriff?" asked Calvin with his face so close to Callahan's that some spittle sprayed Callahan in the face.

Uncocking his pistol, Calvin stood up and dropped it back into the well-oiled holster strapped low to his thigh.

"Well, I can see Micah has made a good choice in his pick of men to take down Scarhead!"

All three raised their glasses and downed the last swallow of beer.

Standing and taking a couple of coins from his vest pocket, Callahan looked at RJ and said, "Let's get out of here and go to my office where we can talk."

Evening found RJ and Calvin on the trail east out of Grand Platte towards a washed out river basin where Sheriff Callahan told them they would probably find Scarhead and his riders holed-up.

"They don't fear nothing so they will have a pretty big campfire going that you should be able to spot from a long way off giving you plenty of time to leave your horses and sneak up on their camp and take 'em by surprise."

Just as Callahan had said, about three miles outside of Grand Platte, both RJ and Calvin smelled smoke a few minutes before they saw the light coming from a campfire.

"Let's dismount here" RJ said, then getting down from his horse and sliding his rifle from its scrub and headed in the direction of the camp. Calvin followed suit and the two were soon only a few yards away from Scarhead's camp.

Gazing out and around the camp, RJ suddenly had the feeling they'd been had.

"Do you see anyone in that camp?" he whispered to Calvin.

Before he could say anything more, the quietness of the night suddenly echoed two gun shots from behind them in the vicinity of where they had left their horses.

Both RJ and Calvin stared at each other when they heard a voice yelling from far off.

"Hey Amigo's, your horses are both dead. You come looking for me Amigo's."

A sudden *snap* of a tree limb and both RJ and Calvin's guns exploded in its direction, bringing a scream and a thud as someone hit the ground. The night once again became silent.

"Ricco. Are you alright?"

"Si brother," came a reply from somewhere up above them.

"One of them is in a tree."

RJ once again gazed out over the campfire. "We have to move from this place, but not knowing where they might be hiding, could be deadly for either one of us."

"I would bet that there is one of them behind that large rock just right of the fire." RJ looked in the direction Calvin was pointing and nodded in agreement.

"I have a rock that I'll throw over there and then make tracks for that rock. You fire towards the right side of it. That should make whoever is behind it move to the left. Wherever the others are, they will probably send a couple rounds in the direction of my thrown rock. Maybe with some luck you can pick out some muzzle blast and locate another one."

"Be careful, Calvin."

"Ole Johnny Blue Coat couldn't get me. I doubt if either one here can either."

With that, Calvin stood, threw his rock and like a scared jackrabbit was gone.

The ten yards or so across the camp to the large rock seemed forever to bridge, but Calvin did it, dove over it and as suspected, one of them was there caught off guard by RJ's shot. Two shots from Calvin's pistol took another one's life.

Five shots rang out from RJ's rifle as he caught a glimpse of muzzle blast from high above and to his left. His five shots were followed by the sound of breaking tree limbs as a body fell to the ground.

"Ricco. Ricco." Once again filled the night, except this time there was no answer.

"Chico, it's me Arturo."

RJ judged the voice to be straight in front of him but far off.

"Hey Amigo's, we will meet again someday. I know who you are and our paths will for sure cross again. Adios Amigo."

A couple minutes went by before RJ heard the far off beating of horse hooves.

"Calvin. Are you okay?"

"Yup." Calvin said, getting up and walking out from behind the rock and in the direction of RJ.

RJ also got up and walked toward the campfire, which had died down quite a bit from when they first got there and tossed on a couple more sticks of wood.

As the two came together, each had the same question on their lips.

"We were set up! But by who?"

CHAPTER 16

RJ and Calvin made their way back to North Platte the next morning with the dead bodies of three tied face down across their horses, which were found just outside of their camp, sorry that Scarhead and Arturo got away.

As they entered the town, several small boys who had been hitting a tin can around with a stick, but stopped what they were doing and ran up next to RJ and Calvin.

"Did you shoot them fella's?" asked one of the boys, running up close enough to poke one of the dead men with his stick.

"Hey, you boys runs along now," Calvin warned.

Lost in thought for the moment, Calvin wondered if these were the first up close dead men those boys had seen.

"Can you remember the first dead guy you ever saw, RJ?"

Reining his horse to a stop, RJ removed his hat and drew his arm across his forehead, soaking up the rivulets of sweat on his shirt sleeve that were starting to run down his face. Replacing his hat he turned to look at the dead men they had in tow.

"Yup, Calvin I certainly do. It was my daddy. I can see him now, lying face down in the dirt next to our corral. Mama told me that he must have had a heart attack." Searching down deep, RJ continued, "Then later on in the box that he was buried in. Mama picking me up so I could touch his face, which was so cold. Seen a lot of dead since then, Calvin. Yep, seen a lot of dead."

Calvin was just about to say something, but the voice of Sheriff Tom Callahan stopped him.

RJ had seen Callahan step thru his office door onto the boardwalk as he was talking to Calvin but didn't let on, now he stood before them with a strange look on his face which RJ picked up on.

Bet you didn't plan on ever seeing us again, did ya sheriff? RJ thought as he looked Callahan in the face.

"Well, now, will you lookie here. It appears you caught up with Scarhead and his boys."

Stepping down into the street, Callahan went to each of the dead and grabbing a fistful of hair turned up their heads so that he could see their faces.

"Don't see ole Scarface to be one of these," he said, stepping up next to RJ who had dismounted.

"No sheriff, he got away along with the other Mexican who called himself Arturo."

"You recognize either of these three?" RJ was hoping that at least one of them had a price on his head and was sure that sheriff Callahan knew who they were.

"Well, that one there," he pointed at the one on the middle horse. "His name is Ricco and he was Scarhead's brother and, like him, he has reward money on his head. The other two I don't know who they are but saw them in town with Scarhead. Five thousand reward money on Ricco though. I'm curious to know how Scarhead and Arturo got away."

"Well sheriff. I'm curious to know how they knew we were coming." RJ saw Callahan's eyebrows perk up knowing the accusing tone of his voice couldn't go un-noticed.

"I don't believe the tone of your voice suggests that I had anything to do with it here?"

"You tell me sheriff?"

"Better make it a good story." Calvin piped in.

"Well, let's go into my office and get the paper on Ricco, then we can talk some over breakfast."

"Food does sound good, RJ," Calvin said, turning around and, once again, shooing the boys away from the dead men.

Three hours later, well fed and the horses rested, knowing that five thousand dollars was being wired to his account, RJ and Calvin set out in the same direction they had followed the tracks of Scarhead's gang out of town the day before.

The sun was nearing noon and the full heat of the day sapped your energy and it wasn't long before both horses showed signs of getting overheated, not to mention RJ and Calvin. They were soon upon the campsite of the previous night's shootout and circling the site looking for any tracks that would lead them in the right direction that Scarhead and Arturo had taken. Making a wider circle they came upon a place that had several large, dried drops of blood. Continuing to circle, they came upon a small creek bed with some small waterholes that still contained some water.

As RJ dismounted, he indicated to Calvin that this would be a good place to let the horse's water and feed on some on the clumps of dried grass surrounding the creek bed."

Walking around in the dried out creek, RJ and Calvin came upon several boot prints and lots of horse prints along with some more dried blood, but larger spots.

"From all the prints here, I'd say that Scarhead and his men had been here for some time and was probably where they had left the horses tied up."

"Yep, and waiting to hear us coming up the trail," Calvin said with a sarcastic tone to his voice. This was the first time that RJ had heard or seen any negative actions from Calvin and wondered if it would be better if they just headed for home.

"What'd' ya say Calvin? Want to head on back to Deadwood and leave Ole Scarhead and Arturo for another time? Won't bother me none if you want to."

"I was thinking that those two are long gone. We don't know this country like they do so to me, we ought to head for Deadwood, get good and rested up and see who else we can hunt down."

"Deal then. Let's go on back to town, have ourselves a nice bath, some good food, a good night's sleep and head on out in the morning. Horses could use some good oats also."

Off in the distance was the cry of a lone coyote.

"Listen to that coyote," said RJ, mounting up.

"Strange, Coyotes are seldom out during the day, especially one as hot as this."

"Well then, what do you make of it?" In their time together in the Rebel army, Calvin had come to respect anything that RJ had to say in regards to the unknown.

"Don't rightly know. Maybe one of them had stayed back and was waiting to see if we would follow them, and if so, to ambush us again. If it is, well, we fooled him."

If they'd gone and investigated what it was that coyote was howling about, they would have discovered the body of a man whom the coyote was standing over calling all the other coyotes in for some food. Being an outlaw, you had no say in the way you would leave this world. The dead corpse of Arturo, who was about to become a coyote's supper was witness to that. Bounty money never to be collected.

During baths later that evening, RJ learned from one of the bath house attendants that Micah had spent quite a bit of time there in Grand Platte. He and Sheriff Callahan was known to spend a lot of time together, and on the occasion when Scarhead was in town, all three could be found playing cards and drinking together. Real chummy, he thought.

"Sometimes when Chico and his brother Ricco came to town, Sheriff Tom would set them up with one of the little Chinese prostitutes who would later be found beaten or with her throat cut."

"How do you know all this about them?"

"I listen and watch with my eyes and ears open and with my mouth shut. I tried to get to you both before you left town going after Chico but there wasn't an opportunity. You have to be careful as to not draw attention to yourself."

The attendant that supplied RJ with information was named Annie and she went on to tell him that on several occasions, men whom she had seen on wanted posters in the sheriff's office often would show up in town and Sheriff Callahan would offer them safe surroundings.

"How did you come about getting and knowing so much about wanted men and their involvement with the sheriff?" RJ at once saw the usefulness of having someone like her to feed him information but then thought that it probably wouldn't be safe for her to send telegrams to Deadwood. Someone for sure would spread the word and that would end up getting everyone killed.

"How would you like to leave here and come back to Deadwood with Calvin and myself? I'm sure you could get a position at one of the many bath houses there or have Martha find you some other job."

"I don't know about that. You see, it's Micah that I gathered information for and he rules the streets of Deadwood. I'm not sure how he would take me not being able to feed him information concerning outlaws that come into town." Getting up from her crouched position, Annie stuck her head around the corner of the bath area and once certain that there was no one to hear she went on to tell RJ what he already knew about Micah.

"I probably shouldn't be telling you this, but Micah is a bounty hunter." She drew in her breath and gave out a little gasp just saying the words, as if they were poison.

RJ didn't let on to Annie that he knew that or that he and Calvin were also bounty hunters.

"Well, Annie, the offer is there. Calvin and I will be leaving tomorrow if you want to come with us you are welcome to."

Calvin had been soaking just listening to RJ but he was aware of Annie's beauty. He noticed the sparkle in her green eyes. The way her breasts heaved up and down beneath her blouse. He was taken in by her and he couldn't help himself from speaking, "Annie, I wish you would consider RJ's offer and come back to Deadwood with us."

Calvin hadn't gone un-noticed by Annie. She had noticed him first when they approached the bath house and wondered if he was RJ's son, not knowing they were very close to the same age and friends, not related. Calvin had retained his youthful looks where RJ had aged so he smiled when she had asked if he was RJ's son.

"No Annie, I'm not his son."

"Could've fooled me by golly." She said, slapping her hands against her legs and turning her head, hoping that they wouldn't see the blushing in her cheeks by her mistake. And now, they were asking her to join them and return to Deadwood with them.

"How would I get to Deadwood? I have no horse or buggy? I have saved up some money but not enough to purchase one, besides, I have never ridden a horse."

All but tripping over himself, Calvin, trying to hide the excitement in his voice spoke up.

"I can purchase both a horse and buggy for the trip back to Deadwood and when we get there I'll just sell it, right RJ?"

"Whatever you want, son!" RJ said, standing up and stepping from the bath not given any notice that he was naked as a jay bird and Annie, paying him no mind. After all, she had seen hundreds of naked men and had learned not to notice or stare at them, although she did notice Calvin's quite generous parts when he stood up as she handed him a towel to dry himself off with.

Stepping up to RJ, Annie went up on tip toes and gave him a tender kiss on the cheek. Turning back to Calvin she did the same, then clapping her hands together informed them that they best be getting along if they expected to find someone at the livery who would sell them a horse and buggy this time of night.

"Yahoo!" escaped Calvin's lips looking at RJ with a big grin on his face that extended from ear to ear.

A deal was made to pick up the horse and buggy the next morning. Annie would have her few belongings packed and ready. Annie agreed to meet them later for supper not knowing at that moment she would be spending the rest of the night wrapped in Calvin's arms.

The next morning was perfect as the three rode out of North Platte. RJ had spent some time again with Sheriff Callahan, this time being a little more forceful. He would have a couple days to figure out just how he was going to approach Micah.

All his plans would go up in smoke once they arrived back in Deadwood.

Chapter 17

The ride back to Deadwood seemed longer than what it had taken them to get to North Platte and if they had any clue as to what had transpired in Deadwood since they had left they might have been in more of a hurry to return, but as it was, they just moped along having a lot to discuss. It wouldn't be until they entered Deadwood and talked to Martha that they would learn what had gone on in such a short period of time. They would also learn exactly what roll Micah had played in what they had encountered in North Platte where Scarhead was concerned.

It was a nice evening in Deadwood and the streets, although alive and busy were the quietest they had been in months. The arrival of the wagon train with new businesses to start up and of course the arrival of new women had cut down on the stress of some major Deadwood figures that flowed on down the chow line to the hired cowboy and the lone miner.

The many saloons were filled to capacity and the saloon noises could be heard up and down the streets as money and drink flowed easily.

Martha, who had been busy since RJ and Calvin had left, walked out of her place and onto the boardwalk.

What a beautiful evening, she said to herself taking in a long, deep breath and scanning the streets, her ears picking up all of the noise generated by horses, wagons, piano playing and the loud laughter coming out through the bat wing doors of the saloons and gambling establishments.

As Martha walked the men she encountered all tipped their hats in acknowledgement plus it is what a gentleman did when addressing a female, although not to whores.

As Martha walked, her thoughts were on RJ and Calvin. She had been told by one of her enlisted girls that something was going on with Micah, and that it concerned RJ, Calvin and the outlaw known as Scarhead. Walking by the alleyway between the bank and the Bella Union Saloon and Gambling Emporium, Martha thought she heard the muffled screams of a woman coming from the back of the saloon.

Hurrying down the alley with blood rushing to her head and her heart pounding, Martha soon was at the end of the alley and at the backside of the Bella Union where she once again heard the muffled screams.

Looking up at an open window, she continued to hear the screams along with the voices of men warning her to keep quiet and to enforce their commands, Martha heard the *whack, whack,* of an open hand landing against the face of the woman doing the screaming.

"That'll shut her up for a spell," she heard one of the men say.

"I need to get in there," Martha whispered out loud knowing that the only way into that room was through the swinging doors of the Bella. Hurrying back to the front of the building, and not giving any thought to her safety, Martha stepped through the doors and at once half the men in the place looked up at her and there was a moment of quiet. The noise of the saloon sounded, to Martha's ears, to be a mile away, although she was standing in the middle of hooting and shouting and wolf whistles. It only took a minute for all action to resume once they had observed who she was. Stepping rapidly to the rear of the room, Martha saw that there was a large man standing outside the rear room's door. This man had a beer mug in his hand and was talking to a rough looking cowboy wearing an eye patch who looked and smelled terrible. The cowboy with the patch saw Martha as she approached and sort of turned and stepped into her path. Martha saw that this man hadn't taken a bath or washed his clothes for a long time.

A muffled scream came out the door and Martha asked in a loud voice, "what's going on in there and who's doing all that screaming?"

Looking directly at Martha, the man with the eye patch spoke up as he took a step in her direction.

"Ain't none of your affair ma'am, so I suggest you turn around and leave." Folding his arms across his chest he repeated the warning. "Ain't none of your affair!"

Once again, a scream came through the door and Martha noticed a smile come across, the face of this despicable man.

"That's where you are wrong mister! A screaming woman becomes my business. Martha went to push her way past not giving any more thought to her safety.

A swift backhand across her face, knocked Martha to the floor. Then a kick to her midsection, took her breath away and Martha tasted her stomach bile as she was about to throw up.

"That's enough, Jake," came the voice of the big guy stepping forward between her and the cowboy named Jake.

"Pick her up and bring her inside."

Martha saw the door open at the same time she was being lifted to her feet. The pain in her ribs and the lack of breath slowed her down, therefore, she couldn't fight back as she was propelled into the room. Once inside she was roughly seated on a wooden chair and surrounded by three cowboys who stood around waiting their turn with the young Chinese girl lying naked on the cot. Atop her was Micah in the act of raping her. With each deep movement, she would scream out and immediately after doing so, one of Micah's hands would come up and give her a stiff whack across the face. Martha saw blood flowing from her nose and out of the corner of her mouth and saw the smirks from those waiting their turn.

Martha took this opportunity to reach for and pulled the pistol out from the holster of one of the men standing next to her. Before he could form any kind of warning, Martha cocked the weapon and aiming it towards Micah, pulled the trigger. A loud, deafening gunshot filled the room and Martha saw a bright red stain appear in the back of Micah's shirt.

The impact of the bullet seemed to lift Micah up and off the girl. Curse words spewed from his lips as he sunk to the floor. With the speed of a mountain lion, Martha was by the girl's side with the pistol now pointing, cocked and ready at the men who had been standing around and were now in the process of drawing their own pistols.

"Don't try it," she warned, as two reach for their pistols. In a split second, Martha had to make a life or death decision as it became apparent they were not going to obey her warning.

Bang! Bang! The colt roared as two lead shots found their targets. One of the men was spun around and fell onto the table, knocking the lamp to the floor where the glass mantel shattered. Lamp oil slowly spread out over the floor and burst into flame. Within a matter of a few seconds, the fire had spread through the small room. Martha grabbed for the girl and pulled her to her feet. Next she grabbed the blanket that was on the cot and wrapped it around the naked girl as they ran from the burning room, bumping into several men, including the one eyed guy. She would have stopped and put a bullet into him for knocking her to the floor, but it was more important to get away from an impending inferno.

Almost like clockwork, a line of men was established and soon buckets of water were being thrown on the fire. Once the fire was manageable, the two dead men were dragged out. Micah, although badly wounded and sustaining burns to his body, survived.

Martha knew that she couldn't take the girl to her place as there would be lots of folk looking for her.

Martha remembered a small creek that had a fairly large overhang of rock that they had passed coming into town on the wagon train. This is where Martha decided to take the girl. Once things settled down, she would go back into Deadwood and gather some things to survive on until RJ and Calvin returned.

Martha was surprised when the Chinese girl spoke to her in broken English.

"I am Fay Ling," she said as she bowed to Martha.

"I'm Martha," she said in return, also bowing to her.

"I know who you are. Nuying told me all about you."

"What brought on what was happening to you back there?"

Martha had ripped a piece of material from her dress and dipped it in the creek and used it to wipe off Fay Ling's face, removing some dried blood from the corner of her mouth.

"I think I asked too many questions. One of the men you shot, I had spent some time with and because I had seen him hang around Micah I asked some questions having to do with what Micah did for a living. I guess he went to Micah and told him about my questions, because soon after I was dragged from my room and brought to the room that you found me in where I was stripped naked and had already been raped by one of the men you shot.

"Micah grabbed me by the neck and asked me who had told me to ask questions about him? I told him no one had told me anything. I told him I knew he was a very important man and I was curious. That's all. He had just started his rape of me when you arrived. I suffered much in the few minutes before you shot him.

Martha saw tears appear in Fay Ling's eyes and run down her cheeks, taking her in her arms, Martha wrapped the blanket tightly around her.

Feeling her small body shaking, Martha thought to herself, *she is still so frightened that she can't control her shaking.* Other thoughts entered Martha's mind as they both stood there in the fading light of day. Soon it would be dark and Martha would make her way back to town under the cover of the darkness.

Martha and Fay Ling moved under the overhang where they both sat down on a large log that someone had purposely dragged it there. Looking around, Martha saw a small circle of rocks that surrounded what appeared to have been a campfire.

It's going to be a dark night, Martha said to herself seeing that there were no moon or stars in the sky to light the night. In the far off distance, the howling of a coyote could be heard, which, along with what Fay Ling had already endured only made her tremble more.

Soon, Martha stood and told Fay Ling that it was time for her to go back to town and see what she could learn and to also pick up some items from her place. Martha was also excited to see what damage the fire had done and if Micah was still alive.

"I have no idea when RJ and Calvin will return, but, until they do, we must not let anyone find us."

When Martha thought it was dark enough and the excitement had died down, she left Fay Ling and made her way back into Deadwood. In the darkness, she could smell the smoke from the fire and when she entered the main street, she saw that there were still some men tossing buckets of water on the smoking building to make sure there were no wayward sparks. Their fast actions had prevented the town from going up in flames, something that was an issue in those days because everything was built of wood. Many of these small towns would succumb to fire.

During lightning storms, men would congregate in town with their water buckets in case lightning were to hit one of the wooden buildings and set it on fire.

Martha was careful to stay close to the buildings as she made her way towards her place. In front of her, standing on the boardwalk watching the action was Nuying.

"Nuying," Martha whispered just loud enough for her to hear. Turning around, Nuying's face lit up when she saw who it was that had called her name.

"Martha!" there was both happiness and concern in her voice. "I've been standing here watching the men fight the fire and saw them pull three men from the saloon. One of them was Micah and they carried him over to doc's office. I had been told that Fay Ling and you were also in there and was worried when you weren't brought out."

"Fay Ling is fine." Martha told her placing her hand on her shoulder. "She has undergone a traumatic ordeal, though." Looking around, Martha led Nuying in the direction of her place, knowing that there might be someone there watching to see if she returned.

"I'm going to need you to go to my place and pick up some items that we will need to survive on for a few days. I also need you to watch for RJ's return and send him to the place I will tell you about."

Martha went on to tell Nuying all she knew up to that point. She told of the heartrending screams that she had heard coming from the back room at Bella's and had gone to investigate.

"Fay Ling was one of the two girls I told you about that could speak and understand some English so they would be perfect to help gather information."

"I guess she showed she understood more than they thought she did and got worried."

Stopping just yards from her place, Martha told Nuying what she needed.

"Before you get me these items, I need you to go see doc and find out how Micah is."

Martha couldn't describe the look that came over Nuying's face, except it looked like she had seen Satan, the Devil himself.

"Whisper my name to doc," she told her. "He is one of the good guys."

"Whew! I was worried there for a minute. So far I have gone undetected and I want to stay that way."

"I know your concern Nuying," Martha said, once again placing her hand on Nuying's shoulder. Nuying simply nodded her head and set off in the direction of doc's office.

I hope that bastard dies right there in doc's office. A wish she hoped for, but one that wouldn't come about, for at that very moment, Micah was sitting up in a chair with doc wrapping a bandage around his chest covering the entrance and exit wound of Martha's shot. He had also bandaged Micah's hands where they had suffered some burns.

"Be a few weeks before your hands will be bendable. Those blisters will have to heal, but if you keep having someone rub that ointment I gave you on them, then they will be one hundred percent again."

"What about my two boy's doc?"

"Both were dead when I checked on them. Someone was a good shot as they both were shot mid chest probably killing them instantly."

"It's not someone, doc! It was RJ's woman, Martha."

"No Chinese girl, either?"

Doc shook his head, indicating there had been no one else brought into his office. Doc was well aware of the where bouts of Martha and Fay Ling. He was good friends with RJ, Calvin, and her and was in on everything the three of them did.

"Well, doc, if you hear anything about those two women you get to me on them, you hear?"

Doc simply nodded and put his hand under Micah's arm and stood him up. Although his legs were shaky, he stood and took a few wobbly steps around.

"Don't know what pains me the most doc? My hands or the bullet wound."

"You were lucky. That bullet went right on through the fleshy part of your side and missed any of your organs." Blinking his eye he finished saying. "Your wounds will heal just fine and you'll be as good as new."

As doc finished talking the door opened and Nuying stepped inside.

"I had heard about Mr. Micah and was coming to check on him and see if he needed me or one of my girls for anything."

Micah stepped up to Nuying and, even though his hand was bandaged, slapped her hard across the face knocking her against the office wall. Doc was about to step up, but thought twice about coming between the two.

"Get out of my sight," he screamed, then doubled over as the pain from his wounded hand shot through his body.

Nuying ran out of the doc's office without being able to give doc the message from Martha.

I will just have to keep a sharp eye out for them myself.

Stopping in at Martha's place, Nuying gathered the items Martha had wanted and stuffed them in a pillow case. She found Martha and told her about Micah and not being able to talk to the doc.

"That's okay, I trust you to be vigilant in your watch for RJ and send him to me as soon as he arrives."

Nuying shook her head, gave Fay Ling a light kiss on the cheek and then was gone into the darkness.

Sitting on the log next to Fay Ling and wrapping them both in the blanket Martha wondered.

What in heaven's name had she and RJ gotten themselves into in this hell hole of a town? Never had I envisioned that such a vile, horrendous place could exist. I pity the young, innocent people who come here seeking their fortune and then get faced with all the atrocities that are lurking in this cauldron of depravity.

Sitting there feeling Fay Ling's body still shivering, Martha turned her eyes, now filling with tears, upward toward heaven, and whispered, "Where are you RJ? Where are you? Please, dear Lord, take care of him."

CHAPTER 18

Two days had passed since the shooting of Micah by Martha. Taking Fay Ling by the hand she told her, "It's time we made our way back to my place." Martha felt Fay Ling hesitate some but walked along beside her.

No one in town paid any attention to the two as they entered town and went directly to Martha's place.

The pounding of horse's hooves coming up behind them forced Martha to turn around and check them out. She was startled to see that the one in front had a large sombrero hanging from his neck by a rawhide cord, duel bandoleers crisscrossed his chest and the many silver conchs decorating his saddle, told Martha he was a Mexican. Looking at his face, Martha noticed the deep scar across his forehead and knew at once whom she was looking at.

"Scarhead," whispered Fay Ling before Martha could. The two of them rode on by. Martha suddenly felt sick to her stomach knowing that this was the man that RJ and Calvin had journeyed to Grand Platte to kill for the bounty on his head, was obvious, still very much alive.

"Oh! RJ," she spoke, "where are you and Calvin?" Holding Fay Ling tighter, she made fast tracks now to her place.

Once inside, Martha went directly to the front window where she pulled back the curtains to watch and see where Scarhead and his rider went to. She was surprised to see him pull up and dis-mount in front of the doc's office.

Obviously someone who knew where he'd be had, made contact with him and told him of the shooting of Micah by the woman called Martha. Nuying had told Martha, she was unable to give doc her message so she had given the message to a young boy, named Travis, who liked to hang around outside the saloons running errands and such for anyone needing something done, for which he collected a few coins each day.

"You can't fool me," Nuying told him. "You're just hoping to catch a glimpse up under a dancer's skirt."

Travis's face turned red and his gaze turned from Nuying towards the ground. Travis had indeed spied up under a skirt or two and one of the dancers had even let him put his hands on her well rounded bosom.

"Thought so," Nuying said, turning quickly so that her skirt rode up some teasing Travis. Nuying looked back over her shoulder and caught the reaction on Travis's face and she smiled to herself.

Travis was given instructions to keep his eyes open looking for the return of RJ and Calvin. Martha had told Nuying it probably wouldn't be too much longer if Scarhead was still alive. She prayed that RJ wasn't dead.

Martha watched Scarhead walk out of doc's office and grabbing his horse's reins, head for the rooming house. She saw him point to the Bella Union and the rider who had ridden with him headed in that direction.

Stepping away from the window, Martha turned to Fay Ling and motioned for her to follow.

"You will be staying here for a while until we see what happens next. Micah isn't going to take my shooting him lightly, even if I am the wife of his friend."

A loud knock was heard at the door.

"I wonder who that could be. Now Martha was a little worried and being very cautious, went to the door and asked who it was.

"It's me Travis and I have some news for you."

Martha opened the door and Travis almost knocked her over coming through it.

"RJ and Calvin are just a little ways out of town," came the excited voice.

After speaking to Nuying, Travis had left town and found a nice spot where he could easily see the road but not be seen himself. It was from there he spotted RJ and Calvin and gave him the warning he was told to.

"RJ told me to tell you not to leave the house 'til he comes in. He said that he was going to wait until around ten o'clock tonight, then he and Calvin would quietly slip in and you are to make sure to unlock your back door for them to enter."

"Are they both alright?"

"Yes, ma'am, they are."

"Well, thank the Lord as far as that goes." Tears of joy suddenly flooded Martha's eyes and she plopped down on the couch next to Fay Ling and wrapped her arms around her. A few seconds passed and then Martha went into the kitchen and came back with two nice shiny gold coins which she handed to Travis.

"You did well, Travis."

With wide eyes, he took them and gave her a big grin and a "thank you ma'am."

Immediately after Travis left, Martha went and unlocked her back door.

"I'll make a pot of fresh coffee for the boys." Martha said, looking at a smiling Fay Ling.

"What do you think RJ will do now?"

"Well, knowing RJ like I do, I'm sure he will go see Micah and find out what he was doing attacking you and then having Scarhead show up and going to see him."

"That reminds me." Martha stepped back to the window and saw that Scarhead's horse was still tied up outside Micah's rooming house. Looking at the front of the Bella Union, she saw that the horse the other fella rode was still tied up in front of the saloon.

Once the coffee was simmering and the back door unlocked, both Martha and Fay Ling sat and made small talk until RJ and Calvin arrived.

"Those two men you killed had already raped me." Fay Ling told Martha. "He punched me very hard in the stomach before he started in on me." Martha noticed, although her voice was a little shaky as she talked, there were no more tears.

"I'm glad you killed those two," Fay Ling told Martha before continuing. "It's too bad you didn't kill Micah also."

Martha got up and filled a couple of cups with the fresh coffee and brought one back to Fay Ling then she went and pulled the curtain back to see it Scarhead's horse was still tied in front of the rooming house. It was.

Turning from the window, Martha looked at the clock. "Nine forty five, " she said. Martha suddenly felt as though she had a stomach full of butterflies. She recalled that this feeling was the same as the first time she had lain in RJ's arms.

Out of the corner of her eye, Martha saw the back door start to open. In another second it opened completely and RJ and Calvin were standing in her kitchen.

Fay Ling watched as Martha jumped up from the couch and flung herself into RJ's arms. It seemed to Calvin and Fay Ling that the kissing and the whispered "I love you's" went on forever.

Soon, all four were seated around Martha's living room sipping coffee and swapping stories

"Well, for sure, Micah has had something to do with Scarhead," recalling all that had transpired. "There are just too many noticeable occurrences between Scarhead and Micah and also between Scarhead and the sheriff of North Platte to be unattached to each other.

"What are you going to do now?"

"You said that Scarhead arrived earlier so that means he must have headed directly here after the attempted ambush." Getting up and walking to the stove, RJ poured himself another cup of coffee. Returning to his seat, he asked about the other rider who came in with Scarhead.

"I'm sorry, but I was paying so much attention to Scarhead that I didn't really notice anything about him."

"You said he went over to the Bella Union?"

Nodding her head in agreement, Martha asked, "Do you want me to contact Nuying and see what she can find out? Neither Fay Ling or myself can show our faces right now."

"I gave instructions to Travis to come by here every hour or so just in case we were to need anything. I'll have him ask Nuying to see what she can find out about him and then come back."

About that time a knock was heard at the front door. RJ and Calvin got up and stood in the back room while Martha went to the door.

"Who is it?" she asked.

"It's Travis ma'am.," Martha opened the door and motioned for him to come inside. RJ and Calvin came back into the room and nodded their hello to Travis.

"Travis, I need you to see Nuying and tell her to get me as much information on that other fella who rode in with Scarhead. Tell her that he is over at the Bella Union."

"Gee, Miss Martha, you don't need Nuying for that, I already can tell you who it is."

Travis had a big grin on his face, knowing that the information she had asked about should be worth a hefty amount of coin.

"Sit down and tell us everything you know about him," RJ spoke. "Don't leave anything out, Travis. I want to know even the littlest details you might have heard."

Travis was about to ask how much his information was worth, but decided that they had always treated him right, so he knew that this would be no different.

Martha got up and went and got Travis a glass of water. He took a couple of sips before starting. "His real name is William

Jackson but because he only has one eye and wears a patch over it, he has gotten the name of *One Eye Jackson*. Some even go further and add the word *Lefty* because he is also left handed." How did you learn so much about him in so little of time?" RJ was curious.

"Your friend Micah has always told me to pay close attention to any new rider that comes into town and once I hear their name or get a good look at his face to go to the sheriff's office and look through the wanted posters and see if there is one. If so, I take it back to him and he gives me two dollars."

"Well then, tell me Travis, is there a poster on this William Jackson?"

"There sure is!" Travis's voice had a lot of excitement in it and he had jumped up out of his chair and reaching into his shirt produced a folded poster which he handed to RJ. Unfolding the poster, RJ let out a very loud "wow."

"Wanted dead or alive." He read, then exhaling continued. "Twenty-five thousand dollars." RJ let a low volume whistle escape his lips.

"What is he wanted for?" Calvin asked with eyes the size of silver dollars. It had been awhile since they had seen that kind of money. "We shouldn't have to split that reward with Micah seeing he had nothing to do with collecting it."

"There's more," the still excited Travis spoke.

"He rode into town with a Mex by the name Scarhead. He also has a twenty-five thousand dollar reward on his head." Without being asked, Travis pulled out from his back pants pocket, another folded up poster, this one on Scarhead.

Calvin looked at the posters that Travis laid out on the table. Both were wanted for all kinds of robberies, rapes, and murder. Both were wanted *DEAD OR ALIVE.*

"It's for sure now, that Micah is friends with Scarhead and has to also be with Lefty seeing they rode in together."

"I say we just go into the Bella Union and shoot that son of a bitch Lefty before the three of them get a chance to tie up together. What d' ya say. RJ?"

There was excitement back in Calvin's voice that in the past RJ had come to enjoy about his friend. An excitement he hadn't heard for some time.

"If we just go over there and shoot him, even though there is little law here, there is a sheriff and he might not take to cold blooded murder."

"I'll just call him out, RJ!"

"On what charge? You can't mention him being wanted. Besides, you know nothing about him, like how fast with a gun is he? You'll go and get yourself shot up if you ain't got some kind of plan."

"Well, come up with something RJ and make it quick. We don't know how Micah is or when those two boys might leave the rooming house and go to the Bella Union to meet their friend."

Before RJ could speak, Martha asked if she could speak.

"We're all ears, Martha." RJ and Calvin spoke up at the same time.

"The way I see it, you two need to stay out of sight 'til you can figure out the goings on between Scarhead and Micah." Both RJ and Calvin nodded at her remark.

"So, this is my plan right this minute, and it will only work as long as Scarhead and Micah aren't around the Bella Union, is when I walk in there and confront Lefty and before he can do anything to me, I'll pull my little pistol from under my skirt and shoot him dead."

It was almost funny to RJ hearing Martha's plan.

"Are you kidding me?" he said, as he went to the stove again to pour himself another coffee only to find the pot empty.

"Hold on there, RJ. What she says might just work."

"You're just as crazy as she is if you think that is any kind of plan at all." Looking at Martha, RJ lowered his head and shook it slowly.

"Listen RJ. Time is short here. As it is right now, none of us can leave here for worry what will happen as soon as Micah and Scarhead get word you two are back and I'm sure he will be looking for a way to get me also. I can even show everyone his wanted poster and collect the money without being called a bounty hunter and having to worry about that."

"It just might work RJ."

"Yeah! And it just might get her killed!" Still shaking his head RJ watched as Martha went into her bedroom and came back holding a double barrel derringer along with the gun she shot Micah with.

"When I shot Micah and the two others, it was out of self-preservation and I didn't twitch a muscle or hesitate for a second." Standing in front of RJ, Martha placed both her hands on his shoulders and forced him to face her directly.

"I'm not scared of the man, RJ."

As she spoke those words, looking her in the eye RJ saw something he hadn't seen before. He saw another side of his beloved wife.

"I just don't want anything to happen to you, don't you understand that?"

"Of course I do, my darling, that's exactly why I won't let anything happen to me."

Taking the two pistols from Martha's hand, he inspected them both then handed her the two shot derringer.

"Pull the trigger first, and see where your shot hit. Then, if you need to aim and pull the other one, remember you only have those two shots and not being a powerful weapon you need to be accurate. A shot in the chest will momentarily freeze him in his tracks and that will give you time to aim for his forehead before pulling the other trigger." Looking at her and then placing a light kiss to her lips, he handed it to her, gave her a playful slap on her rear end and told her to once again be careful.

Grabbing the poster off the table, Martha folded it up and stuck it in her blouse between her shapely breasts, turned and without any more conversation walked out through the front door and headed in the direction of the Bella Union. Behind her, looking through the front window, all of them stood watching her as she made footsteps of what RJ hoped wouldn't be her death.

Come back to me alive and well, were the immediate thoughts going through RJ's mind.

The lamplights that lined the street offered a shadowed glimpse of Martha entering the Bella Union.

"She just entered the saloon," whispered Calvin, and you could hear everyone take in a deep breath and hold it as they waited for the muffled sound of Martha's derringer. RJ hadn't bothered to close the front door so that he could hear when she fired the weapon.

As Martha stood for a moment just outside the doors to the Bella Union, she gave her head a little shake to clear out any thought of being scared and palming the small weapon, pushed open the swinging doors and stepped inside. She immediately noticed how loud it was inside.

Hadn't sounded that noisy from the outside, she thought. Her eyes scanned the room looking for a man wearing a patch over one eye. She didn't have to look far, because there, standing not ten feet from her, was the one eyed man staring in her direction.

Walking in his direction and taking the poster from between her breast, Martha opened it up just as she reached him.

"William Jackson!" she yelled at the top of her voice bringing everyone's attention to her, and at the same instant, bringing up the derringer at point blank range she put the barrel right against his shirt in the middle of his chest and pulled one trigger. A surprised look came over his face as the pain reached his brain, but only lasted a split second as Martha quickly raised the weapon up to insert the barrel into his mouth, which was opened wide in a scream of pain as Martha's first shot entered his body. Martha pulled the second trigger. Although it was a small caliber weapon, the shot went into his head and exited out the back, spewing blood, brain matter and hair onto some of the patrons standing at his back.

Not knowing exactly what was taking place, those that heard the shots, or felt the discharge, scrambled to get out of there, and in their rush tearing off one of the swinging' doors.

RJ and Calvin saw several men come running out of the Bella Union and guessed that Martha had accomplished her deed or at least attempted to.

From the corner of his eye, RJ caught movement coming from the front of the rooming house as Scarhead came out the door and was moving quickly toward the Bella Union.

Both RJ and Calvin stepped through the door and with their guns drawn shouted out Scarhead's name.

Quickly RJ said to Calvin, "Let's take this Mex alive."

"You got it RJ"

Before Scarhead had time to draw his pistols, both RJ and Calvin placed a couple well aimed shots hitting Scarhead first in his left shoulder, then his left leg dropping him to the dusty street in a pile of screaming Spanish.

From inside the rooming house, Micah was standing by the window and saw what had just transpired outside. Cussing and shaking his head, Micah returned to his bed where he lay down, staring up at the ceiling.

"Now what?" he whispered along with his cussing. . . .

CHAPTER 19

Almost three months after their arrival into Deadwood, another murder would take place, one that would define Deadwood's tainted history.

As RJ suspected, Micah's wound had healed and he had made an agreement with RJ not to bother Martha or Fay Ling, an agreement that RJ was skeptical about. Although RJ and Micah had been friends in the past, RJ and Calvin decided a late night visit was needed to guarantee his promise.

They informed Micah that they had their suspicions concerning him and Sheriff Callahan. "And one more thing, Micah," RJ said, stopping and turning to address him one more time before leaving, "Calvin and I will do our own Bounty Hunting from now on. That way we can be assured that you aren't setting us up again."

Calvin, who up to this time had been quiet, walked over, drew his pistol, and holding it up and under Micah's chin, warned him a second time, "You will also not bother any one of our friends, girlfriends, wives or whomever else we tell you not to. Your reign of terror on the folks of Deadwood is over."

Still holding his pistol pressed up under Micah's chin, he put a little more pressure on it which had Micah standing on the tips of his toes.

"Have we made ourselves clear?"

With a confirming nod from Micah, Calvin un-cocked his pistol and dropped it into his holster, then nodding to RJ, Calvin opened the door and he and RJ exited Micah's room, confident that there would be no more trouble from Micah.

Scarhead was behind bars and RJ and Calvin split the twenty-five thousand dollar reward money, which gave Calvin the funds to purchase building materials and hire a couple helpers to start building his house. All had been quiet for quite some time. The hot summer days dragged on interminably, which probably accounted for a little action in Deadwood, that is, until the evening of August 2nd.

The Nuttle & Mann's Saloon was a much frequented spot for Bill Hickok. *Lady Luck* had followed Bill on a number of occasions, but as with anything where *luck* is involved, there comes a time when it runs out. That time came to Bill Hickok as he was seated at a card game at that saloon.

Not being one to sit with his back un-protected, Bill liked to sit where his back was always to the wall, but, on this particular night, his desire and drive to play cards overcame this long enforced rule of his and he took a chair at the only card table that had a seat available, the only problem being it left his back toward the swinging doors.

As the deal went around the table, Bill was feeling pretty confident as he had been showing two black Aces and two black 8's. Before he had a chance to play the hand out, a young Jack McCall came in through the bat wing doors, drew his pistol, leveled it point blank at the back of Bill's head and pulled the trigger. Bill Hickok would never play out his hand, but it would go down in the history books of Deadwood known as the Dead man's Hand.

Jack McCall would be set free this time, but would be eventually tried again and hanged.

Seated at that table this particular evening was a man whose face was hidden by layers of caked on dirt and wearing bushy facial hairs. His hands were as steady as two stately cedars standing against the strong winds of a northerner, and whose cold black eyes were just that, COLD black eyes.

Eyes that had seen the death of nine men, caused by his lightning fast draw. Eyes that had looked into the blueberry color eyes of a whore he had been having pleasure with just before he drew his knife and slit her throat.

Now, as Jasper Arnett sat there with blood splattered on his face from the exit wound caused by Jack McCall's bullet, his cold black eyes showed no signs of movement. Jasper Arnett was a wanted outlaw with a ten thousand dollar reward on his head, dead or alive.

What in the hell is wrong with people and what in the hell is this town coming to where a man can't enjoy a friendly game of cards without someone else blowing his brains out.

Jasper folded his hand, stood and pushed away from the table. If he had any kind of warning, Bill Hickok would still be alive and Jack McCall would be the one lying dead, but that was not the case.

It was time now for Jasper to wander on over to the rooming house where he was staying and to have a meeting with Micah.

Micah had removed the reward poster on him the minute he had seen it a short while back, figuring that RJ would pick him as their next bounty to be collected, but now, with all that had gone on between them, Micah now had another use for Jasper.

Jasper had heard some rumors about Micah circulating around the trail that he might be a bounty hunter, so as he knocked on his door, he lowered his right hand to rest on the handle of his pistol, knowing that if Micah was gonna open the door and blast away, he didn't have a chance.

Instead of the door opening, Jasper heard a low voice call out, "come-in."

The room that Jasper stepped into was a very large one. The wood flooring had some nicely designed rugs laid about. There were two large windows adorned with some fancy, laced curtains with some red roses sewn in them for color. A large four poster bed was at the center of the room and there was a small table with two chairs, in one of those sat Micah whose face was clouded in cigar smoke.

"Have a chair," said Micah, rolling the cigar to the side of his mouth. With his right hand, he instructed Jasper to have a seat. In the center of the table was a lone whisky bottle and an empty glass which he also pointed at.

"Pour yourself a shot of one of the finest whiskies in Deadwood."

Jasper, took off his hat and laid it on the table. Taking the bottle, he'd un-corked it and poured himself a shot, then motioning with the bottle to Micah's empty glass. Micah nodded.

"I do believe you can pour me another," Micah said, picking up his empty glass. Jasper filled his glass, then set the bottle down. Picking up his own glass, he hoisted it in a salutary gesture and downed the drink with one swallow.

The amber brown liquid was one of the best tasting that Jasper had ever had. Setting his empty glass down, he un-corked the bottle again and poured himself another, but before he had a chance to raise it to his lips, Micah reached over and put his hand on his arm stopping it from being raised up to his lips.

"Let's talk. There will be plenty of time for drinking."

Releasing his hold on the glass, Jasper pulled his hand out from under Micah's and leaning back on two legs, Jasper crossed his arms across his chest and waited for Micah to begin.

"What happened to Bill Hickok today was terrible." As he said those words, Micah actually felt a little twinge of sadness for his friend. "I just lost a good friend and business partner." Looking across the table at Jasper he shook his head. "Deadwood's a town with no law."

"The way I hear it, is that you are one of the big reasons it's like it is. Seems that you have your own way of dealing with things that border on the verge of craziness."

"I guess if you call dragging a whore around town crazy, then I guess I would have to plead guilty as charged." It was now Micah who raised his glass in a silent salute before downing the liquor. "If people think you are a little crazy, well that just helps to keep things under control. They never know what you are going to do next."

"Let's get down to business, Micah. What do you want from me that you yourself can't handle?"

"We have a bounty hunter in town. The only thing that has kept him from dogging you down is that I removed the reward poster on you. No one in town knows who you are. You can be John Smith for all anyone knows."

"So, what's that to me?"

"I need you to kill him and that hot headed wife of his, Martha."

Hearing her name, Jasper raised his eyebrows and asked, "Is she the woman I heard shot you and killed two others who were in the middle of a good rep?"

Dropping his chair back down on all four legs, Jasper picked up the bottle and with his teeth pulled the cork out, spitting it across the room. He then tipped the bottle to his lips and poured a mouthful of the liquor, enjoying the slow burn as it flowed down his throat.

"I want you to call him out. Everyone in town needs to know that he is a bounty hunter and deserving to die."

"What about the woman who shot you? You said you wanted her dead too?"

"On second thought, I've decided to let her live for a while longer." He had other plans for her that he had just thought about.

"Once RJ is out of the way, we'll take Martha and her two little Chinese girls out of town and have some fun before killing them too." Jasper nodded his head with a big grin on his face hearing that. *Been a long time since I've had myself a woman's pleasure.*

What Micah hadn't planned on or have any knowledge of was that while RJ and Calvin were in North Platte they had seen a wanted poster on Jasper Arnett and had just witnessed him going into the rooming house.

"I'm sure that was Jasper Arnett, RJ," an excited Calvin told him after seeing him go into Micah's rooming house.

"No way for me to make a mistake here. Those black eyes gave him away." Calvin had walked right up to Jasper as he was on his way to meet up with Micah.

"You yourself, RJ, had pointed out his eyes that day we were looking at wanted posters and you mentioned that they could be spotted from a mile away, well, I wasn't a mile away but only a few feet, and I tell you it was him."

"What do you suppose he and Micah are up to?"

"Well, Calvin, knowing Micah and what we have done to him, he knows he can't do anything to us himself so he's concocting up some plan to get rid of us and not draw suspicion to himself."

"What are you boys up to?" was Martha's voice. Calvin and RJ turned to and RJ stood up and leaned in and gave her a loving kiss on her cheek.

"We just saw a wanted man go into the rooming house to have a meeting with Micah."

"What makes you both so sure he went in to see Micah? Couldn't he have just gone in to rent a room? After all, it is a rooming house."

"Could be, but my sixth sense tells me something else is brewing."

"RJ's sixth sense has kept us alive in instances where we should've been killed or captured," Calvin told Martha.

Since the shooting of Micah, Martha had been staying in town at one of the other rooming houses on RJ's insistence so she hadn't gone out much or heard about the murder of Hickok or this cowboy RJ and Calvin were talking about.

Letting out a little laugh, Martha asked, "Need me to put some lead in him for you?"

Both Calvin and RJ laughed along with Martha.

"Might not be a bad idea RJ." "Not a good one either, "came RJ's reply.

"I was just making a little joke," Martha said, walking up to RJ and putting her arm through his and giving him a big hug. It had been some time since RJ and Martha had had any time together. They had talked a little about having a child but decided to wait until all this played out, besides RJ had told her, *Deadwood is not the kind of town I want us to raise a kid in.* Martha had agreed, knowing that RJ was right, but at the same time wondered where else he had in mind. After all, he had started building their home here.

RJ looked at Martha then over at Calvin. These were the two people he cared the most about in the whole world *I don't know what I would do if anything ever happened to either of them.* In his mind, he knew just how close he had come to losing Martha had she not been quick enough when confronted by Micah and his group. Even now, he knew that Micah wouldn't rest 'til he had settled the score with her regardless of his agreement.

What worried him the most was lately, Calvin seemed to fall back into a daze and sometimes he would just cry out loudly clutching his head between his hands. RJ knew that Calvin still needed some kind of medical attention and he was hoping that he would be able to have found a qualified doctor in Deadwood. Someone had shot the old doctor. The town had been waiting for a new one for a couple of months now. With Deadwood's reputation, he would have thought that doctors would have been swarming to set up a practice, but that was not the case yet.

Their attention was once again centered on the front window when they heard a loud voice call out for RJ. Standing in the street not twenty feet from the front door was the figure of Jasper Arnett.

"Hey, RJ Bounty Hunter," the loud voice shouted again. "I hear tell you are looking for me."

"I never said nothing, RJ."

"I know, Calvin." *So this is how Micah is going to play this out. No matter what happens, I will be marked in Deadwood as a bounty hunter, so my life will be useless if I go out and draw against Jasper. Win or lose, I'm a dead man.*

RJ felt the grip on his arm by Martha tighten. RJ turned and looked into her face and saw how soft her features were. How her sparkling eyes were now filling with tears at the thought of something terrible happening to this man she loved so.

"What are you going to do, RJ?" Martha's voice wasn't any more than a whisper. RJ felt the tremor in the hand that held his arm.

"Well, I'll tell you both what I'm a gonna do!" and before either RJ or Martha could ask, Calvin reached for the door knob, twisted it and stepped out into the evening's warm humid air, coming face to face with Jasper.

"You RJ?" Jasper asked, sizing Calvin up and down and stopping his gaze on his right hand that was loosely sitting on his pistol butt.

"That's who you were calling out for wasn't it?"

Inside the open door, RJ couldn't believe what was going down and was just about to walk out in the street and face Jasper, worried for his friend Calvin, but as he started to step out the door, he felt the tug of Martha's hand on his arm stopping his forward movement.

"Well Bounty Hunter, there's a fifteen thousand dollar bounty one my head, dead or alive. You gonna claim it?"

"NO!" Came a shout from the rooming house door when Micah realized that Jasper had the wrong man.

Pausing for a moment, hearing the voice of Micah from the doorway of the rooming house, Jasper noticed the slightest hand movement of Calvin's gun hand and when he did, he also drew his weapon with the speed of a trained gun slinger. Even though Calvin was fast, he didn't even clear leather before he felt a hot burning sensation in his chest. All movement ceased. His right hand fell loosely to his side dropping his pistol in the dirt. The loud boooom of Jasper's pistol was echoing in his head as his eyes started to glaze over, not even allowing him the sight of the hard dirt road that was approaching fast as he fell face down onto the street. He never heard the second and third boom, boom created by RJ's six guns ending the life of Jasper Arnett but a split second from saving the life of his best friend.

Martha, not heeding RJ's warning ran from the doorway to the fallen figure of Calvin. Kneeling beside his body, tears filled her eyes and ran down her face as she turned him over hoping that he would open his eyes or at least see him take a breath. Neither happened.

Martha felt RJ as he knelt down beside her. RJ reached over his body and picking up his hat, RJ shook the dust from it and softly laid it over Calvin's face.

The past twenty-five years went racing through RJ's mind in the next several seconds.

An eternity seemed to pass before Martha felt RJ's arms around her lifting her up as several of the town folk came over to lift Calvin's body up and carry him over to the undertaker's office.

RJ and Martha stood in the street and watched as he was being carried away.

Martha felt RJ release his hold on her, check his gun and reload the two spent cartridges.

Returning the pistol into his holster, Martha heard the whispered words from RJ as he walked toward the rooming house door where Micah was still standing, now watching as the figure of RJ walked in his direction.

CHAPTER 20

Micah had watched the whole scene from his bedroom window before running to the door when he saw that a mistake was being made. Then for a split second felt a little bad for the death of Calvin but was snapped out of his thoughts when he saw RJ rush through the door and put two bullet holes into Jaspers chest.

Now he watched as RJ stood up and looked in his direction.

"I know what you're thinking, RJ." Micah said out loud as he hurried back to his room. He gazed around it and realized there was no place for him to go, he would have to stand and face RJ and knew that RJ was no contest for his gun hand so he turned back around and walked to the door.

Looking outside through the door Micah saw Martha running up to catch RJ. He watched as she wrapped her arms around his neck and pulled his head down and she put her mouth up to his ear and whispered something. When she was done and had released her grasp on his arm, RJ looked once again towards the rooming house, shook his head a couple of times then turned away and headed for the undertaker's. He continued to watch as Martha walked back to her place.

"Damn, I wonder what she told him," Micah said, slapping his hands on his trousers noticing for the first time they needed washing along with his body. "My God."

Looking once again outside, Micah saw that the street was cleared of the two dead bodies, and a couple of skin and bone dogs lolled about licking at the blood stained dirt trying to get some kind of nourishment from the blood that had started to dry there.

By this time, Micah was pretty much healed and knew that it was time to say goodbye to one of the places he had stayed at the longest. Taking a chance that RJ would not come looking for him that night. The next morning with the crowing of a rooster alarm, found Micah saddled and leaving the livery from the rear. Deadwood had been a profitable venture for him, but now he would have to go on to others.

Our paths will surely cross again. These thoughts were interrupted by the sound of metal hitting the dry, hard, dirt. He had ridden out of town and was passing Boot Hill cemetery where Pedro was busy digging a lone grave.

"Whoa boy," he said to his horse pulling back a little on the reins. Micah sat there watching Pedro dig and was reminded just how quickly one's life could come to an end.

Removing his hat and wiping his sweaty brow on his shirt sleeve Micah sat for another minute before replacing his hat, then putting boot heels to the horse's flanks, he clicked his tongue a couple times and quickly rode out of Deadwood not bothering to look back.

As Micah rode, RJ was just waking from a restless night's sleep. Taking Martha's advice, RJ had slept on his decision as to what he was going to do about Micah and was no more convinced as to what to do than before he went to bed. He only knew that now, he wasn't going to go and burst into Micah's room and start blasting away like he was gonna do the day before.

I owe it to Calvin to get our questions answered. And there were many.

Martha had sat and listened as RJ went on and on telling the story of what had transpired in Grand Platte and the sheriff there.

"I just know that Micah, Sheriff Tom Callahan, Scarhead, and God only knows how many others are all in cahoots with one another." Pacing back and forth in front of Martha, RJ went on.

"Look at that fella Jasper. Where do you suppose he came from?" Both RJ and Martha realized that it was a question that also needed to be answered.

RJ had fallen asleep in Martha's arms, now as he woke up, Martha was nowhere in the room, but there was a still, hot cup of coffee for him next to the bed on the night stand.

Smiling to himself with thoughts of Martha and knowing that their home was being built and should be ready to move into before the first snow, RJ sat up, planted his feet on the floor and reached for the cup of coffee.

Coffee's, still plenty warm and strong just the way I like it. Smacking his lips with that thought, RJ stood and wandered over to the window. Looking out the window, his face being heated by the morning's rays, making their way in through the open curtains, RJ couldn't believe his best friend, for so many years, was dead and would be buried this very morning.

Some time was spent last night talking about him to Martha. They laughed together and shed a few tears together, something RJ was not comfortable with, but he couldn't help it.

"There's nothing wrong with a man shedding a few tears from time to time," he was told by his loving wife as she wrapped her arms around him as tears streaked both their faces.

Finally RJ needed to make some decisions concerning Micah and opened up to Martha.

"I just know he's behind having something to do with the shooting of Calvin, although it was me that he called out, and had not Calvin rushed out he might still be alive today."

"Yes, that is true, but you might not be. In a way, you owe your life to Calvin. He showed just how much he loved you." Then she quietly quoted a verse from the Bible. . . "Greater love hath no man, than to lay down his life for his friend."

RJ set his coffee cup down and started to dress. Martha had laid some clean trousers over the back of the chair for him as Calvin's blood was on the other. Getting dressed, RJ had made the decision to confront Micah and see what he had to say about everything that had gone on starting with Sheriff Callahan in Grand Platte, right on up to the previous day and the shooting of Calvin.

Buckling his gun belt around his waist and pulling up his pistol, he spun the chamber making sure it was completely loaded. Satisfied, RJ dropped it into his well-oiled holster, picked his hat off the hat rack where Martha had hung it, placed it on his head and walked from the room, not really sure what the next few minutes would bring when he confronted Micah.

The morning and the main street of Deadwood was already alive with the sounds of a large town awakening from a night's sleep.

As RJ stepped onto the dusty street and made his way towards the rooming house where Micah was staying, he stopped in his tracks when he saw the front door of the rooming house open and tensed up not knowing what to expect.

What he expected turned out to be the least expected, as RJ watched, Martha appeared through the door and noticing him, headed towards him.

As Martha approached, she noticed the questioning look on RJ's face.

"This morning, Fay Ling was just finishing up with her servicing one of her regulars when she noticed Micah riding out of the livery stable on his way out of town. She thought that was something I would want to know about so she came and fetched me. You were finally sleeping so I didn't bother to wake you, but instead made you a cup of coffee, laid out some clean clothes and left to go see for myself what Fay Ling had told me. You must have woken up as soon as I had left."

"I take it that Fay Ling was correct seeing you walk from the rooming house?"

"Yes, she was RJ. Micah was gone, but he had left some things behind and I was in hopes of coming across something that would point in the direction he was going."

"I take it you didn't find anything that could help?"

With a smile on her face, Martha extended her hand. In it was a small black book.

"What's that?" asked RJ reaching for it.

"It is some kind of diary! There are lots of names in it. I didn't have a chance to look at all of them."

Taking the little book from Martha's hand, RJ thumbed through some of the pages.

"Look here!" RJ exclaimed. "There's mine and Calvin's name written in it, along with Sheriff Callahan's." Still flipping through its pages, RJ came across Scarhead's name and also Jasper's.

Showing one of the pages to Martha, RJ continued, "See this page with Jasper's name? His name has a line through it and so does Calvin's." Realizing this meant they were dead, RJ once again felt anger and sadness at the same time.

"Any other names you recognize?"

Closing the book, RJ told Martha they needed to get in off the street where they could have time in private to really go through it.

"Why don't you go back to my room? I'll go and get us some breakfast and bring it back and we can go through it together. Maybe bring over Nuying so she can hear some of the names and see if she recognizes any."

"That's a good idea," he exclaimed, seeing Martha was already walking away to get their food and to find Nuying.

Later, as the three of them sat around the small table in Martha's room, RJ had taken a piece of paper and written down all the names that were mentioned in the little book.

"These names were written in Micah's book. Some had lines drawn through them. See if you recognize any of them?"

"Randy Dalton, Cochise County; Drew McCalla, Arizona; Everett Pike, Denver, and he went on and on till he had read the last name. Those with lines drawn through them also had dollar figures after them with the word collected.

"I bet those are some of the outlaws Micah had tracked down, killed and collected a bounty on."

Martha and Nuying nodded their heads in agreement.

RJ watched for any expression on their faces which could be a sign of recognition. At the mention of Jack Cloud Martha spoke up.

"Does that name sound familiar?" It was Nuying who asked the question.

"I'm pretty sure that he was in the brig at Fort Collins." Thinking back the best she could Martha told them, "There were several outlaws in the brig while I was there but I never paid much attention to their names."

RJ read off several Mexican names trying to pronounce them the best he could, causing both Martha and Nuying to give off a little laugh. One of the names, Arturo stood out.

"Arturo! That's one of the Mexican names I heard called when Calvin and I were ambushed outside of Grand Platte."

RJ read off several more names and as he did, his mind pondered why Micah would have left such a valuable book behind.

"If I was a bounty hunter, this book would be like a bible to me. It seems that he took pains in trying to keep track of known outlaws with prices on their heads. So, why would he leave it behind?"

"I found it under the pillow on his bed. Maybe he just forgot he had it there."

"Well, he must have just updated it cause both Jasper's and Calvin's names had a line through them."

There was a slight rumbling noise heard in the room and all eyes turned towards RJ.

Smiling and rubbing his stomach and to the amusement of all, RJ said, "I guess that is my stomach's way of telling me it is time to dive into that plate of bacon and eggs you brought in with you." All agreed and for the next fifteen minutes the only sounds in the room were those of the occasional burp, fart, or lip smack.

"That book is going to come in mighty handy once I get ready to hit the trail again." RJ spoke after swallowing his last bite of food and washing it down with a big swallow of coffee.

Martha just sat there. She knew that RJ had to leave to go make some money and now to also get Micah, but she was hoping that it wouldn't be this soon.

"Sure isn't gonna be the same out there without Calvin by my side."

Getting up from the table, Martha walked over next to RJ and placed her hand on his shoulder. "He'll be with you, just not as a living body. You'll hear his voice as a whisper in the wind blowing through the tree tops. You'll see his face next to yours as a reflection in the many creeks you'll kneel beside for that drink of cool water. RJ smiled as he listened to Martha and the visions of her sentences came to life in his mind.

"Then sitting around your campfire at night you'll hear him speak through the voice of a lone coyote." RJ remembered the many nights he and Calvin would sit and listen to the far off cry of a lone coyote yearning for another to answer.

Listening to Martha and feeling her soft, comforting touch on his shoulder, RJ knew that he would be ok, that life for him would change some without Calvin, but he would be ok.

Soon talk was directed once again on Micah.

"During the war, Micah was ruthless in his tracking down of the enemy once he set his mind to it. He won't let this here Deadwood happening slide. He will be out there and a danger to us all if he isn't dealt with."

Pushing back from the table, RJ stood and scratched an itch on his ass before continuing.

"I would imagine he will head to Grand Platte, where he has a friend in Sheriff Tom Callahan." Gazing at the wall, he said, "If he has been there, I'll get it out of ole Tom!"

Four sets of eyes focused on him when he said that because they all knew exactly what RJ was talking about.

"If he doesn't seem surprised to see me then I will know that Micah has had some kind of contact with him and my showing up there was something expected."

Remembering a name he had read in Micah's book that had a circle around it RJ thumbed through it searching the pages.

"There!" he said, stopping and pointing at a name. Charles Allen was written in large print, circled and after his name was written five thousand dollar reward, D O A. Next to that was written Grand Platte, Nebraska.

"Can't get any clearer than that," RJ exclaimed, rubbing his hands together.

"This Charles Allen fella will be frosting on the cake if he is still around there. Sheriff Tom Callahan will know, but I suspect Micah will have already taken care of that business."

Having not only the knowledge of where Micah might be headed, but also the name of a wanted outlaw who had a price on his head only sparked RJ into wanting to leave right away.

"There are a lot of things needing tending to before you leave," Martha told him, seeing the excitement in his eyes and hearing it in his voice. "Your leaving will just have to wait one more day."

It was settled that tomorrow RJ would leave for Grand Platte.

RJ knew that with Micah out of town, Martha didn't have to worry about anything happening to her in his absence, so he quit thinking about that and concentrated on what he had to get done before he left.

As the day wore on and the sun rose higher in the sky, RJ noticed that it had lost some of its summer heat and, for a moment, visions of winter's cold fingers entered his mind.

He had been cold before. Back east during the war, he had never witnessed being so cold before. More soldiers suffered from frostbite as much as they did from the enemy's lead balls. Many regiments surrendered to the Union Army just to be able to have warm blankets, food and shelter of which the Union Army always seemed to have and word spread through the many Southern camps informing the soldiers that if they surrendered all would be made available to them and a lot of them did.

Not only had RJ and Calvin lived through those freezing eastern blizzards and sub-freezing temperatures, but they had lived through the Colorado winters as well. Now with the summer sun cooling down, he was once again reminded about the cold weather he was told about coming to South Dakota and the Great Plains where he was headed.

RJ and Calvin had journeyed to Grand Platte so he knew about how long it would take him to get there, but not knowing what he would encounter once arriving there and where the trail would lead him was a big question in his mind as he finished making his preparations for the journey ahead.

As RJ was walking towards the Union Belle for a cold beer, he was accosted by a large black dog showing his teeth and foaming at the mouth. RJ noticed the animal's many ribs that told him this animal was starving and it looked like he could easily become his next meal. Instantly, RJ's memory went back to the time that he and Calvin was approached while on the battlefield by a hungry dog and the way Calvin had talked to him suddenly returned.

Calvin had told him that there was something in the animal's eyes that told him he didn't want to hurt him but needed something to eat. RJ had watched as Calvin took a small piece of food from his backpack and slowly approached the animal speaking in a soft, low voice. Once the dog had feasted on the few morsels given him by Calvin, t*hat dog and Calvin became inseparable after that. Calvin could tell you the number of times that that dog had saved their* lives, and the day that a Union cannon blast ended his life, and now here he was faced with that same predicament.

Remembering a piece of jerky he had in his vest pocket, RJ took it out and slowly crouched down and extended it to the animal speaking softly as he remembered Calvin doing. Although a low growl continued from the animal, he slowly approached RJ's extended hand holding out the jerky.

RJ noticed that as he approached, the hairs on his back, relaxed and he thought he picked up a slight wagging of its tail. Cautiously, the dog's nose came in contact with the jerky, then sticking out its tongue took a couple licks before taking it from RJ's hand. What happened next surprised RJ as the animal cautiously moved forward and licked the empty hand that was in front of him never taking his eyes from RJ's.

The animal suddenly stood up and bared his teeth and emitted a loud growl, at the same time RJ heard a voice behind him say, "Looks to me like you have a friend there."

Standing and turning to face the voice, RJ saw the face of an old man whom he had never seen before.

"I've been watching that dog from yesterday when he first appeared. Like you, I figured him to be hungry, but he wouldn't take any food from me. No, sir, wouldn't even eat any I left for him." As they both watched, the big dog turned and sniffed the scraps of food that had been left for him and eat them.

"Well, now. Will you look at that," the old man said. Then, once again the dog faced them and gave off a low growl.

"Seems like he is protecting you."

It was true. The animal did let RJ know someone was behind him.

Just like he had my back, like Calvin always had.

Turning away from the stranger, RJ looked down on the dog. He was now almost right in front of him sitting and had a slow wag to his tail.

Turning around to speak more to the stranger, RJ was faced with his back as he walked away. Turning once more to the dog, RJ said, "Well, ole boy. If you don't have a home, how about taking up with me?"

Immediately the dog stood up, wagged its tail and licked RJ's out-stretched hand.

"Well, looks like it's settled then. Let's go introduce you to Martha and get you something more to eat, then I figure you have to have a name."

As the two walked, RJ lifted his eyes towards the sky and whispered out-loud.

"You still have my back don't ya, Calvin."

Chapter 21

Martha was curious to see what RJ had outside after he returned and told her that he had something to show her.

She was not prepared for the large black animal who, the moment she walked through the door, was on his four feet with back arched and hairs standing on end.

Martha turned to RJ in horror, afraid she was going to be attacked by the big animal. RJ spoke up and the dog at once sat down and wagged its tail.

"Where in the world did he come from?" Martha asked, watching RJ as he approached the big animal and kneel at his side and playfully scratched him around the neck.

Running his arm across his sweaty forehead, RJ relayed the story of how he was walking toward the Union Belle to get himself a cold beer when this big black dog appeared in his path with teeth bared and foaming at the mouth. He then went on to tell her about the strange man who appeared out of nowhere.

"Well, remember RJ, that Calvin always said 'everything happens to us for a reason and there is a season for everything.'"

"What do you make of this?" he asked, watching as Martha extended her hand and actually was able to give him a pat on the top of his head, which continued into a scratching motion back and forth behind his ears.

"What do we have for food inside that we can feed him?" At RJ's mention of food, the dog stood up on all fours. His ears perked up, and both RJ and Martha noticed his tail wagging vigorously. Mouth open and tongue out, the big dog appeared to be smiling.

"Looks like he understands the word food!"

"I think so," RJ said, turning to open the front door. As soon as he did, the dog bounded through it and was found inside sitting next to the same chair that Calvin always sat in whenever he and RJ was there to eat.

Martha and RJ looked at each other in surprise, and shrugged their shoulders.

Martha found some scraps left over from last night's dinner, and cutting them up, put them in a bowl which she set down in front of the big black dog.

The dog sat there and made no movement to eat the food which Martha had placed before him.

"What do you suppose he is waiting for?" asked RJ.

"I don't know. Maybe he's waiting for you to tell him it is ok to go ahead and eat?" Looking at Martha, RJ turned back to the animal who had his eyes on him. Pointing to the dish, RJ said. "Go ahead. Eat boy."

Immediately he stuck his nose into the bowl and started to wolf down the scraps that Martha had cut up.

As they stood there watching him eat, Martha asked RJ. "I suppose you need to find a name for him?"

"I was hoping you could help me out there. You remember Calvin's dog story during the war? Well, I was hoping you'd remember that dog's name."

Were you thinking about naming him the same name?" Martha, looked down at the dog who had finished the food and once again scratched him behind the ears, bringing a wagging tail and open mouth, with his tongue hanging out. RJ couldn't help but notice once again like he was smiling at him as Martha continued her scratching.

"If you remember," Martha stated, "you and Calvin were tucked down inside a hole that you had dug so that you were not in plain sight of the enemy soldiers. Calvin said that a cannon ball thundered overhead landing not more than ten feet from where you and he were hidden. The explosion of dirt burst into the air, showering you both with its debris. At the same time, he said that a large black dog was hurled into that hole you two were in as part of that debris."

"Thunder!" RJ yelled out, startling both Martha and now the dog. As if this had always been his name, Thunder jumped up and placed his front paws on RJ's chest and gave his face a couple very wet licks.

RJ couldn't help but wrap his arms around Thunder's neck and gave him a big bear hug.

"He's as tall as you are!" Martha exclaimed. She had moved back a couple of steps when Thunder jumped up on RJ.

"Do you think he could be part wolf, judging from his size?"

RJ had thought the same thing when he first saw him. "If he's not, he sure could be."

RJ let Thunder give him another lick before taking his front paws and saying "down", put them on the floor.

Thunder then went to the front door, turned and gave off a loud woof. RJ took it as a sign he wanted out.

Once again, looking at Martha, RJ went and opened the door and watched as Thunder walked outside and lay with his body across the entrance as if saying, "Anybody wanting in, has to come through me first."

As RJ and Martha stood there, Martha wrapped one arm around RJ's waist so that she could feel his closeness. Together they just stood in silence. It wasn't long before those feelings took over and RJ scooped her up in his arms and headed for the bedroom.

Martha was all giggles as RJ's one hand tickled her ribs as it made its way to her ample bosom.

A while later, a loud shrilled voice at the door awoke them. They had fallen into a blissful snooze and now awoke, still wrapped in each other's arms wondered who was screaming out front.

Getting out of bed, Martha, who was missing the least amount of clothes was dressed first and pulling the divider curtain to the room, made her way to the door. Opening it, Martha found Nuying pinned against the front wall by Thunder who had jumped up and planted his two front paws either side of her chest, forcing her back against the wall.

Martha couldn't help but notice how menacing the huge body of Thunder looked next to Nuying's. His bulky form next to RJ's didn't look half the size as it did next to Nuying's.

"Thunder, get down!" she commanded, not knowing if he would listen to her or not. To her amazement, he pushed himself off Nuying and sat in front of her still shielding Martha and the front door from this stranger.

RJ appeared, and at once, Thunder stood and walked to him. RJ reached down and stroked his head.

"It's all right, boy. This is our friend Nuying." Walking over to Nuying, RJ gave her a slight hug in hopes that Thunder would acknowledge her as a friend.

"What did you want, Nuying?" Martha asked.

"There is a young cowboy in the Bella Union who has had too much drink, causing all kinds of trouble with the girls. I'm afraid that two or three of the men are going to hurt him if he doesn't stop and leave the girls alone."

Martha looked at RJ who was already walking back in to retrieve his pistol and belt. When he returned, he asked, "Where's the sheriff?"

"No one knows," she told him.

As RJ stepped down off the boardwalk onto the street, Thunder jumped down next to him and looked up as if waiting for his orders.

"You can come with me boy." At once, Thunder gave a big wag of his tail and bounded off in front of RJ, then stopped once a few feet ahead until RJ was walking next to him.

"Where did that dog come from?" asked Nuying, as she and Martha stood watching the man and dog walking toward the Bella Union together.

"RJ brought him home this morning. He said he was walking and this black dog blocked his path so he gave him a piece of food and then brought him to my place where we fed him, then gave him the name Thunder after another dog that Calvin had found during the war."

Turning away from Nuying, Martha continued to watch them walk.

"There's something very special about that dog." Martha said.

Thunder and RJ were only a few steps away from the swinging doors of the Bella Union when they flew open and a man came flying through them followed by three others who had drawn their pistols and was blasting away at the man lying in the street.

With the speed of lightning, Thunder was flying through the air with his teeth bared landing on the outstretched arms of the three firing their pistols. The weight of Thunder and the surprise he brought to the three, as he landed on their arms, jarred the guns from their hands, which gave RJ time to slam his pistol into the side of one of the three's heads, knocking him to the ground. Thunder spun around and was now in front of the other two with back arched, teeth bared and ready to attack if he was given the order to do so from RJ.

Martha and Nuying were already kneeling at the crumpled form of the young cowboy lying in a dead heap on the dry, dusty street. When RJ turned and looked down at Martha for some kind of sign, he saw her look at him and shake her head, signaling he was dead.

"I gave that little whippersnapper plenty of warning to leave them dancers alone." One of the men told RJ. "But he continued anyway."

"You didn't have to kill him. Now pick up your guns and your friend there, and get out of here."

RJ knew that he didn't have any authority over them and the sheriff being nowhere around wasn't gonna cause them any more trouble.

Standing, Martha asked several of the men standing outside to pick up the dead man and carry him over to the undertaker's.

Martha's mind was filled with mixed emotions as she watched the body being carried. *No one knew who he was. He will be buried in a un-marked grave in Boot Hill and forgotten.*

Martha turned away and saw RJ bend down rubbing Thunder's back. "You two make a hell-of-a-team." She said, putting her arm around Nuying and heading back to her place.

RJ and Thunder looked up at her. Martha thought for a moment how much Thunder's eyes looked like Calvin's before he turned his head away as if he had read Martha's thoughts.

"You have nothing to worry about now, Martha," came Nuying voice. "In China, we would say that Thunder is a good omen sent by the spirit world as a protector. Just look at how he and RJ seems to know each other.

Martha found that what Nuying was saying was intriguing and asked her to continue and tell her more.

"You heard RJ mention an old man that showed up from nowhere, that he had never seen before, and how when he turned back to ask him more, he had disappeared."

"What does that mean?"

"The old man was the dog's spirit master. He was there to make sure that his dog was going to be accepted by RJ and vice-versa. When they accepted each other, he walked away. We believe that at times of excessive danger, he returns to intercede knowing just how the situation is going to end, so as to protect the human master, he will give the command even if it means death to the dog."

Martha re-told the story of how Calvin and RJ had a dog who appeared to drop out of the air brought in by an exploding cannon ball and how that dog had saved the lives of Calvin and RJ on several occasions, and that on the very last day of battle, an exploding cannon ball ended that dog's life.

"What do you think of the story of Calvin's dog and what happened to them during the war where he was concerned?"

Stopping and taking both of Martha's hands in hers, Nuying quietly and with much humility answered her question.

"I believe that the old man was Calvin and the dog was the same dog that was in Calvin's story during the war, and the reason he turned away from RJ was that he became emotional because of their past relationship and the shortness of time since his death."

Pulling Martha in even closer, she told Martha that she could not share anything she was told with RJ.

"I will tell you this that as long as RJ stays close to Thunder he will be safe in all he does and everywhere he goes. Why you can't share that with him is because he might become too dependent with that knowledge. He needs to build that relationship himself with Thunder."

As Nuying finished, RJ and Thunder approached. "I need to finish getting ready to leave. I've decided that Thunder just might make a fine traveling companion."

Martha was pleased with that news since her talk with Nuying who now looked at Martha with a knowing smile on her face.

"That's great!"

"Well, I just have a feeling that Calvin would want me to."

"What do you want me to pack for food for him?" asked Martha.

"I don't need to take anything. He will eat the same foods, I do. What I can shoot and cook will be fine for him to." Thunder leaned up against RJ's legs and rubbed the length of his body against him.

RJ watched as Thunder then went over to Martha and did the same thing. Next, Thunder once more jumped up on Nuying's chest, pinning her once again to the wall. The difference this time was that he licked her face before pushing off her and setting her free from his huge body.

Martha looked at Nuying with a smile that was one of knowledge as to what she had just witnessed. Then, with that knowledge, Martha stood on tiptoes and planted a light kiss on RJ's cheek.

"We have work to do, Thunder, let's leave these two gals and get to it."

As they walked away, Martha smiled to herself, no longer worried for RJ's safety.

Look after him Thunder, bring him home safe.

Looking over at Nuying, then toward heaven, she whispered. "Thank you, Calvin."

Chapter 22

Early the next morning, as RJ was saddling up to leave, a slight breeze blew into town kicking up some dust and, even though winter months were still some time away, RJ felt the coming of cooler weather. His plan was to ride into Grand Platte, Nebraska, confront Sheriff Tom Callahan and get to the bottom of what had transpired the past couple of days where Micah was concerned. He'd also want to know if he had any dealings, or knew of the outlaw with a five thousand dollar reward on his head, who went by the name of Charles Allen.

Last night had been a restless one for RJ. Even though Martha was beside him, he got little sleep, thinking about everything that had taken place in the short span of time.

"Just what will you do, once you track down Micah?" Martha wanted to know.

"I kinda hope that I don't find him. I don't think he will ever return to Deadwood, but, if we want any kind of life free of watching over our shoulders, he has to be dealt with now."

"I want you to know that I won't worry about you so much seeing that Thunder will be going along with you.

It's amazing how quickly Martha has taken to Thunder and Thunder in return. Several times during the night, either she or RJ had gotten up and found Thunder lying across the entrance to the room. She had watched RJ crouch down next to him and Thunder sitting up to lay his head across RJ's lap.

Now, as RJ finished saddling up, Thunder had stood by his legs wagging his bushy tail as if he knew that there was a journey ahead and he was ready for anything that was about to take place.

Nuying and Fay Ling brought over a grain sack that had some food packed in it and handed it to him and then went and stood next to Martha.

Finishing up, RJ stood next to Martha and wrapped his arms around her and gave her a big kiss. Once done, he turned towards Nuying and Fay Ling and tipped his hat. "You gals take good care of Martha. I'm counting on you."

Stepping up into the saddle, and turning once more to give the three a nod, RJ spurred his mount and the three watched him ride out of Deadwood closely followed by Thunder.

"Don't you worry none," Nuying told her, "that big dog will lay down his life if need be."

"I hope so, Nuying, I hope so," whispered Martha, turning away and walking back into her room.

Leaving Deadwood and passing what was to be his and Martha's home along with a camp for Calvin, RJ walked his mount over to the newly dug grave of Calvin. Thunder had followed him and as RJ stood there with hat in hand, he watched as Thunder circled the mound of dirt. Stopping, Thunder pawed the loose dirt which covered the grave. RJ thought he saw a tear form in Thunder's eye before he came and sat next to him

"You act as if you know who is in there big fella."

Thunder looked up at RJ and gave off a little whimper, then stuck out his tongue and gave RJ's hand a couple of licks.

"Well, Calvin, I'm sure gonna miss you this time around," RJ said, looking up and then back at the fresh grave of his friend. RJ tried to think of a time when he had gone anywhere without his trusted friend and couldn't think of one. Reaching down, he gave Thunder a rub on the top of his head before turning and climbing up into the saddle. Thunder was already at the feet of the horse. As he was leaving he had a feeling that there were eyes on him. He stood up in the stirrups and gazed around. RJ noticed that Thunder had also stopped and he saw the short hairs on his back rise up.

A couple moments passed before RJ figured that no one was watching them even though he had, had that feeling.

"Okay Thunder let's get to it!" RJ put spurs to flank and his mount took off like a shot followed closely by Thunder.

RJ enjoyed a burst of speed from time to time and this was one of those times. Thunder must also be enjoying the sudden run as he was bouncing up and down with every stride he made. Soon, RJ reined up and was moving at a moderate pace, one of which Thunder seemed comfortable in keeping.

It wasn't long before RJ noticed the actions of Thunder. Just like Calvin did at times, he raced on ahead and then sit in the middle of the trail waiting for him to catch up.

Could there actually be some kind of spirit world where, when you passed on you got a chance to return to a time and a place of your choosing, but just couldn't return in human form but something of your own choice? RJ shook his head to rid it of those kinds of thoughts because he didn't believe in that sort of stuff, although the past couple of days had him questioning them.

The morning soon turned into noon. RJ noticed the difference in temperatures as he rode and was not anxious to see colder weather just a month or two off as he recalled the freezing temperatures he and Calvin experienced during the war. Calvin used to say, "It's colder than a well digger's ass." A saying that always brought a smile to RJ's face.

At night sitting around the campfire, RJ would talk to Thunder as he sat close to him. RJ scratched his back and talked to him just as he and Calvin used to do.

Sometime during the night, RJ was awakened by Thunder's low growl. He reached for his pistol just as all hell broke loose.

Two Pawnee Indians, who had chosen not to live on the reservation set up by the white man, had stumbled onto RJ's camp site and were just about to use their knife and tomahawk to kill him, when one of them was attacked by Thunder.

Thunder had jumped on one of them forcing him into the other so they both were off balance and fell into the still orange coals of the campfire, kicking up lots of hot ashes and sparks. Both screaming as their bodies were burned by the hot ashes. RJ was able to get a good aim at one of the Indians.

BAM, BAM, his six guns roared and he saw his target go limp. The second Indian was back on his feet, but Thunder had a grip on his leg. A loud whistle from RJ stopped Thunder and he let go of the Indian's leg, this offered RJ the clear shot he needed. Again, his six-gun roared and spewed out its deadly lead finding its target. Seconds later, Thunder was standing next to RJ.

"Thanks boy!" RJ said, reaching down to rub Thunder's head. Then he crouched down and wrapped his arms around the big dog's neck. Thunder accepted the affection only for a moment before bounding off to inspect the two dead Indians.

The rest of the trip to Grand Platte was uneventful.

Entering Main Street, RJ and Thunder were met with a lot of staring. Not too many had ever seen a dog the size of Thunder and RJ would also learn that his showing up here was expected.

Reining up in front of the sheriff's office, RJ dismounted and wrapped his horse's reins around the hitching post next to a big grey.

RJ motioned for Thunder to sit outside while he entered Sheriff Tom Callahan's office.

"Well, I'll be a son-of-a-bitch!" exclaimed Callahan seeing RJ walk into his office. Standing, he walked out from behind his desk and offered his hand to RJ.

RJ hesitated for a minute, then clasped Callahan's hand in the traditional hello.

"What brings you back here so soon?" Callahan asked, pointing to a chair, instructing RJ to have a seat as he walked around his desk and took up his own chair.

"I'm looking for an outlaw who goes by the name Charles Allen. He has a five thousand dollar price on his head." Gone was any pretense of letting on he was a bounty hunter.

"Sounds to me like you have yourself a pretty tough job and by all means a dangerous one."

Noticing the stack of posters on Callahan's desk, RJ asked, "Wouldn't have the poster on this Charles Allen, would you?"

"Before I answer that question, where's that partner of yours?" Scratching his head and flipping back his long hair, Callahan was curious to see if RJ would lie to him or not. He had received word as to RJ's coming and the death of Calvin.

Slowly bowing his head and in a whispered voice, RJ told the story of Calvin's death.

He had thought of not telling Sheriff Tom Callahan the truth, but decided he probably already knew and by not being truthful, he might not get the answers he needed if, in fact, Callahan knew.

"I'm generally sorry to hear that," responded Tom. "As to a poster on Charles Allen, you can quit looking."

"Why is that?" Questioned RJ

"Well, that Charles Allen fella, went and got himself killed about two weeks back. He was cheating at cards or something like that and the other players threw him out of the gambling hall. But of course, Charles, having also too much to drink, burst back into the joint with his pistol out. Before he could get off a shot, several of the men inside drew and plugged him cold dead."

"What will become of the bounty money?"

"Well RJ, the government has decided that we lawmen can claim the reward monies if no one else does, such as you bounty hunters. So I claimed it. Sure was nice having five-thousand dollars deposited in my account."

"Yeah! I bet it was."

Picking up the stack of posters from his desk, Sheriff Callahan fanned them out and offered RJ the opportunity to look at them and see if anyone looked familiar or if there was someone in particular he wanted to go after.

"Here's all the posters that I have at present. You're welcome to any of them."

RJ slowly went through the posters stopping on one in particular. "Chico Morales," he said aloud, "Scarhead."

Looking at Callahan, RJ spoke, "He escaped from the jail in Deadwood not too long back. How did you get this so quickly?"

"That's an old poster," responded Callahan. Then thinking back asked, "You were tracking him before weren't you?"

"That's right I was. Still am if he crosses my path." Deciding he was going to see what Callahan might tell him, he continued. "I'm on the trail of someone who I think you know." RJ watched as Callahan looked up from the poster of Scarhead.

"And who might that be?" Callahan knew just who RJ was going to name. Micah had spent a day there in Grand Platte before moving on to Ogallala where he told Callahan he was going to be if and when RJ came looking.

"You know damn well who it is! Now I want you to tell me all you know about Micah, where he's at and what part did he have in the killing of my friend Calvin?"

"I don't know what you're talking about! Sure, I know Micah but that's all."

RJ stood up and walked to the door. Turning back towards Callahan, said, "We'll soon see about that." Opening the door, RJ let out a whistle to which, Thunder came bounding through the open door that RJ held open for him.

Thunder took a quick look at RJ and then continued towards Callahan, jumping up on his desk, with his muzzle and teeth bared drooling saliva, stuck it in Callahan's face.

"What the hell?" were the only words that came from Callahan's mouth.

RJ was struck by this sight, especially how big Thunder appeared standing half crouched on the desktop.

The slight movement of Callahan's gun hand brought a renewed growl from Thunder.

"I'd be mighty careful about what movements you want to make." warned RJ, closing the door.

"Now, let's get down to answering some questions, shall we?" Beads of sweat had formed on Callahan's forehead and RJ watched as sweat ran down the length of his nose to drip off the end. Thunder's own head being close enough to lick off the drip if he had a mind to.

RJ suddenly smiled, thinking that if he were to let Callahan stand, he would probably see a big wet spot on the crotch of his pants, or a brown one on his rear. Maybe both.

I know that I would have pissed my pants when this big black dog jumped up on the desk if I were the one sitting in that chair.

"What in the name of Moses are you smiling about?" asked Callahan, wondering when this would be over.

"Not important. I need you to start talking and tell me what you know concerning the whereabouts of Micah."

"Will ya get this thing, uh, animal out of my face first?"

RJ placed his hand on the haunches of Thunder and told him to sit, which he did, still in the center of Callahan's desk, but not as threatening, but with ears perked-up just waiting for his next command.

"Micah paid me to send you on the trail so that you would be ambushed and killed. He didn't tell me why, only to arrange it. I was surprised to see you two come back leading the horses of the three dead."

"You must have gotten word to Micah before we returned to Deadwood, right?"

"Yes. That's right. I sent him a message, but he never replied."

Tom Callahan slowly reached up and removed his hat, then removed his bandana from around his neck and carefully, under the watchful eyes of Thunder, wiped the sweat from his brow.

"Where did you get this dog?"

It was a question that RJ answered with a, "none of your business".

"He just looked a little bit like a dog that used to hang around the saloon a few years back. Watched old Scarhead pistol whips him once for being in his path on the way to the saloon. After that, no one could get next to him. Up and disappeared one day."

As Callahan told that story, RJ noticed the short hairs rise up on Thunder's back and he reached over to stroke him while telling him that it was all okay. Thunder turned his head and looked into RJ's eyes. RJ noticed a sadness in them as if he were remembering that pistol whipping.

"Where is Micah now?"

"I don't rightly know," came Callahan's answer. An instant later he felt the teeth of Thunder's bite on his left shoulder, tearing through his vest and shirt. Thunder then shook his head in a ripping motion that helped sink his teeth through Callahan's skin all the way to the bone.

Callahan's scream only lasted for a split second before RJ pulled out his pistol and hit him right between the eyes knocking him out cold.

RJ noticed Thunder released his bite and looked over at him with what appeared to be a smile on his face. He gave RJ a lick and jumped down from the desk. Thunder walked to the door and RJ walked over and opened it for him. Somehow Thunder knew that Callahan would answer any questions that RJ put to him once he woke up from RJ's pistol hit.

Once he awoke, and rubbing his forehead, Sheriff Tom Callahan told RJ that Micah was waiting for him in Ogallala. He also told him that Micah had left there with two brothers wanted for numerous robberies and rapes throughout the county.

"Micah will no doubt have them set some kind of trap for you so you had better watch every curve and your back, at the same time."

"If it is okay for a lawman to collect the reward money, then why didn't you apprehend these two brothers?"

"Because they rode in with Micah. I didn't have a choice but to let them off."

"I know that you probably have instructions from Micah to let him know when I leave here." Callahan nodded his head.

"Last time I left here, it wasn't very far before Calvin and I were ambushed. Was that the best area to set up an ambush, or do you know of a better one that I should be on the lookout for?"

"About halfway between here and Ogallala, you will come upon a river. Now, there is only one good place to cross it. You'll see. It's well marked and the trail you'll be on leads right to it. On the opposite side is a large rock formation, this is called Lookout Rock. You have to pass right by. It is there that I would probably set up an ambush." Then thinking for a second, Callahan told him. "There's another spot you could cross, but it will be about ten miles out of your way. You could cross there and then follow the river on high ground which would put you above the rock formation where the two brothers would probably be waiting."

RJ had one last warning for Callahan before he left. "If this is another one of your setup and I'm not killed, remember this. I will return with Thunder, and when he attacks you I won't command him to stop."

"I've told you all that I know, RJ."

"I want to believe you sheriff."

Walking out of the office, Thunder was on his feet ready for whatever he was commanded.

RJ remembered the grey hitched next to his and spoke back into the room. "Why does this grey look so familiar?"

"Probably because it belonged to Micah. He wanted you to see it and know that he was here and what I have told you about his going to Ogallala is the truth."

Leaving the door open, RJ stepped off the boardwalk, went over to his mount and untied him. Climbing up into the saddle, RJ was reminded of another time not too long ago when he and Calvin was right here in this same place. As his mind started to wander, a loud bark brought him back. He looked down at Thunder and saw a familiar look in his eyes. Before he could think about those eyes, Thunder was up and on his feet running down the street, stopping only to look back as if to say, "Are you coming?"

Chapter 23

As RJ rode along, he couldn't help but notice the actions of Thunder. He would run up ahead, out of sight, and then sit and wait for RJ to catch up with him. Then, he would look back over his shoulder, wag his large bushy tail and bound off again out of sight.

RJ's thoughts were of Calvin and how he would ride ahead to check for any disturbance or signs of the enemy soldier. Now he watched as Thunder seemed to be doing the same.

"Maybe there is something to this likeness and Calvin's spirit being in this large dog." RJ spoke out loud. The whispering breeze through the treetops seemed to be speaking to him.

Thunder's barking and growling spurred RJ into a fast gallop. Rounding a bend in the trail, he saw Thunder blocking the path of a very large man on horseback with his barking. The man was cursing the large dog. Seeing RJ approaching, the man started cussing at him.

Thunder had stopped his barking and growling once RJ appeared.

This huge man on horseback has to be Fat Arthur Duggan. RJ thought to himself. He had seen his poster in both Deadwood and just a few hours ago while going through the posters in Sheriff Callahan's office.

"Are you Arthur Duggan?" asked RJ, watching what this man was doing with his hands.

"Who the hell's asking?" came the rough voice of Duggan.

RJ thought for a minute before answering.

"Names RJ Murdock. I just came from North Platte, where I had some business with the sheriff there."

At the mention of sheriff, the fat man raised his eyebrows and slid his top coat back where he could rest his hand on his six-gun.

This movement didn't go un-noticed by either RJ or Thunder who suddenly jumped up, and taking a big bite of the fat man's hand, pulled him off his horse. As he was falling, he pulled out his pistol and fired a shot that winged Thunder's right ear.

The ten-thousand dollar reward for Fat Arthur was the last thing to go through RJ's mind as he heard Thunder's yelp at being shot.

RJ's own pistol was clearing leather as he jumped from his mount and landed only a few feet from where Arthur had landed. RJ's pistol roared, sending lead into the guts of this fat man. Another crack of RJ's pistol, puts another one into his chest, hitting his heart, killing him instantly.

RJ looked over at Thunder whose ear was running blood. RJ went and got his canteen, then he un-tied his bandana, poured some water on it and wiped off the blood from Thunder's ear where the very tip had been shot off.

"Well old boy, you probably saved my life. Had it not been for you pulling him off his horse, he might have shot me." RJ found himself with his arms wrapped around Thunder's neck with his face buried in his fur. Thunder put up with this added affection for a short while, then jumped up and out of RJ's grasp.

RJ walked around the fat man wondering what he was going to do to transport him back to town where he could claim the ten-thousand dollar reward money.

Remembering the Indians, he and Calvin had seen around the fort in Colorado on their journey to Deadwood and the contraption they called a travois strapped to their horse and even dogs, RJ went about finding two sturdy tree limbs he could strap to the Fat Man's horse to make himself one of those travels'.

Once assembled, RJ rolled the dead man onto it and lashed him down.

RJ was about a day's ride from town. As he entered town a couple of the local boys who had been hitting a can with sticks came running up beside him, poking the dead man. RJ was just about to say something to the boys when Thunder gave of a loud bark stopping the boys in their tracks. RJ turned back with a smile on his face.

Two hours later, having done all that was required to claim the reward money and making sure that it got wired to his bank in Deadwood, RJ sent a message off to Martha.

The whole town was basked in the reflections of reds, yellows, blues as the sun went down and the sky said its own brand of Goodnight for all to enjoy.

RJ sat on a bench outside the telegraph office with Thunder at his feet and reflected on the life he had chosen. If not for Thunder's companionship he would probably head on back to Deadwood, collect Martha, and either head west to California or South to Texas, where he and Calvin often mentioned as a place they wanted to journey to.

As if he was reading RJ's thoughts, Thunder rolled his head backwards and looked up into RJ's face, then lowered his head so it rested across his lap.

RJ noticed the silence that had taken over the once noisy street and rising from the bench headed to the rooming house where he had a bed reserved. He was told he could not bring the dog in with him so he patted Thunders head and left him sitting outside the door. Thunder was more than happy to take up watch over him.

Next morning, RJ and Thunder once more headed out of town toward Ogallala and hopefully finding not only Scarhead but also Micah. He knew that along the way there were gonna be two brothers to tend to.

RJ would have to rely on Callahan's directions and that didn't settle too well on his mind, and he was thankful to have the big black dog along to keep a close watch on his movements, looking for signs he had detected danger.

The nights on the trail were the loneliest now. Although Thunder proved to be a good trail buddy he wasn't Calvin and RJ soon became more and more aware that once he had taken care of Scarhead and Micah his days of bounty hunting would be over. Martha had shared with him her desire to have a child, and even though he was older he kinda liked the idea.

Almost before he knew it, the trail opened up just like Callahan had described to him that it would.

"Gotta head west now, Thunder." RJ said, as if Thunder knew which way west was. To his amazement, Thunder bounded off to his left, which was the direction they had to take.

Just as Callahan had told him, the river, he noticed, was deep and because of that it was impossible to cross.

RJ continued riding, keeping his eyes out for any kind of movement indicating a trap. He was also looking for the place Callahan had told him about where he would be able to cross.

Soon, he heard Thunder barking, but not from in front of him, but off to his right. Looking across to the other side of the river, RJ saw the big black dog on the opposite side of the river.

"Looks like you found that crossing place," he said, looking up ahead to see where he crossed.

It wasn't long before he saw several small islands that would make crossing the river possible. Thunder stood on the bank and watched as he crossed without any problems.

Once across, RJ looked around for the trail that would lead them up and out of the draw and put them above Look Out Rock and out of any danger that might be awaiting them if the two brothers had indeed camped out there awaiting his arrival so that they could kill him.

Thunder had taken to staying within sight of RJ, but as they drew near to the ambush area, Thunder bound ahead. It wasn't long before RJ rode upon him sitting in the middle of the trail.

Dismounting, RJ flipped the reins over a couple tree branches and took his rifle from its Scabbard.

Slowly, both he and Thunder approached the area above Look-Out-Rock, and sure enough, he saw one of the brothers looking out over the river crossing.

"Where do you suppose the other one is?" he whispered to Thunder.

With the speed of a Bob Cat, Thunder took off and within a few seconds there was loud barking sound and the screaming of the other brother as Thunder had detected him and was now biting the living daylights out of him.

RJ saw movement from the corner of his eye and at once swung his rifle's sight onto the moving figure.

KaaaaaBoom, sounded RJ's rifle as an ounce of lead entered his target's chest, dropping him in his tracks. Now RJ started to run toward the sound of dog and the other man, worrying that Thunder might get shot. He had nothing to worry about. By the time he reached the two, Thunder had torn the throat out of his victim.

Thunder bounded over to RJ and leaped up and planted his front paws on his chest almost knocking him over backwards. His big black bushy tail wagging

"Good boy, good boy!" was all Thunder needed to hear. He had taken out one of the bad guys, now man and dog celebrated the only way they knew how.

A short time later, rummaging through their camp site, RJ found a couple of unopened tins of meat along with several apples and some beef jerky which he fed to Thunder.

RJ decided that there was no way to bury the dead so he dragged them next to one another and piled what loose stones he could find on top of them.

"Probably should have just left them to the wild animals! What do you think, Thunder?"

Thunder looked at RJ and wagged his tail. To RJ, this tail wagging had become Thunder's way of agreeing with him.

RJ hated not to be able to collect bounty on the two, but he wanted to get on the trail and find Scarhead and Micah, so, once he was done, he went to his horse and mounting once again, spurred his mount in the direction of Ogallala.

The sooner I take care of Scarhead and Micah, the sooner I can return to Deadwood and Martha. Thoughts of Martha brought a smile to RJ's face, remembering her warm body next to his.

Thunder was off in the lead and RJ felt that he didn't have to be quite so tense, so he relaxed and enjoyed the day.

Collecting the rewards on both Scarhead and Micah and, if they were to sell the property they owned, then he and Martha would have plenty of money to move on.

At one time, RJ thought he and Calvin would try to track down the notorious James Gang and collect the reward monies that were on each of the James's heads along with its members, but now as he rode on without Calvin, thoughts of pursuing them were all but nonexistent. That was something that Calvin had talked about and might have happened if he were still alive.

I sure wish I had gotten a chance to question those brothers. I'll bet they knew exactly where Scarhead and Micah were holed up. After all, Ogallala was a pretty big place and knowing Micah he had already gathered a few followers so there would be no way for me to enter town without someone's eyes seeing and getting that information back to Micah.

As the day wore on, RJ was full of thoughts as to how to go about not getting himself killed.

RJ knew that by this time, Micah had probably received a telegram from Sheriff Callahan informing him of the deaths of the two brothers. He was pretty certain their bodies would have been discovered by now.

When he hadn't returned a second time to North Platte, and the brothers not returning, he was pretty sure that Callahan would have sent someone out to investigate and they would have discovered the two stone graves.

Later that evening while he and Thunder sat around a small campfire, RJ's thoughts were again centered on Micah and the way of preventing his death and Thunder's.

I need to find Scarhead first. I'm pretty sure that Micah would use him as a front line of defense along with whoever else he could find was willing to act as a bodyguard.

Lying at his boots next to the fire was Thunder. Although he had his head on his outstretched paws, his eyes were wide open and ears erect, ever watchful and listening for danger.

Darkness set in fast, and before RJ knew it, it was pitch black. There wasn't even a star in the sky to offer any kind of light.

"I hope you can see in the dark?" RJ said jokingly to Thunder. The moon was nothing but a sliver in the sky and offered no light at all. Not even critter noises could be heard. Nothing moves on such black nights. RJ tossed a couple pieces of wood on the fire. Some sparks escaped and went heaven bound trying to light up the sky.

It was at this very instant that RJ saw Thunder stand, crouching down with his back hairs raised and his teeth bared as a low growl escaped his throat.

RJ had his pistol drawn and was trying to hear any kind of sound coming from the direction that Thunder was facing.

"Whoever is out there had better speak up and make yourself known as a friend or outlaw." RJ had stood up and had taken a few steps away from the glow given off by the hot bright red coals of the campfire.

"It's me Mr. RJ," came the voice of someone RJ knew very well. Thunder also recognized it and went bounding in its direction. Very soon, Thunder reappeared in the light of the campfire with Nuying holding onto his tail.

"What in the world are you doing here, Nuying?" asked RJ, stepping up to her and giving her a big hug. "And how in the hell did you find me?" he queried.

RJ indicated a place for Nuying to sit. He went to fetch his canteen and uncorking it, handed it to Nuying who looked like she had been through hell.

Taking a small drink, Nuying handed the canteen back to RJ and started to tell him her tale.

"Shortly after you and Thunder had left, Martha got a visit from one of the pan miners who had a small claim up in the timber line. He told her that he had seen three men, including one whom he recognized as Micah, on horseback heading into the upper timberline area known as Eagles Ledge. He told her that he followed them and there is a large overhang of rock where they are holding out."

"How did you come to track me and Thunder down?" anxious to hear her story.

"Martha told me that she had to follow you and try to catch up with you with this news."

"I told her that I would go instead. She argued some, but then gave in." RJ listened intently, not wanting to miss a single detail of Nuying's story.

"I asked around to see if anyone was headed to North Platte and found two wagon haulers that we're headed there that let me ride along if I would cook for them during the trip."

Looking down at the ground, she added. "I think they were expecting other privileges other than me just cooking for them," still looking at the ground, she continued, "I tried to fight them off, but the two were too strong so I quit fighting and did what they wanted me to do."

"Nuying. I'm so sorry to hear that." RJ was next to her with his arm going around, her shoulders and pulled her face into his chest to comfort her. Pushing back from RJ, she said,

"I know what they look like and if I ever see them around Deadwood again!" she took her finger and ran it from ear to ear indicating she would slit their throats. Continuing her story, she said, "Once in North Platte, I looked up the sheriff there and told him who I was and asked if he knew who you were. He said he did and that you and a big black dog were on the trail to Oogaallaala. RJ smiled at her attempt at pronouncing the city's name. I told him that I needed to catch up to you that there was a crisis in Deadwood that you was needed for, and he let me borrow a horse if I promised to return it on my way back."

"Was that sheriff's name Tom Callahan?"

"Yes. That is what he called himself and the way he looked at me gave me the willies." For the first time since meeting Nuying, RJ noticed her beauty and understood why any man couldn't help but give her an up and down at meeting her.

The voice of a lone coyote perked up Thunder's ears and he bounded off into the blackness in the direction from where it had come from.

"How did you manage to find me at this hour and in such blackness?" RJ motioned for Nuying to sit back down.

When I came upon two stone graves and uncovered part of one to see if it was old or new and found it to be a new one it gave me hope of finding you."

RJ watched a shiver go through Nuying's body and realized for the first time that the night was not just black but also brought a chill with it. Getting up and going to his saddle, RJ untied his bedroll blanket and returned with it and wrapped it around Nuying's shoulders.

"Thank you," she said in a low voice snuggling down into the blanket.

Off in the distance, they heard the cry of the coyote again. This time it was answered by a much louder voice and RJ made it out to be that of Thunder.

"Sounds like Thunder has responded to the call of the wild." Nuying said, turning her eyes in RJ's direction.

RJ noticed a shy smile on her face, which was reflected off the fire.

"It would sound that way," he agreed.

"What happened to the horse Callahan let you borrow?"

"Once it got pitch black and I could no longer see the trail I got off and started to walk, afraid the horse might step in a hole or something where he or I could receive some injuries. He is only a short ways back down the trail."

RJ's thoughts were scrambled, not knowing now what he should do.

There's no doubt that Micah would send one or more riders into Deadwood to case it out and report back their findings. What would he do then? Would he dare show his face in Deadwood? Would he sneak down under the curtain of darkness and harm Martha?

All these thoughts went racing through his head and he didn't have any answers right now. Looking over at Nuying, RJ saw that she was sound asleep, sitting there wrapped in his blanket.

Although his thoughts were muddled, looking at Nuying, RJ suddenly felt the same weary feeling and he sort of scrunched down under his hat and closed his eyes.

Maybe if I can get some sleep, I will be able to think straight and have some answers as to what to do next. These were the last thoughts on his mind as RJ's eyelids closed and sleep overtook him, the many questions floating around in his head would have to wait to get answers in the morning.

Off in the distance, but within his sight of RJ, Thunder also snuggled down next to his new found companion. Not a coyote, but a big, beautiful wolf. A slight whimper left his lips as he lowered his head to rest on his front paws.

Chapter 24

It became pretty clear to RJ the next morning that he needed to track down Scarhead.

"I don't think Micah will show his face in town. I think there are enough town people who now want to live respectable lives and Deadwood has started to become a different kind of town in the past few months that they will take care of him. Besides, Martha is there and she sure isn't frightened of him anymore."

"So, we go looking for Scarhead?" Nuying had made up her own mind, seeing what she had gone through to get here, that no matter what RJ said, she was going with him. End of story as far as she was concerned.

RJ lifted his eyebrows at Nuying's "we" and turned to face her. For the first time he noticed the smoothness of her skin, the sparkle in her green eyes, which was not a trait of Chinese women. He slowly scanned down her body and thought to himself how proportioned she was. He knew that after all she had been through, all he would have to do is say the word and she could be his.

A brushing against his leg brought him back from his thoughts of the moment. Looking down, Thunder had stepped between them and the wagging of his big bushy tail told RJ that he needed that familiar pat on the head.

"Where have you been to all night?" RJ questioned as he bent down and scratched Thunder's head

Nuying crouched down and wrapped her small arms around Thunder's neck and talking to him just as though he was her best friend, echoed RJ's question.

"So, where have you been all night, uh?"

Thunder jumped up and gave a loud bark as he bolted to the edge of their camp. It was then that both Nuying and RJ spotted two big black eyes staring at them from the brush.

"Well, what have you got there, Thunder?" asked RJ as he gave off another loud bark, this time the response was the appearance of the female wolf who looked at them both and quickly turned and bound away into the woods followed by Thunder. RJ and Nuying just stood and watched as they disappeared.

"I'll be damned!" was all that RJ could come out with.

Nuying broke the silence with her question.

"How do you know that Scarhead is in Ogaaa, Ogaaala, lalllaa?"

"Ogallala!" RJ completed the word that Nuying was having trouble with.

"Yes. Ogaaaallaaaala."

"I don't really. I was told that Micah was there so I just took it that Scarhead wouldn't be far away."

"Well, RJ. You know now that Micah isn't in Ogaaaalllllaaalaa so why do you still think Scarhead is?"

Stopping dead in his thoughts at Nuying question, RJ realized he had once again been taken by the lies of Callahan.

"Why! You lousy, rotten son-of-a-bitch!" RJ said in an angry voice as Nuying's statement sank in.

This sudden loud outburst from RJ startled Nuying and she jumped back a little.

"I should go and kill that snake-in-the-grass just like I threatened him when I was here last time."

Nuying watched as RJ paced around their camp, mumbling to himself, pounding one fist into the other, kicking up dirt with his boots. His antics were those of frustration at being misguided for a second time and not seeing it himself.

Thunder had heard the loud voice of RJ, and seemingly out of nowhere was back in camp and by RJ's side.

Once RJ settled down some, Nuying asked what he intended to do.

"I'm not going to waste time traveling to Ogallala and discover that Scarhead isn't there. We'll head back to Deadwood."

"What about Sheriff Callahan?"

RJ thought for a moment, then decided they would circle Grand Platte so that Callahan wouldn't see that they were headed back to Deadwood and Micah's plans were about to fail.

"What we have to do now, is find your horse."

"I left him not too far back on the trail."

"He should be right on the trail, if not maybe the ones belonging to those two I killed will still be around."

If I was going back into Grand Platte, I'd take those two back and collect what reward monies were on their heads.

Heading back, RJ let Nuying ride and he walked along beside her. Out in front, Thunder bounded along. About two miles later, Thunder took off running. Both RJ and Nuying watched and listened. Pretty soon, both heard the bark and the thumping of horse's hooves on the hard packed trail. Sure enough, up the trail came the horse Nuying had gotten from Callahan, followed closely by Thunder.

"Good boy, Thunder." RJ said, grabbing the reins of the horse.

"We can stop here for a breather if you want to?" RJ said as he walked around the animal talking to him in a calming voice.

"How much further is it to where those two are buried? We should keep going 'til we reach that place."

"I judge it to be only about another mile or so. You're right. We'll stop there, find their horses and have something to eat. There is a stream there so that the horses can water."

So far, Nuying had surprised RJ. *Not only had she come all the way from Deadwood by herself, suffered at the hands of the haulers who had given her a ride, and found him in the dark of night, used some common sense where Micah and Scarhead were concerned, now continued to show him she was also smart to the ways of travel.*

Nuying had noticed a surprised look on RJ's face with her suggestion of waiting later to stop and spoke up, "I heard you once ask Martha how I come I spoke such good English. I was sold as a little girl to a trader who was coming to America. Once here, I was put in a school to learn the ways of this country and the language so that I could help him in his business dealings. As I said, he was a trader and there was a lot of money to be made by buying goods in China and selling them in this country."

"What kind of goods did he market, where he would need a young girl who knew the language?"

"Once I learned the language, I would go with him to camps where there were lots of young Chinese girls that had been smuggled into this country from China. I would make the buying deals with the sellers who were always American and later on would also help sell them."

Surprised at her story, RJ motioned for her to continue.

"I am not happy with what I have done. I have seen many young girls beaten, tortured, raped and killed, because of me."

"You were doing nothing more than what you were brought into this country and schooled to do." RJ walked over next to Nuying and put his arms around her.

"You are the only person that I have ever told concerning my past."

"You know that you can tell Martha. She thinks of you as a younger sister!"

"When we get back, there is a lot I want to share with you both. You have been my friends and should know everything."

Back in Deadwood, Martha waited for any word from either RJ or Nuying. She had sent a telegram onto Grand Platte in hopes that RJ would receive it. She knew that he would look up the sheriff there so that is where she had sent it to, not knowing all that had gone on between him and Sheriff Callahan concerning not only Micah but Scarhead.

Now that Nuying had gone, Martha relied on Fay Ling to go do errands she couldn't, because she still didn't want to be seen.

Fay Ling told her that two young men were over at the Bella Union asking questions about her and RJ. She heard that someone had seen RJ leave and that's what they were told.

"Well it's for sure then that Micah knows RJ isn't here."

"What do you want me to do?" asked Fay Ling concerned for Martha's safety.

"I don't think there's anything right now. I can't see Micah coming into Deadwood now with everything that's gone on."

While Martha was in town wondering what Micah might be up to next, Micah was in an old line shack where he was now nursing the bullet hole in his side put there by Martha. It had opened up with the ride from Ogallala.

"What in the hell is taking those two so long?" Micah growled, not really directing it to anyone in the room.

"If I thought I could go into town I would," Scarhead remarked as he daubed the fresh blood from Micah's side. The bullet hole looked mighty red to him, and was surrounded by pus, indicating it was infected.

The two who had ridden into town came from Ogallala with their cousin Trip, who sat in the shack listening to Scarhead and Micah.

Trip Cord was a noted gunslinger who had joined up with Micah and Scarhead a couple years back and had, by chance, met up again only a few days back in Ogallala with his cousins. All three were running from a new brand of bounty hunters, known as the Pinkerton's. These were a group of lawmen that the railroad had hired to capture or kill the train and bank robbers known as the James Gang.

"Hey Trip, why don't you ride into town and find those two cousins of yours and kick their backsides back here with the whiskey and bandages that they were told to get pronto!"

"I'm not a go-for-boy," a defiant Trip informed him. "Go into town and find them yourself."

Since they had met in Ogallala this time, neither Scarhead nor Trip were able to get along. They were just plain ornery to one another and that was about to come to a climax.

"I've listened to your bull for the last time!" shouted Scarhead turning away from Micah, drawing his pistol as he did.

Trip saw the movement as Scarhead started to draw his pistol and went for his own pistol but Scarhead had the advantage.

Scarhead's pistol exploded in his hand. Lead and smoke escaped from the barrel of his pistol just as Trip's finger reached his own, but he knew it was a split second too late. Trip's eyes opened wide as he saw the cloud of gun-smoke escaping the muzzle of Scarhead's pistol. Trip never felt a thing as the bullet from Scarhead's pistol hit him directly in the mouth, breaking teeth and putting a nice round hole through his tongue, as it continued out the back of his head killing him instantly

"Now what in the tarnation did you go and do that for?" Micah asked, looking at Trip through the cloud of gun-smoke as he fell face first onto the hard dirt floor creating another cloud, this one of dust.

"I told that son-of-a-bitch the next time he wanted to mouth off to me I was going to blow his brains out." Given off a snort and dropping his pistol back into his holster, Scarhead finished his sentence, "just keeping a promise."

"Well, mister, that promise just cost you a thousand dollars!" Looking over at the lifeless body of Trip then back at Scarhead. "That was the advance I had to give him to come along."

Scarhead stepped over Trip's body and reaching down into his shirt pocket came up with a handful of bills and, fanning them in his hand, he turned and tossed them at Micah.

"Whatever is there is all you're gonna get." He turned around and walked out the door, leaving a bleeding Micah bent over to pick up the bills off the floor.

If it wasn't for Micah's injury, Scarhead would never had dared do what he just had. Scarhead knew very well what Micah was capable of doing with a pistol and had seen firsthand the speed at which he could draw it. Now his only worry from Micah was getting shot in the back.

A few minutes passed before Scarhead walked back into the room.

Micah was sitting on the edge of the straw bed bent over holding his side. He looked up when he heard Scarhead walk through the door and enter the room. "What da'ya think we should do with Trip's body. If those two cousins of his return and find out he's dead, they're gonna wanna know what happened and I ain't in any mood to take any of their crap.

"I suppose you could drag him away from this shack and throw some branches over him, then we could tell them that he rode into town and they must have missed him on the trail or in town."

"They might believe that seeing as all he could talk about was getting himself a bottle and a whore."

Scarhead went over and bent down beside Trip's body. Taking ahold of one of his feet, he proceeded to drag him out of the shack. Once outside, he tied his rope around him and with his horse dragged him out and into the timber line where he covered his body with some old dried up tree branches.

Where the dirt floor had soaked up some blood, he simply kicked the dirt around mixing it up until it wasn't noticeable.

"That should take care of that," he said. "Can't notice a thing."

As the two sat there and waited, Trip's two cousins were doing what he had talked about wanting to do.

In town, Carl and Vincent had drank a couple of beers and purchased a bottle of whiskey and were headed for doc's office when they were met on the street by a couple Chinese girls who offered them both a good time for two bits apiece. This price was so low and they were so attractive that the two couldn't resist and followed them to a small shack out back in the alley, not knowing they were sent by Fay Ling to find out anything they could.

A short time later as the two walked towards the doc's office with big smiles on their faces, the two Chinese girls were in Martha's room with Fay Ling telling them all they had found out.

"So, there are six of them, and as we had already guessed, Scarhead is one of them."

The most troubling news was that Sheriff Callahan was friends with Micah and knowing that, assumed that he wouldn't give RJ her message that Nuying was to deliver to him.

Fay Ling told Martha that the two were named Carl and Vincent and they had a cousin who was in a shack outside of town with a well-known outlaw named Scarhead and another guy who was paid to come along as his protectors.

"They told me that this other guy was injured and his name was Micah."

All this news was as Martha had already thought of and wondered if Nuying had made it to Grand Platte and was headed back or if that sheriff might have hurt her anyway once she gave him Martha's message.

Martha was told that the two had purchased some bandages and some pain medicine from Doc. The one named Vincent was the only one to have ridden out of town with the other one taking a room at the rooming house.

"He is sitting outside in front on the bench talking to old man Harris."

"Well, if he thinks he can get any information from old man Harris, he is sadly mistaken. Why, half the time he doesn't even know his own name."

Martha went to her front window and pulled open the curtain and looked across the street. Sure enough, the one known as Carl was sitting on the bench with old man Harris next to him.

Martha was amused watching old man Harris's hand movements. RJ had often said. "I wonder if you were to tie old man Harris's hands behind his back, could he still talk." As she observed, those hands were in motion now, and she wondered what they were saying.

As she turned from the window, Fay Ling noticed a worried frown on her face.

"Don't you worry none, Martha, I'm sure RJ and Nuying are okay. Why, I bet they are on their way back here at this very moment."

Martha, looked at Fay Ling and tried to smile as she nodded her head.

Fay Ling wasn't too far off with her statement, for at this very minute, RJ and Nuying were less than a hundred miles from Deadwood, the only problem being is that their trail was being blocked by a Mexican outlaw named Juan Garcia who had his pistol out and aimed at them.

"You are the two who came from Deadwood in search of a Gringo named Micah, Si?"

"That's right," answered RJ. "Who are you and what's the idea with the drawn pistol? Do we know each other?"

Waving his pistol back and forth, Juan told him, "I been paid five-hundred pesos, Amigo, to catch up with you and the senorita and to make sure you don' make it back to Deadwood." Eying Nuying up and continued down. "I must say it's a shame to shoot such a fine lookingggggg. . ." He never finished his sentence. From out of nowhere, Thunder came flying through the air and buried his teeth in Juan's throat knocking him from his horse and ripping his throat open as he fell. Once on the ground, Thunder fiercely shook his head, which tore Juan's head from his body.

"Thunder!" RJ shouted loudly. Thunder dropped the head and walked over towards where RJ had dis-mounted. He walked with his head low and his usually wagging tail, now still and hanging between his hind legs. As he approached, he saw a big grin come over RJ's face and heard his voice, not in anger but praise.

"Good boy, Thunder, Good boy."

CHAPTER 25

On their way back to Deadwood, RJ rounded up the two horses belonging to the two dead that he had buried with stones.

These two horses and Juan's along with their hardware will bring me a couple of thousand dollars once I get to Deadwood, and along with the money taken off of Juan that makes for a good day's pay.

The rest of the trip back to Deadwood proved uneventful until they were a couple of miles out.

RJ had tied the three horses behind Nuying's and on this part of the trail they were riding single file, with him in the lead.

Turning around, he spoke to Nuying, "I wonder where that big black dog has gone off to? I ain't seen or heard nothing from him for a while."

As Nuying was about to say something, she saw RJ's face suddenly grimace in pain, and at the same time she heard the loud report of a gunshot. RJ was lifted up and out of his saddle as the bullet hit him in the left shoulder, at the same time yelling for her to get down. Two more gunshots were heard scattering all the horses, leaving both RJ and Nuying searching for cover that they found behind a fallen tree.

"Did you see where those shots came from?" RJ's voice was racked with pain as he scanned the timber line and saw a quick reflection of what must have been from the ambushes rifle. "Did you see that reflection? Could have been a rifle," he whispered to her.

Sticking her head slightly out and over the tree they were behind, to see if she could see anything, the sharp sound exploded once again, spewing wood slivers, not two inches from Nuying's face, forcing her to quickly pull back her head." I saw the puff of smoke that time," reported RJ.

"What now?" Nuying asked. RJ noticed how calm Nuying's voice seemed.

RJ had no idea who was shooting at them or how many there might be.

"Where is Thunder?" he whispered, hoping that all he believed him to be was true.

Vincent sat behind a large rock formation with an eagle's eye view of the large fallen tree that sheltered both RJ and Nuying.

"I know I hit ya, you sons-a-bitches!" he said aloud, scanning the fallen tree through his rifle's sight for any movement.

Vincent had returned to the shack with the bandages and whisky and had bought Scarhead's story about his cousin Trip leaving for town.

Bet them two are having themselves a mighty fun time right about now, he thought, thinking about Carl and him together in such a wild town as Deadwood.

Vincent and his brother Carl had never experienced a place quite like Deadwood before, but their brief time there together with those two little Chinese girls fired him up to return, but first he needed to take care of the business at hand.

Noticing a slight movement from behind the tree, Vincent let loose with a round and saw it hit the tree and kick up some wood. This was the shot that hit just a couple inches from Nuying's head.

Vincent figured that the noise he heard from behind him was caused by Scarhead coming to help him out hearing the gunshots. As he turned to say something, he was aware of, for only for a split second, the size of the mouth and the whiteness of the teeth that were about to sink into his face.

Instinctually, he squeezed off another round from his rifle, giving off a partial scream before the teeth sank into his cheeks, and knocking him over backwards at the same time, Vincent would feel the pain of the bite until his throat was torn out, causing almost instant death. Thunder had once again saved his new found friend, RJ.

RJ thought he heard a slight yell just before hearing another gun shot. Taking the chance to look over the tree and up at the rock formation where he knew the shooter was, he caught the sight of a big black something he knew had to be Thunder. In another moment he called Thunder's name and saw him jump up onto the rocks before bounding down toward him and Nuying.

RJ stood up, then knowing that at least, for the time being, there wasn't anyone else up there or Thunder wouldn't be on his way down.

Nuying looked at the shoulder wound and told RJ that it had gone all the way through. Having him lift his arm indicated that the bullet hadn't hit any bone.

As Thunder appeared, he bounded over to RJ and jumped up and planted his front paws squarely in the middle of his chest with such force it propelled him backwards and into Nuying who couldn't keep her balance so that the three of them ended up on the ground with Thunder on the top pressing RJ's body tightly into Nuying's.

RJ and Nuying just lay there laughing as Thunder attempted to lick both their faces at the same time. To RJ, it was truly a happy time as his mind drifted back to that day he met Thunder and what the old man had spoken to him before walking away and disappearing.

"Thunder! You're truly amazing. Where did you come from anyway?" RJ said, as he fluffed up the fur on his neck.

If only he could speak. I'm sure Calvin has his hand in here somehow even though I don't necessarily believe in such things.

RJ's thoughts were interrupted by the volley of lead and gunfire. All around him, shells were exploding, kicking up dirt and rock, some splinters hitting him in the face drawing blood. He felt a bee sting and realized he had been hit in the foot. Thunder had disappeared again, with the sound of the first shot.

Rolling onto his side to get his body behind the tree, RJ caught the sight of Nuying running into a clump of trees where he also thought he caught the glimpse of Thunder.

Good boy, Thunder. You somehow got Nuying out of harm's way.

It dawned on RJ that he was once again in a bad position. Held down by what had to be at least two people with rifles and him with a lousy hand gun.

As RJ laid there he couldn't help but notice how quiet the day had become. The exploding gunfire had scared away any birds or other creatures and now it was deadly quiet.

If only I had my rifle. RJ thought, knowing it was with his horse which took off with that first gunshot.

The air was once again filled with gunfire, but RJ didn't feel any lead hitting around him. Changing position, he saw a blur of black off to his left and knew that it was Thunder and he was running hell-bent in his direction.

BAM, BAM, BAM RJ heard the rifle fire and saw dirt explode all around the racing Thunder.

As his dog got close enough for RJ to see real well, he noticed something had been tied to his body.

"Gawd dang, if it ain't my rifle! I'll be a son-of-a-gun," he said loud enough that his words seemed to echo through the air with the repeated gun shots.

RJ's mouth dropped open as he watched in amazement at the speed which Thunder ran all the time avoiding the many bullets kicking up dirt around him.

RJ had to extend his arms and half-catch Thunder as he tried to stop him from a full run. Bullets were now splintering wood from the tree he was behind. Untying his rifle, RJ cocked it and popping up, let go with a volley of his own in the direction he had seen gun smoke.

As he guessed, his volley produced a retaliation from the two high above him.

Now, scanning the area, RJ was quite sure he knew exactly where they were.

About a hundred yards from where those two are is an old line shack. I bet that is where they have been holed up. I wonder just who it is. Is it Scarhead? Micah? Or some other hired guns?

Thoughts raced through his head. He knew that before long it would start to get dark and he would have a chance to move but so would they.

Thunder suddenly bounded off back in the direction from which he had come. Following him was exploding lead and splinters of rock. RJ watched as he disappeared back into the clump of trees where he was pretty sure Nuying must also be.

He wasn't sure exactly what he was going to do once it got dark other then make it over to that clump of trees and hope Nuying and Thunder would be there.

We'll need to stay close to Thunder. There is no way anyone could sneak up on us with him around.

As afternoon turned into evening, RJ was grateful for the evening's coolness and the chance he would have to move around.

When he looked up on the ridge and couldn't see the large boulder, he knew that if they were still there, that they couldn't see him either. Cautiously he stood up. When no fire came his way, he moved slowly towards the grove of trees which he had mapped out in his mind while it was still light out.

RJ felt something bump into his legs and realized that Thunder was beside him. "Hey big fella," he whispered. In the blackness he pictured Thunder's face turning up to look at him when he spoke.

As they walked, RJ was aware of Thunder's body pushing him in the direction he wanted him to go. Soon, RJ heard the whisper of a female's voice, and looking in its direction, he made out the shadow of Nuying. "Come quickly!" she whispered, grabbing ahold of his hand.

RJ had forgotten the foot wound he had sustained until now. He let out a loud groan as he stepped forward with his weight on his injured foot. Immediately he stopped dead in his tracks and pulled on Nuying's hand stopping her.

"Aarrrgggghhhhhh!" he groaned, straining to hear any sounds coming from the direction of the large boulder. RJ realized that in the quietness of the night, his groan would have traveled as far as the boulder giving off their location. No sounds were heard, so RJ tugged on Nuying's hand indicating they should continue.

Before long, Nuying had led them to where she had the horses tied up. During the time RJ was being held down by rifle fire, she had located the scattered horses.

"I think we'll stay here until daylight," whispered RJ. "I think those fella's are gone anyway." RJ was pretty sure of his assumption.

About midnight, the cloud cover that had blocked the night light from the moon and the stars opened up and the night was basked in a haze-like glow from the moon.

RJ's plan now changed.

"I'll leave Thunder here with you while I go and see if there is anyone staying in that shack. If you hear the sound of gunfire, get on one of those horses and head to town as fast as you can. Find Martha and she will know what needs to be done."

"Be careful," she whispered in his ear, stepping on her tip toes. She watched as his shadow soon faded away.

RJ didn't know quite what he was going to do once he reached the shack if he saw someone there. RJ had nothing to worry about.

Sitting in the shack, Scarhead and Micah had also heard the gunshots. Vincent, having returned from town, had left earlier to find a location that he could look out over the road leading to Deadwood for a man and a Chinese woman riding together.

Now hearing the gunshots, Micah remarked, "Sounds like our boy has found himself one man and one Chink woman."

Scarhead stood up and was going to leave, but Micah's hand stopped him. "Let's wait a spell and see what happens."

"Well, I'm going outside where I can hear better. That report didn't sound too far off and if Vincent needs some help he just might call out."

"Suit yourself, but you're leaving that whiskey bottle in here."

Scarhead raised the bottle to his lips and drained almost half of what was left before handing it over to Micah. Using his shirt sleeve, he wiped off his mouth, turned and walked out the door.

It wasn't long before he walked back in and told Micah that with the last gunshot he had heard he had also heard a loud scream.

Standing on wobbly legs, caused not only from his injury, but from the whiskey he had consumed, Micah followed Scarhead from the shack and both headed in the direction Scarhead pointed.

In only the matter of minutes they were at the boulder looking at the dead body of Vincent.

"Look at that!? Micah indicated, pointing to Vincent. "He's had half his face and throat ripped off."

"What do you suppose did that, a wolf or a mountain lion?"

Before Scarhead got an answer, he heard noises coming from behind the big fallen tree that lay next to the trail several hundred feet below where they stood. When he glimpsed something black moving, at first he thought it might have been a bear but then he also heard voices.

Pointing down towards the tree, Scarhead raised his rifle and let off several rounds. When Micah saw movement he did the same. That continued throughout the day and into evening 'til it got too dark to see anything.

"Let's get out of here. Can't see nothing anyways," Micah suggested. "Pitch black. Let's make our way into Deadwood under this blanket of darkness and see if we can locate Carl."

As quietly as they could, they led their horses away from the shack and down a small path which led them back to the main road. They continued to walk their horses until they were sure they couldn't be heard riding away.

As RJ made his way through the trees, he became aware of someone behind him. Turning around, he saw that Thunder and Nuying were following him. RJ stopped and let them catch up to him. He was going to give them hell and send them back, but seeing Nuying with a rifle in her hands, he changed his mind.

Can always use an extra rifle if need be.

"Do you know how to shoot that thing?" he asked, pointing to the rifle she carried.

"Yes, I can." Nuying remarked. "I told you there are many things you and Martha don't know about me."

"Well, Nuying. I guess, once this is all over, we just might have to have that sit down talk."

Nuying didn't respond but instead pointed forward as a signal to get going.

Insight of the shack now, RJ looked around to see if there were any horses in and around the shack. He saw none. Thunder had taken the lead and was pawing at a large pile of tree branches. Bending down, RJ removed several limbs before discovering the body of a dead man. Uncovering it, he noted that it wasn't Micah or Scarhead.

Instinctively, RJ wondered if there was reward money posted for him.

Turning to Nuying, RJ said. "Stay here with Thunder. I'm gonna get closer to the shack." So leaving her and Thunder, RJ crept to within a few feet of the open door. Knowing now that no one was there. He stood and entered the shack. Then walking back out, he called for Nuying and Thunder.

"Looks like no one's home."

"Who was that dead man back there?" asked Nuying.

"Don't rightly know," answered RJ, realizing he still had his pistol drawn so he returned it to his holster.

Looking around inside the shack, Nuying discovered the old bloody rags and some medicine.

"Looks like at least one of these men was injured, RJ. Look at these bloody rags."

RJ once again felt the hurt in his foot so he sat down and removed his boot to examine his injury.

Thunder, having smelled the blood from RJ's injury, walked over and started to lick his wound. RJ let him, knowing there was healing in that saliva.

During the war there were dogs kept just for this reason. Something about their saliva helped keep a wound from getting infected.

As RJ sat there with Thunder licks his wound, his thoughts went back to the war when Calvin was still alive and had just found his own Thunder.

Reaching down and scratching Thunder's head, RJ whispered, "Is that you Calvin?"

Chapter 26

Under the cover of darkness, Micah and Scarhead entered the back alley which ran next to the livery stable where Micah had a friend who slept in one of the horses stalls. That is now where they headed.

Entering the stable, one could hear the snoring of someone in a deep sleep. Following the sound, Micah soon came upon the sleeping Jesse Harris.

"Wake up," Micah said, bending down and shaking Jesse.

"What the hecccccckkkk!" Jesse mumbled being awakened from such a deep sleep.

"It's me. Micah."

"I'll be a son-of-a-gun." Jesse said, shaking the cobwebs of sleep from his brain.

"What are you doing back here? You might rightly get yourself hanged."

"I need you to get woke up. There's something I need you to do for me."

"Well, at this time of night, I reckon I need a cup of black coffee and a shot of whiskey?" said Jesse, stretching his arms above his head, giving off a loud yawn, which Micah gathered could have been heard all the way to the other end of town.

Extracting several coins from his breast pocket, Micah handed them to Jesse. "Go over to the Bella Union and get yourself a couple shots of that rot gut you like so much. Then go to the rooming house for some coffee and see if there's someone there who goes by the name of Carl. If he's there, bring him back here with you. Do you understand?"

Taking the coins and nodding his head, Jesse told him. "Understood, Micah."

Micah and Scarhead watched from the stable as Jesse crossed the street and walked into the Bella Union. What they didn't see was Fay Ling leaving the back door of the saloon several minutes later. Not far behind Micah and Scarhead was RJ and Nuying, with Thunder leading the way.

"Thunder is staying pretty close this time," Nuying remarked. He had always run along up front but never within sight. Now he stayed close, as if sensing some kind of danger.

Rounding the horseshoe curve in the road, RJ looked over at the structure of a house almost finished and ready to move into. And looking off to the right of that one was a pile of lumber that Calvin had purchased to start his own house.

"Looks like your house is almost finished," remarked Nuying pointing to the structure.

"Sure does, Nuying," said RJ, reining his horse to a stop so he could look at what would be his and Martha's home. "Much has been completed since I've been gone."

Looking once again at the pile of lumber which would have been Calvin's home, RJ's emotions almost got the better of him. Suddenly, Thunder bolted ahead and ran to the pile of lumber, then to the mound of dirt which covered the body of his best friend Calvin. Both Nuying and RJ watched Thunder as he slowly paced back and forth by the grave, raise his head and gave off an eerie sounding bark, almost a howl. He paced for another few seconds before walking back to them.

RJ and Nuying rode up to the barn, which had already been completed, and got down from their mounts. RJ led all the horses into the barn where he fed them some oats.

"Do you think you can get to Martha, in town, without being seen?" asked RJ.

He hadn't got a "set in stone" plan yet, but knew that Martha had to know that he and Nuying were both safe and alive and

Nuying had a better chance at doing just that without being noticed.

Not only Martha, but Micah and Scarhead were also awaiting word on RJ and Nuying.

RJ knew that if Nuying were to get to Martha, she had to ride fast.

"You need to be in Deadwood before it gets light out," RJ told her. "If you're seen by anyone that Micah might have paid to let him know if you or I show up there, we won't be able to surprise him."

"Do you think he's in Deadwood, RJ?"

"He very well could be, Nuying." Finishing, he said, "I just hope he's not."

Nuying assured RJ that she could get into town and to Martha without anyone knowing, even if Micah was in town. Nuying entered Deadwood while it was still dark, although the moon did light up the night some.

Getting down from her mount just outside of town, Nuying made her way to one of the cribs outback of the Bella Union. Listening outside of one door after another, listening to sounds that would indicate that there was action going on inside. She came to one door and was satisfied that whoever was there was alone, she gave it a light knock.

The girl's name was Jing-Wei. Nuying told her to go see Martha and relay the message that both she and RJ were alive. "Bring back any information you can in regards to Micah and Scarhead."

"I have some news right now," she told Nuying. She listened to Jing-Wei as she recounted the earlier happenings.

"I told Martha that they were looking for her and RJ. Their names were Carl and Vincent and that they were brothers hired by Micah. They said they were staying outside of town in an old line shack. They also told me that Scarhead and Micah were staying at the shack with their older cousin Trip.

"They left and went to get some bandages and pain medicine from doc, also some whisky to bring back to the shack." Remembering the one that stayed behind, Jing-Wei told her "his name was Carl."

Nuying knew that these two had to be the ones riding with Scarhead and Micah, and hearing that one of the brothers stayed in town, she surmised the two dead men were Trip and Vincent.

"I need you to go fetch Martha now."

Still having no idea that Scarhead and Micah were holed up in the livery stable, Jing-Wei simply walked up the street to where she knew Martha was. This didn't go unnoticed by Micah, who watched intently 'til she walked back out the door and continued on back the way she had come.

"Git out there and follow her, Carl," commanded Micah.

Instantly Carl was on his feet heading in the direction of the alley next to the Bella Union. He had been there earlier with his brother so he was familiar with where he was going.

Never having seen the Chinese woman that Micah was looking for, he didn't recognize her as the one now standing not fifteen feet from him talking to the girl he had followed, besides, they all looked alike to him.

"Who are you?" asked Nuying, surprised to see that Jing-Wei was followed.

At the same time, Carl noticed she had a rifle in her hands and that it was pointed straight at his midsection which caused him to come to an abrupt halt.

Thinking fast, Carl answered, "My name is Carl. I was out walking and saw this here little Chinese girl and remembered her from earlier and was just wanting to get some more lovin', so I followed her here." He gave her a big grin.

"Well then, step up closer so I can get a better look at ya."

As Carl took a step towards Nuying, out of nowhere the figure of something big and black came around from the back of one of the cribs and before he could move, was attacked by it. As always, Thunder went for the throat and within the blink

An eye, Carl lay in the dirt, dead, with his throat ripped out and blood soaking into the dry dirt.

Back in the livery stable, Micah and Scarhead watched as the Chinese girl walked into the alley closely followed by Carl.

"I think...." Micah had started to say when he heard some footsteps from the back of the stables. Motioning for Scarhead to follow him, Micah headed for the rear of the stables. Stepping out back, Micah saw the backside of a woman walking briskly and knew that it had to be Martha.

Hurrying as fast as they dared so as not to make any sound, Micah and Scarhead followed her 'til they could hear voices. A few more steps and they would be around the backside of the Union Bella and amongst the many cribs that the whores would render service to their customers in. It was here that they had followed Martha.

As Martha approached, she had to step over the dead body of Carl. She walked up to Nuying and gave her a big hug, glad to see that she was alright.

Stepping into sight, not twenty feet away, Micah and Scarhead made their presence known. All eyes turned and looked towards them. At the same time, Thunder appeared and with a loud growl went flying through the air. His wide opened mouth set on Micah's throat.

BOOM, sounded Scarhead's drawn pistol and Thunder seemed to freeze in mid-jump before falling to the hard ground not three feet from both Micah and Scarhead's feet.

Although Nuying had her rifle up and ready to fire, Martha had stepped into her line of fire preventing her from taking a shot.

"How about you dropping that rifle?" Came Micah's voice, as he and Scarhead stepped over Carl's body, not paying any attention to it what-so-ever.

"I said, drop that rifle!" In the blink of an eye lid another BOOM went off. This time it was Micah's pistol and both Martha and Nuying watched as a big red hole appeared in the middle of Jing-Wei's forehead, the impact propelling her backwards before she crumpled to the ground.

"Now!" Micah repeated, pointing his pistol at Nuying. "Drop the friggin' rifle!"

As Nuying dropped the weapon, several voices were heard coming from the front of the alley getting louder as they drew nearer.

Micah nodded to Scarhead and he turned to level his pistol at the first person to round the corner. Stopping dead in their tracks, at being confronted by a pistol aimed at them, the men simply threw their arms into the air, turned and ran.

Laughing, Micah remarked. "Looks like you have a lot of support with those guys."

"It's me you came here for!" Martha pleaded. "Let Nuying walk away." Looking at the dead girl, Martha looked back towards Micah and with fury in her voice started for him.

Instantly, Micah's pistol swung up and connected with the side of Martha's head, knocking her down to the ground but not out. Through her fuzzy eyes, she was sure she saw a slight movement of Thunder's tail.

Grabbing Martha by the arm, Micah pulled her to her feet and shoving her, then Nuying forward, instructed them to walk into the livery stable paying no attention to Thunder. As they came out of the alley, five sets of eyes watched as they headed for the livery.

Once inside the livery stable, both Martha and Nuying had their wrists bound and with a long rope, which Micah had flung up and over one of the rafters and then being tied to their hands, he hoisted them up till just their toes barely touched the stable floor.

Scarhead had stepped next to Nuying and was running his hands up and down her suspended body, paying close attention to her shapely breasts, pinching one then the other nipple forcing her to cry out. He was about to do the same to Martha but was stopped by Micah.

"You don't lay a hand on this one," He threatened Scarhead through bared teeth. "When the time comes, she's mine."

"You filthy pig!" screamed Martha at Micah, spitting in his face. "Just wait till RJ gets here."

"And just how is a dead RJ going to help you? His ghost maybe?" This was followed by an ungodly hard slap to her rear end. This time it was Martha who cried out.

"Your husband RJ, Calvin and myself had a good thing going at one time. Then RJ got greedy and didn't want to pay me my dues for information I fed him. That left me having to make a hard decision. Having Calvin gunned down, I thought would set RJ straight as to our partnership, but it only soured it."

"You're going to find that trying to kill RJ isn't going to be as easy as killing Calvin."

Martha's outburst caused her to suffer another hard slap to her rear-end. This time she was ready for it and refused to cry out.

Angered beyond control or reason, and starting to feel the pain in his side from a bullet hole, put there by this woman, Micah looked around for some kind of switch. Spying a buggy in one of the stalls, he went to see if there was a buggy whip. Finding one, Micah returned and stepped in front of Martha showing her the switch.

Without any warning, Micah laid the switch across her breast.

The instant pain forced a cry out from Martha's lips.

"You think you can hold out screaming? Think again." This time the switch was laid across her rear-end. As Micah had predicted, Martha cried out in god awful pain.

Tossing the switch to Scarhead, he nodded his head toward Nuying. Reading the silent gesture from Micah, Scarhead laid three hard hits to Nuying's back side before ending with one across her midsection and breast.

Micah figured that their screams were being heard by anyone who might still be up and about. Turning his attention to the open livery front, Micah walked out onto the street and shouted at the top of his lungs.

"If anyone of you know where RJ is, go tell him I have his wife and I'm getting angrier by the minute having to wait for him to show his face."

To make his point, he motioned for Scarhead to lay the switch once again to Nuying's breast causing her once again to cry out in pain.

While all this was going on, behind the Bella Union, Thunder was just coming to. Scarhead's bullet had grazed his head, knocking him out. Now, as he came to, he looked around and not seeing Martha or Nuying, he stood up and shook himself violently trying to clear his head from the injury he had sustained.

Thunder's ears perked up when he heard the loud voice of a man talking and then the crying out of a woman's voice. Thunder knew that he had to fetch RJ, and that time was of the essence.

RJ, sensing something must be wrong seeing that Nuying hadn't returned was already making his way into town.

It was slowly getting daylight and RJ knew that this day was going to be one he would tell his kids about if he and Martha ever had any.

RJ had a worried look all across his face as he rode. Nuying not returning and Thunder nowhere to be found had him worried sick.

Suddenly, out of nowhere in the path ahead of him, raced Thunder. Dismounting and bending down, RJ was met by a very happy dog who for at least a minute kept licking his face. Once he stopped, RJ was able to get a closer look at him and noticed the dried blood on his head, then the actual injury.

"That's a nasty wound you've got there, big fella," he said, followed by, "where is Nuying or Martha?"

At the mentioned of their names, Thunder broke out of RJ's grasp and bounded toward Deadwood.

Just outside of town, RJ was met by a couple of the men who had gone to investigate the shooting behind the Bella Union and who also witnessed what was happening in the livery stable where Martha and Nuying were being held and beaten by Micah and Scarhead.

"We're no gunslingers or else we would have helped out," said one of the men hanging his head in shame.

"That's ok. What matters now is that you had the sense to meet me before I rode into Deadwood and was faced by the situation at hand."

Although RJ was aware of just how non-human, at times, Micah could become, he had seen something in Sheriff Tom Callahan's office that he hadn't known about Micah.

While sitting in his office looking at some posters he had come across one for Micah. Either Callahan had overlooked it or, had left it in purposely for him to find, he wasn't quite sure. Now he reached into his saddle bag and removed that poster.

Although there wasn't a picture of Micah, his name was mentioned alongside several others. Wanted for his part in the Massacre at Lawrence, Kansas during the war, where he rode alongside William Quantrill, there was a twenty-five thousand dollar reward on his head, dead or alive.

All that time we had heard he was dead, he was, in fact, very much alive and riding with Quantrill. Well, if I get out of this one alive, Micah just might be the last bounty I collect. Now it made sense to him concerning the nickname of Mad Man Micah and how he had acquired it.

RJ's thoughts were interrupted by the loud, blood curdling scream of a woman and made it out to be Martha's. The hair on his neck and head rose.

Thunder jumped up when he heard it too, but looked to RJ before he moved.

It was light enough out so that RJ could see Micah and Scarhead standing in front of the livery stable from his position upon entering town.

RJ had witnessed the speed of the draw of both Micah and Scarhead, so he wasn't planning on facing them down.

Knowing the atrocities Micah was wanted for told him that he would show absolutely no mercy in getting what he wanted, and right now it was him that he wanted.

"Scarhead will be a problem," he said to himself.

At the mention of his name, RJ saw Thunder's ears perk up, the hairs on his back rise and his lips curl up baring his sharp teeth, and before RJ could see anything more, Thunder bounded off like a shot not bothering to wait for RJ's command.

RJ had stayed back in the shadows of the buildings not giving himself away trying to work out a plan in his head.

Without giving it any thought, RJ found himself looking up into the sky and talking to Calvin.

"Well, Calvin, quite a situation I've gotten into this time. If you can hear me, give me some sort of sign." As he finished, he felt a strong nudge on his legs. Looking down, and coming from nowhere, Thunder had materialized next to him and next to him was the figure of the big wolf Thunder had introduced him to.

"Is that you, Calvin? And who's your friend?" It was a stupid question because RJ didn't believe in such nonsense, but this wasn't the first time that Thunder had come out of nowhere to be by his side. He remembered what Martha had told him when they had talked about the big black dog.

"Believe what you want to believe about him. If you want to believe that somehow Thunder is Calvin in dog form, that's fine."

Once again RJ heard the loud voice of Micah calling out to him. This time RJ was in a position where he observed Micah as he stepped just outside the front doors of the livery. His eyes also saw the hanging figures of Nuying and Martha better, now as it was getting quite light out.

As Micah finished calling out, RJ saw Scarhead step away from the hanging body of Nuying before raising his arm and bringing the switch once more down across her already cut and bleeding breast. Nuying screamed a scream that would wake the dead and every hair on RJ's body stood on end.

A movement in the upstairs window of the rooming house caught his attention. Looking directly at the window, RJ once again saw the curtain being opened slightly and a person's head appeared.

"I'll be a son-of-a-gun!" RJ whispered, recognizing the face as that of the old man who had spoken to him that morning when Thunder appeared. Looking down at Thunder, RJ saw that he also had his eyes fixed on the figure in the window. Looking back up at the figure, RJ could have sworn he saw the man nod at him before once again disappearing. Looking down and expecting to see Thunder and his friend was an empty space, but had no time for thoughts.

Once again, RJ focused his attention on the two in the livery stable, and seeing Micah about ready to take the switch to Martha, he called out in a loud voice.

"Micah!"

Immediately at the sound of his name, Micah turned away from Martha and focused his attention on his old friend.

"I was beginning to think you weren't going to show." Then hunching his shoulders, he stepped away from Martha and started walking towards RJ. Looking back, he motioned for Scarhead to follow.

"Glad you showed up, RJ I was just getting ready to taste your wife's charms." This brought looks of disgust from Martha.

"No need to do that now, seeing I'm here standing in front of you."

"You're right about that point. Yes, you're for sure standing right in front of me." Micah looked RJ up and down as if sizing him up.

RJ watched the movements of Scarhead very closely. He had stepped out onto the street and had moved maybe ten feet from Micah.

"Before I kill you, you need to answer a question for me. Will you do that?"

"Ask away."

"What happened between us anyway?"

"I'll tell ya Micah. Was going to anyway."

RJ thought he felt Thunder's body press hard against his leg and looked down to once again see nothing. RJ suddenly felt a presence around him, which calmed his nerves and brought to his mind the times he and Calvin had spent target practicing and learning how to quick draw.

"I'm waiting for that answer now," came the loud voice from Micah.

With a calmness in his voice, RJ started. "Remember back when you told me you first came to Deadwood and the things you had done so that the town's people would be scared of you? Remember?"

A big grin came to Micah's face. Spitting out a stream of spittle, he nodded his head.

"Oh yeah. They're still scared of me. Look around RJ. Do you see anyone on the streets? Of course not. Frightened little kids, the lot of them. What's that got to do with you and me?"

"Remember you telling me about the whore who stole money from some of her clients? You set up a trap to catch her red handed with a client's money? Turned out to be your money?" Micah nodded his head in agreement once again.

"You didn't even know that whore's name, did you?" Showing signs of increasing anger now, RJ continued to speak in that same calm voice, "Well that whore's name was Abigail Lewis."

"So? Your point?"

"Lewis was her married name. Her maiden name was Murdock."

Micah raised one of his eyebrows at the mention of Murdock, knowing that was RJ's last name.

The thoughts that went through RJ's mind now were almost in slow motion. He was standing next to Calvin as he explained that you didn't have to draw your pistol all the way up and aim it at your target, but simply pull if up and out of the holster and just point it in the direction of your target, then with your finger, pull back on the trigger and with your left hand reach across and use a fanning motion on the hammer. He demonstrated this several times and that is what RJ had practiced over the months.

"No one will ever be able to out gun you." Calvin would say giving him a couple slaps on the back. All this returned now as he stood there facing Micah and Scarhead.

Just before he knew that it was time to draw, he glimpsed up at the window. No one there, instead he felt the old man's presence beside him along with that of Thunder and his lady friend.

"That's right, Micah. Abigail was my sister."

With the speed of a lightning bolt, Micah drew his pistol and so did Scarhead.

RJ's hand was as fast as lightning also and as smooth as a new baby's bottom. Pulling back on the trigger and at the same time he pointed it in Micah's direction as his left hand came across and fanned the gun's hammer twice before changing direction and pointing at Scarhead. His left hand never stopped its fanning motion until all six shots had been made.

Looking through the cloud of gun smoke, RJ saw both Micah and Scarhead in the process of falling down dead to the ground.

As RJ holstered his pistol, he felt the familiar nudge against his leg. This time when he looked down, he was greeted by the face of Thunder. No old man, no wolf companion, just Thunder.

EPILOGUE

Three years had passed since "The Big Shoot-out" as it had come to be known. RJ and Martha had started a hardware store and it was a profitable operation, so much so that RJ had stopped bounty hunting, as he now had a son to look after.

Calvin Jeremiah Murdock or CJ for short had just turned two and was already running around outside their home and getting into all kinds of mischief.

Fay Ling had moved into their home as a nanny to CJ, as both RJ and Martha had a business to run, even though she was expecting another child, secretly hoping it was a girl this time but knowing no matter what she or he would be loved.

Nuying, with the support of Martha and RJ, decided she would go back to China, where she could help out the most, to try to eliminate human trafficking.

One day, she watched as a wagon came into town being led by three men on horseback and another two sitting on the seat. It stopped in front of the Bella Union and ten Chinese girls were unloaded. She found out a little while later that one of the girls had just turned ten. It was this sight that made her decide she had to do something.

Martha and RJ bought her boat fare and since she had been gone, they had received only two letters. In the last letter they had received from her, she stated that she had been arrested and in a sort of prison, where she managed to smuggle the letter out. They could only imagine what she had to do to get someone to help her. "I see no daylight or anyone from the outside." She went on to write, "Every day about fifteen men, some of them guards tie me naked to a wooden bed where they take turns raping me." Martha cried the day the letter came. Now, almost two years since that last letter, Martha was surprised when a lone wagon entered the streets of Deadwood. Driving that wagon was Nuying and aboard it were ten small Chinese children, she had smuggled out of China with the help of a very rich American who thought he was purchasing these young girls. Nuying would set up an orphanage of sorts where she would continue to take in and protect anyone she could.

The big dog Thunder disappeared shortly after the gunfight to the dismay of both Martha and RJ.

The day he disappeared, Martha and RJ had gone into town to church. Thunder didn't follow them this time, but sat on the porch watching them as they pulled out in their wagon. When they arrived back home, Thunder couldn't be found. Later, Martha went to the farm about three miles away and asked Colleen if she had seen Thunder.

"Why yes, I did," she told her. "He came walking by with some old guy that I'd never seen before. He was running around the old man, in circles, barking and playing, and the old guy had a stick he would throw and Thunder would run after it. I went to the edge of our drive and just watched them till they were out of sight"

Martha re-told the story to RJ.

Some night's sitting on their front porch, RJ and Martha would listen and often hear the call of a lone animal. It wasn't one of a dog or a wolf, or a coyote and they would just look at each other and smile a smile that needed no words.

In 1879, Deadwood experienced a devastating fire that had destroyed three hundred businesses, including RJ and Martha's hardware store.

The gold boom was over and now only a small mine was giving up its last remaining ounces of gold. A lot of the burned out businesses decided not to re-build and were in the process of packing up their households and leaving Deadwood for the west coast.

Because RJ and Martha, too, had lost their hardware store in the fire, they also had decided to pack up. The summers in Deadwood were much too hot and the winters, too cold.

"Calvin and I had talked a lot about Arizona and Texas as somewhere that we always wanted to go."

"Well then, flip a coin. Heads, Texas and tails, Arizona." RJ flipped the coin and it landed on heads.

"Looks like Texas has won out."

Today found them with a packed wagon ready to head for Texas.

Leaving town, they had to go by their home. As they were passing, both looked for one last time at their home.

"Once we arrive in Texas, we'll re-start our hardware business and we'll have another house. It may take some time, but we'll do it, I promise."

Martha looked at RJ just in time to see his facial expression change. Following his eyes, she found herself looking over at Calvin's grave.

"Oh my!" She exclaimed. Sitting next to Calvin's grave was the big black dog, Thunder.

RJ was about to call him when he had a change of heart.

"He's knows we are here, and somehow I think he knows where we're going. When we go now, if he follows, that's great."

"And if he doesn't?" asked Martha.

"Then he doesn't." RJ replied. "Someday he may decide to visit Texas. He wasn't really my dog to begin with."

As they now passed, RJ saw Thunder stand up and turn toward the road, but instead of bounding towards them, he just stood there and watched as they disappeared around the horseshoe curve and out of sight.

E. C. Herbert with N. C. McGrath

For the last time, RJ raised his eyes heavenward and spoke softly, "Save a spot for me up there, will ya Calvin?" As he said this, he heard the distant call of Thunder and knew that all was going to be okay.

THE END

Elmer, better known as Al to associates and friends, was born in a little town in central Florida known as Polk City in 1950.

He grew up moving between Florida and New Hampshire. In his youth he enjoyed playing cowboys and Indians and watching westerns on TV such as, The Lone Ranger, Rawhide, Roy Rogers, The Rifleman, Maverick, Tombstone, and several others. As he grew older he put aside this enjoyment for other interests.

Traveling through the Southwest on business he realized he was in the part of the country that he loved as a youngster. This sparked a renewed interest in the Old West.

Getting down-sized and out of work with time on his hands, Al started to read "dime store westerns" and was transported back to those days. His most read author is Ralph Compton. His interest in reading soon led to a desire to write. "New Dawn at Twin Arrows" was his first novel.

Ghost Riders of Bloody Creek follows his love for the old west. "I was born a century too late." Al confesses. "I would have loved to have walked the streets with my childhood cowboy heroes."

Made in the USA
Coppell, TX
07 December 2020